TAKEOVER

KINGS OF THE BOARDROOM
BOOK ONE

NANA MALONE

COPYRIGHT

This is a work of fiction. Names, characters, places, and incidents either are the product of the author's imagination or are used fictitiously, and any resemblance to actual persons living or dead, business establishments, events, or locales, is entirely coincidental.

Takeover, Book 1 in the Kings of the Boardroom Series

COPYRIGHT © 2024 by Nana Malone

CHAPTER 1
GWEN

The wind whipped around me in a furious torrent as I eased open the balcony door, trying to get a reprieve from the noise at the benefit. I only needed ten damn minutes to myself.

It was impossible after the catering fucked up, and I fixed the flowers, and I stopped a senator from getting into a fistfight with a D-list actor. But it was my mother's birthday. Earlier, my sister Morgan had managed to sneak in a bottle of champagne, so I could do the ritual even without her.

The blast of wind was strong enough to make me wobble a bit, and I sucked in a sharp breath as the wind snuck around the opening of my peacoat and wrapped me in its chilly embrace.

I closed the balcony door behind me and dragged in a deep, frigid breath. It was March. Where was the goddamn spring weather already? I went out to the rail of the stone balcony and set the champagne down, sighing as I pulled out the little makeup compact full of glitter. "Happy birthday, Mom."

She would have been fifty today. I could still see her bright shining smile every time she saw me and Morgan. And the best part about

1

Mom was that she always made time for each of us to have our individual identities with her. She and Morgan used to go to the park every time it was one of their birthdays, just the two of them for a couple of hours.

For me and Mom, we always had a moment to make our glitter wishes. The one unimpeachable wish that we would share with each other and no one else.

I uncapped the makeup pot, took a swig of champagne, and poured the glitter into my hand. "I miss you, Mom. And my wish for you, on your fiftieth birthday, wherever you are, is that you know you are missed and that you are surrounded by love."

Then I opened my palm and blew the glitter into the air.

Unfortunately, that was when another gust of biting wind hit, and much of the glitter hit me in the face and blew back onto the balcony.

Somewhere in the shadows at my right, someone coughed. "Oh, for fuck's sake, glitter?"

I whipped around, brandishing the partially drunk champagne bottle as a weapon. "What the fuck?"

A man stepped out of the shadows, and my breath caught. He was tall. Ridiculously tall. Tall enough to make me take a wary step backward. I could already see where the sparkly glitter had hit him on his sharp Italian-cut suit. There was even a touch of it on his sharp jawline.

His shoulders were broad, like a swimmer's shoulders. The suit was tapered and fit snugly, showcasing his broad chest. And the fabric hung like a dream and looked like it would be buttery soft too.

"Start talking, or I'll start whacking."

He chuckled low. "You're not going to do much damage with that champagne bottle, especially if you keep pouring it out like that."

My arm holding the bottle had tipped over. And he was right. Champagne was spilling.

"Fuck."

The bottom hem of my Christy Brown dress was wet, and I cursed. "Damn it, I said start talking."

"You're the one who came out and covered me in glitter. Who carries around glitter anyway?"

"None of your goddamn business. Tell me who you are before I show you how handy I can be with a bottle of champagne."

"Well, aren't you a violent little thing?" he murmured, his voice like silk down my back.

I held the bottle higher and his hands went out. "Relax. My name is Atticus. I was here first. I just didn't let you know I was out here because... Well, you looked like you needed a moment."

Holymotherfuckingshit. Atticus fucking Price. I'd glitter-bombed *the* Atticus Price. Freaking excellent.

The man had only been on the cover of *Forbes* three times in the last year alone. Pendragon Tech was at the forefront of cutting-edge prosthetic technology, and they'd gotten into the renewable energy game three years ago when he'd taken over as CEO.

I lowered the bottle. "You're not here to attack me or something?"

Even in the shadows, I could see the hint of a smile as he stepped forward. And this time, the step I took back was pure self-preservation.

One thing was glaringly obvious; the *Forbes* photographer should be shot. They hadn't done the man justice. I didn't have much else to go on because the man was usually a cipher. He attended these kinds of things, wrote a check, and vanished. You rarely saw him in a society page, and it was rare to see his name on any of the gossip sites.

Good Lord, even in the moonlight and shadow, I could tell the man was gorgeous. Like stupidly gorgeous, with a chiseled jaw that looked like it was cut from stone and the kind of cheekbones that would make any model jealous. He had deep-set, shrewd, ice-green eyes, a straight Roman nose that looked like perhaps it had been broken once or twice, complimented by a high brow only slightly covered by a curling lock of dark hair, and lips full enough to make you fantasize about kissing him.

Sure, all of that made him handsome. On the verge of too hand-some. But there was a rugged edge to him that made him intrigu-ing. Still, it was a sharp-edged ruggedness that warned you to be wary.

Everything, save the thick, softly curling lashes surrounding his cold, shrewd eyes, was both a magnet and a warning beacon that cautioned while he was pretty, he was also dangerous.

"So you stood and watched? I might have saved my ritual for later."

"Casting a spell on the rest of the world?"

"If I thought casting a spell would work on the nepo babies and sycophants in there to make them donate more, I might try it."

He smirked. "Nepo babies and sycophants, huh?"

Easy. He's here, so he's likely one of those nepo babies.

"Would you categorize anyone in attendance differently?"

His amused gaze swept over me. "Okay, so you're not enjoying the benefit then?"

Enjoying was the wrong word. My family had put on the Hearts and Hope Benefit every year for the last ten years to honor my mother. At seventeen, I had been placed on the board and put in charge of pulling it off. I loved this benefit. The fact that Becks Incorporated would no longer be able to afford to play host sliced through my already shattered heart.

I didn't tell him that though. Instead I feigned bravery.

"The benefit is great. It raised a lot of money for heart disease. I just don't like the song and dance. I wish that the people in there actually cared and weren't just here for an expensive meal, a tax write-off, and the see-and-be-seen aspect of it."

He cocked his head as he studied me. "You certainly have a strong opinion."

"I *do* have strong opinions. You seem surprised."

"Let's call it refreshing." The corner of his lips tipped up into what could only be described as a slightly insolent smirk. It was like he didn't give anything away without you working for it. I wasn't interested in working that hard.

"I want to go back inside," I said. "If you'll excuse me."

The leash he kept on his oh-so-precious smile loosened, and one escaped, rooting me to the balcony. Christ almighty. It was better for the world that he didn't release them that often. A smile from him was paralyzing.

"Oh no, you don't. You blasted me with glitter and then basically called me, what was it? A nepo baby and sycophant."

Way to insult the donors, Gwen. "I mean, I don't know you. So you tell me, *are* you a nepo baby or a sycophant?"

There it was again. Another smirk. "According to you, I probably fall under the nepo baby category. Can I ask who you are?"

I lifted my chin. "I'm Gwen."

"Is that it? Just Gwen?"

Just my luck, he was probably one of my father's business associates. And given the financial troubles we were in, I probably didn't need to make it worse. "Just Gwen to you, Mr. Atticus Price."

"You have my full name. How is that fair?"

"The world isn't fair, is it now?"

He flashed me a grin, and my heart stopped. Hell, time stopped. That grin should be illegal. When he bestowed it upon you, everything around him went dead still and it was all you could see.

That made it easier for people like him to prey on you. Like vampires. Wasn't that part of the lure? They stunned you with their beauty, and that made it easy to pounce.

I lowered my champagne bottle. "So, you're not trying to take over my spot?"

He cocked his head. "Why do I get the impression that you wouldn't ever wait for anyone to dismiss you?"

I stood up a little straighter. "You'd be right."

"You are fascinating, Just Gwen."

"I'm glad you approve. Enjoy the benefit." Then I turned. I had a speech to give. The last one I was ever going to give in my mother's memory.

And instead of rehearsing a proper goodbye, I'd ended up bickering with some idiot on the balcony.

Not just any idiot. Atticus Price.

I knew Pendragon Tech and their reputation for corporate raiding. I didn't know anything about Atticus, but his company's reputation was well earned. Which made him, despite his beautiful face and sexy godlike smile, firmly in the look-but-don't-touch category. I had enough on my plate without salivating over a man, even if that man was somewhere between an avenging angel and demon all in one. Besides, I knew what shattering heartache men like that could cause, and I made a vow to stay away from the likes of him. Besides, I couldn't go back if I wanted to. I had a speech to give in my mother's honor.

And given all the buzzing from my clutch, everyone was looking for me.

I had messages from my sister, Morgan, my best friend, Lance, my father, and my stepmother. It was time to perform. I had to report for duty. It didn't matter how I felt.

I slipped my feet into the shoes I had ditched before going out to the balcony, and my toes were almost grateful because at least now they were covered. I still had the bottle of champagne in my hand as I hurried down the hall and made a hard turn and ran straight into my sister. The force of our contact almost knocked me on my ass.

"Easy does it, Gwen," Morgan said. "Come on. You have to go give this speech. I still can't believe we won't be doing this benefit anymore."

"Yeah well, I think we've got bigger problems."

I didn't know how much Morgan knew about the trouble Becks Incorporated was in. Our dad had made a series of investments, attempting to grow too fast, and now we were struggling. I spent most of my days trying to find investors. Someone had to give us an influx of cash.

Morgan was still in school, and I didn't want to worry her. She'd struggled so much when mom died. She hadn't spoken for a solid year. My father had been a useless wreck, so I'd had to take care of her. I'd been the one sitting with the nanny in her speech pathology appointments.

But we'd worked hard and with therapy, she was more and more like the Morgan I'd grown up with. She would survive a slight emotional jostle. At least I hoped she would. I might crumble under the weight of saving my company and having to go back to that terrified worried place emotionally.

Besides, our grandfather had left us trust funds. I'd used mine to start a small software company a few years ago, and much like my father, I had struggled. But once Morgan graduated, she'd have access to hers and she would never have to depend on my father for anything.

The tech bros had not exactly been supportive of a woman-founded software team. And finding other investors had been diffi-cult, though the software was superb. Our pride and glory was our predictive AI algorithm.

So much so that my father had decided to invest in us, pulling my company in as a subsidiary of his own. But he had over extended himself, and now he was trying to sell us off. So there was that.

"You ready?" Morgan asked, pulling me out of my haze of self-pity.

I found the strength to smile at my sister. "Yeah, of course."

"That's my Gwen, always prepared."

I could hear the door of the balcony opening behind us, and I purposely dragged my sister along as she turned to try and look at who was coming off the balcony.

"Was there someone out there with you?"

"Nope." I lied tightly.

Morgan laughed. "Okay, then why are you running from there? Slow down."

"I'm just in a hurry to get on stage, okay?"

"Right. You don't want to tell me who was out there?"

"Nobody important."

"Oh my God, Gwen, did you meet someone out there?"

"Morgan, I have more on my plate than thinking about whether there's a swipe left on someone or not."

She rolled her eyes. "It's swipe right. And obviously, the fact that you don't know that by now says a lot about your dating life."

"Which we're not discussing."

"I know. I just want to see you happy."

I turned to my sister and clasped her hands outside the enormous double doors into the rear of the ballroom. "I appreciate you, and I love you, but I don't date."

She sighed. "I know. I'm just saying it might do you good to have some fun. Your birthday is coming. Maybe it's time to loosen up a little."

"I will take that into consideration. Later. Look, go find dad and Clarissa. I'll see you after I'm done."

"Okay, break a leg."

She whirled around again, and the doors opened. A waiter carrying two trays loaded with champagne narrowly missed Morgan, caught his toe on my foot, and went sailing down behind both of us.

The clatter of glass and bottles made us both jump back. "Oh, shit."

We both bent to help him, but Morgan shoved me away. "You have to get on stage. Go."

"Fine." Once I knew the two of them had it well in hand, I stepped around the mess and walked in, shoulders back, poised and ready.

But as I stepped out on stage, I couldn't shake the prickle of heat dancing up my spine. I didn't even have to look up to know I'd find an ice-green gaze on me.

CHAPTER 2
ATTICUS

T<small>HERE WAS ONLY ONE MOMENT OF HESITATION BEFORE</small> I <small>ATTEMPTED TO</small>
follow "Just Gwen" into the hallway. *My little lioness.*

The fact that I tried to fight the compulsive tug toward her was
laughable. From the moment she'd stepped onto the balcony with
her champagne, I'd been mesmerized by her lithe movements. The
slope of her neck, the way the moonlight made her medium brown
skin shimmer with moon beams, and of course the way that her
sleeveless dress had hugged every single curve.

The white of the bodice was covered in black symbols of some kind
and picked up strains of the color blue, sort of a reverse bleed or
reverse ombre, ending in the train of the dress deepening to a dark
peacock blue. The effect was stunning.

Her hair had been tucked into a braided updo with several curly
strands escaping to frame her face. And fuck me, that face.

Her eyes were wide, lifting at the corners , and her lips were full
enough to give me a legion of inappropriate ideas. "Just Gwen" had
the kind of unforgettable siren-like beauty that dragged you in
whether you wanted to come or not.

11

I searched the hall for her, but she was already gone. I heard a commotion to the left by the stairs just as my brother approached. "Where the hell have you been? We need to make a move right now. I've located James Becker. We need to talk to him."

"Yeah, I'm coming. Did you see the woman come in from the balcony?"'

Micah's brows rose. Eyes that were a darker mirror to mine assessed me shrewdly. "What woman?"

"She was just here. Tall, maybe five foot seven or eight, white dress that hugged her body to fucking perfection. Her dress made her look like a peacock."

"You're sure you saw her? Talked to her?"

I knew what he was getting at. "Yes. I didn't bloody imagine her. The damn woman glitter-bombed me."

His lips twitched. "Glitter-bombed?"

I gestured to my suit and my hair. It was almost as if that was his first time looking at me properly.

"You're serious?" he asked.

I knew what he was getting at. I wouldn't be the first Price to lose my shit. "Yes, asshole. I'm not making her up. She had gorgeous luminescent brown skin and an ass that probably will cause me problems."

My brother chuckled softly. "Um, no, I didn't see her. But you're waxing poetic about some woman. Are you sure you're okay? Did you hit your head?"

I snarled at him. "No, I did not fucking hit my head. Her name is Gwen something-or-other. Get Pierce on it."

"You want me to get Pierce on finding a woman for you? Last I checked, you had women coming out of your ears. Not to mention, we're supposed to be out here convincing Becker that you're marriage material."

I rolled my eyes and headed toward the stairs, only to see several waiters picking up remnants of a discarded tray and a woman marching down the hall. Just not *my* woman.

Your woman?

That thought gave me some pause as I looked for Gwen. The other woman turned slightly before heading into the ballroom, and from the profile, she resembled Gwen, but she was definitely not her. She was shorter.

"Fuck." I turned back to my brother. "What were you saying about Becker?"

"We're at his table. We need to get in front of him. It looks like he wants to make a deal with Bronson Jacobson."

I ground my teeth. Fucking Bronson Jacobson had been a thorn in my goddamn side for years. The fucker was my constant shadow. He'd gone to Harvard with me for grad school. And then we'd both interned at Google where I'd gotten to see his supposed work firsthand.

Typical nepo baby tech bro. He was lazy, shady, and cut corners. But his parents had a fuck-ton of money, so he always seemed to land on his feet. And while I generally didn't pay him too much attention, he saw himself as my perpetual competition. So when he found out Pendragon was going after new technologies, specifically, our artificial intelligence applications, his company started doing the same.

"What does Bronson want Becks for?"

"Like us, he wants that algorithm. The software that the facial recognition is built on is what he's after. While we want to use it in building better modeling for prosthetic integration, he wants to use it for commerce and likely military applications since he got that NSA contract last year."

I muttered a soft, "Fuck," under my breath.

"Yeah, so let's fucking get in front of Becker right now and change the narrative. Oh, and please put on the face."

I followed my brother back down the other hallway toward the ballroom, where I apparently had to put "the face" back on. What-ever the fuck that meant. I knew how to play the game. I'd been playing it my whole life. I learned from the manipulative master himself. "Don't get your hopes up. If rumors are right, he's not selling unless the sales comes with marriage to one of his daughters."

"Which makes me worry about what the daughters look like. But it might be a win-win."

"Nobody forces my hand, ever."

I hadn't realized I was searching for the woman from the balcony when we walked in until I saw a flash of white as everyone was milling about. She was near the stage, talking to someone. Oh yes, Dr. Riza Hamann. She was one of the experts who had done the introduction at the beginning of the benefit. Talking about the research, the good work that they were doing and had done over many years. Excellent. Riza could tell me who she was.

She flashed a smile at the doctor, and my gut tightened. Jesus Christ. She had a smile like that? Not that she'd used it on me. No. I'd gotten her brandishing a champagne bottle. And what was with the goddamn glitter? I glanced down at my suit, and I could still see a couple of patches of it as it clung to me. I knew better than to touch it though. Because that was the way with glitter. My goddaughter, Emery, loved this stuff. Every time I left Gavin's fucking house, I was covered in it. It stuck in your hair, on your fucking skin, in your orbit until it saw fit to leave.

Micah glanced at me. "Mate, brush off the glitter, would you?"

"There she is. That one there." But as I pointed, someone stepped in the line of sight as Micah tried to see.

"Who the hell are you talking about?"

She had shifted out of sight again. "Never mind. Where's Becker?"

"There he is."

James Becker walked with the assumed power of a man in control of his life. However, I knew that he was bleeding money and needed an infusion. Or better yet, he needed to sell off his research and development arm. He couldn't sustain it. They were a small tech company. There were some things they did well, but they'd been over-extending themselves for years. I knew even an influx of cash might not save them, but selling off their R&D arm would. My brother and I walked toward him, and many of the guests parted, knowing exactly who I was and to give me a wide birth.

There was a woman with him, and her eyes went wide when she saw me. She was about his age. Maybe a little younger. Tawny skin, hair piled in an updo. She tapped her husband on the arm, and he turned and gave my brother a knowing smile.

"Micah Price. I have to say, you are persistent."

My brother flashed a grin that was so easy for him to find and access. "James Becker, you are a difficult man to get a meeting with. You know my brother, Atticus."

I reached out and shook his hand. Becker's brow lifted for a moment. "Atticus Price. Interesting seeing you at the benefit. You don't usually do these charity gigs."

"When my brother told me that it was difficult to get a meeting with you, I figured, what better way to have a casual conversation."

Becker nodded. "There was a time, Price, when I came to you. Or have you forgotten?"

Ah, so this was personal. "I was aware. However, at the time my father was in control of the company. He no longer is. I am, and I'd appreciate a moment of your time."

I wasn't used to asking for anything. But I had to stop him from going to Jacobson, whatever that took. *Even if it means marriage?* I had to let him know that I wasn't fucking around and it was in his best interest to give me what I wanted.

Pleasantries were exchanged, and then I saw *her*... "Just Gwen" was walking up to the stage. Her stride was confident. Her shoulders back. And then she approached the podium. Several guests started to mill to their tables.

She spoke to someone downstage, and then Riza joined her and spoke into the microphone. "If everyone will just take their seats, I have a special guest I would love to introduce you all to."

Riza gave a delightful introduction about a woman who had done a lot of charity work, traveled a lot, tirelessly raised money for their cause, and then called her a friend.

Yeah, yeah, give me a fucking name.

"Allow me to introduce Gwenyth Christin Becker."

The fuck?

My blood went cold, then molten hot. The woman with James clapped just a little bit harder, and I frowned. Christ Almighty... their *daughter*?

Becker however, was paying no attention to the stage despite his daughter going up to speak.

"If you want my time, I'm telling you now, Price, I'm not entertaining any offers for Becks Incorporated that don't come as a *full* partnership."

My gaze skittered to him and then back at the woman. I could see it in the chin and the jawline. She was Becker's daughter. *Fuck.*

"What do you mean by full partnership? Of course, we wouldn't be in partnership. We would be acquiring." He needed to say it.

He shook his head. "You're missing the point. Becks stays in the family. If you're not interested in that kind of partnership, there's nothing to discuss."

A spike of fury at his demands had me narrowing my gaze. My brother bumped my knee with his, telling me to calm the fuck down.

This man was using *her* as his bargaining chip.

On stage, Gwen started to speak, and her voice ensnared me once again. "Thank you so much for the warm welcome, Riza. Ladies and gentlemen, I would love to say thank you so much for once again attending the Hearts and Hope benefit. I can only hope that today, on what would have been my mother's fiftieth birthday, we raise money for other women like her who don't get to celebrate birthdays with their family."

And then something happened that I didn't expect. Her words wrapped around my cold dead heart and squeezed. She had been doing some kind of ritual for her mother. On her birthday. Why do the benefit today? He didn't give a damn about honoring her.

The woman next to Becker sat in rapt attention as she listened to Gwen. But Becker was talking to Micah. The two of them were making arrangements for a meeting. My brother, ever the magician. He could talk anyone into anything, whereas I was the blunt instrument.

I turned to Becker. He'd been jerking us around for months. He obviously wanted a better deal than he was entitled to. But knowing who his daughter was made a difference.

A big one.

"Pendragon is prepared to meet the terms you put forth. But our patience is running thin."

Becker lifted his brow and sat back. "You're serious?"

Was I? I'd just met the woman.

But the idea of Becker marring her off to anyone else, made my fingers curl into fists. I found what I hoped was more of a smile than a snarl. "I'm always serious."

"Then perhaps we can come up with a scenario that benefits us both," he said, leaning back in his seat looking like the cat that swallowed the canary.

"Fine. Friday then. Let's get something on the books."

I didn't give a fuck about him. Our terms would benefit Pendragon and that's all I cared about. But if it meant access to Gwen, then for once, I was willing to negotiate.

To my brother, I leaned over and muttered, "Make a donation."

He gave me a small nod. "We already made one. The standard two hundred thousand."

Without taking my eyes off her, I said, "Make another for five million."

I could feel the heat of his stare, but I wasn't paying attention to him. Instead, I gave my full attention to Gwenyth Becks, letting the seductive smoke of her voice settle in my bones.

With the meeting with Becker secured, I placed a call to my head of security, Pierce Trent. "Yeah, boss?" was his terse response.

"Get me everything you can find on Gwenyth Becker."

"Full work up?"

"Down to who her high school bully was. I want it all."

CHAPTER 3

GWEN

THE LAST PLACE I WANTED TO BE THIS FRIDAY MORNING WAS MY FATHER'S office.

I'd always hated my father's office. He'd taken minimalist to a whole new level. The words cold and barren were an apt description. The only saving grace was his view of the city.

The other problem was the temperature. The chill of his office was legendary.

He kept it at a balmy sixty-two because he felt like it kept everybody alert. The problem was, it certainly didn't keep him alert. His lack of concentration during long meetings was also notorious.

When trying to get my father to make a decision, I had to be quick about it. The effort of keeping my father on task today, however, was Herculean. I could tell that his mind was somewhere else. We'd only been at this for fifteen minutes, and his attention span waned already. Of course the office was frigid, just like he liked it, and I shifted uncomfortably in my seat across from him.

I knew he didn't keep it this cold because he liked it like this. This was about power. He wanted everyone to be just a smidge uncomfortable in his presence.

"We need to discuss the investment opportunities on the table," I said. "At Turn Tech last month, several venture capital firms showed real interest in my team's algorithm. I know we don't want an investor, but we're about to run out of time and funds if we don't accept an offer. Or if you have another plan, I'd like to hear it."

I placed the file on top of the three others I'd brought that needed his signature.

"The first thing you'll see is the data I pulled from accounting and our operational budget." I knew that should get him focused. I'd bombard him with information, then make a quick ask and move on. He admired efficiency.

"Now, as we've discussed, we want someone minimally invasive. Hands off. I have options for—"

He put up a hand. "There's no need to discuss this further."

My heart started to race, and my lungs fought for air. No. He could not give up. "Look, we're on the same page about not looking to sell. It's the family company, Becks Incorporated. But we have hundreds of employees to consider, and we have to fight. We can't just let all of this fall apart."

There was another part I didn't say out loud. The truth of it all was that he had over-gambled, over-expanded. And honestly, I'd started digging and delving into areas that he didn't have the expertise on. We were better when we were small. Agile. There were departments that were definitely overspending. And the sales team needed to be reined in. But we could do this. We just had to be smarter. I couldn't let him sell us off piecemeal. For starters, everyone would lose their jobs. Some of my team had been with me since just after college. They'd bet on me. They deserved to have me fight for them.

And then there was the obvious problem of parts of my software falling into the wrong hands. Artificial Intelligence had so many applications. Some of it could be used to do amazing things, but some of it could be used to do shitty things. Even something like facial recognition was a hot-button topic because of how those models had been built and who was building them.

I'd only ever wanted to help people. But there were people like Bronson Jacobson who only cared about his pockets. And I would die before I'd just lay down and hand my life's work to him.

We couldn't just give up. "There are things we could do. I've still got some meeting with VC's coming. I know there are some partnerships. I spoke to Wexler and Co.'s CEO; they would love to do a partnership and license my software. We have options. I just need a little time. Selling is ridiculous. You haven't even tried yet. I mean, *really* tried."

He shook his head. But before he could speak, there was a knock at the door. "At last," he muttered.

I glanced toward the door. "What are you talking about?"

He didn't answer me but instead called out, "Come."

Teresa, my father's executive assistant, opened the door. "Sir, Gwen, Mr. Price is here to see you."

My stomach fluttered at his name. Hell, what was wrong with me? The Ice King made the long-dead butterflies come to life. I really was fucked in the head.

He was the last kind of man I needed. The kind I'd learned not to trust. The kind of man who could eviscerate me and my life.

But, like a fool, ever since the benefit a few nights ago, I couldn't get him out of my head. That slight upturn to his lips just at the corner, it wasn't a smile. Because God help you when he actually did smile. The damn thing was lethal.

But never mind what he did to the butterflies in my stomach. What the hell was he doing here?

My father pushed to his feet and straightened his tie. Why the hell was he trying to impress Atticus Price?

You know why.

We needed investors, but Pendragon Tech? They were notorious for their acquisitions. Carve up and sell off. Fire everybody.

My stomach roiled. I had to find another investor. His company could fix everything for my father, but what would that mean to my employees? My people?

Maybe I was over reacting. Maybe there was another reason he was here. But one glance at my father told me otherwise. "You can't be serious," I said flatly.

My father ignored me, going to meet Atticus. But Atticus's gaze was on me, and the same crackling sizzle I'd felt the other night came back like a blast of wind.

You know better.

I knew better.

Men like him are dangerous.

Men like him *were* dangerous.

But still, there I was, like a moth being pulled to the flame.

Well, this moth would rather cut off her own wings than fly into that fire. But there he was in all his beautiful glory while the sizzling prickle danced down my spine. How could someone so strikingly handsome have the absolute warmth of an arctic penguin? Rigid as stone and zero heartbeat.

Yeah, well, at least he doesn't sparkle like a damn vampire anymore.

My lips twitched, and I bit the inside of my cheek. Unfortunately, he seemed to notice that, and he cocked his head slightly, the corner of his lips lifting as he watched me. "Ms. Becker. We meet again, Gwenyth."

"It's actually *Christin*-Becker."

My father stiffened, and I internally danced my little dance of victory. Dad couldn't stand it that Morgan and I had hyphenated surnames, but our mother had insisted. But still, I watched, stricken, as the two of them shook hands. What was he doing here? Wasn't it enough that he'd barged into my dreams? Wasn't it enough that I hadn't been able to stop thinking about him?

You never should have touched him.

No, I shouldn't have. But there he'd been, dusted in glitter. It wasn't intentional, honestly.

And of course, my father, being my father, started off trying to unsettle him. Which I appreciated because he was sure as shit unsettling me. "Let's hope you have something interesting to say, Price."

My gaze swiveled between the two of them, and then the sickening realization hit. My father was selling research and development to him. "Dad, you can't be serious."

"That's enough, Gwen."

"Dad—"

He cut me off. "Leave us. We have *actual* work to do."

I prayed for a sign that my father was joking, that maybe he was just humoring Atticus, but he wasn't.

"Dad?" I tried to find a hint of the father I had known once. The one who had been kind and listened. That man had vanished the moment my mother got sick.

"I run this company, Gwen, and have done so for far longer than you've been alive. I make the decisions."

Atticus's assessing gaze met mine. There was something there. It looked like fury. But why would he be angry at me? I hadn't even done anything yet.

And just what do you plan on doing with him?

Not the point.

"Dad, R&D is *my* department. Before we were your R&D, it was my startup. You can't just expect me to stand by idly while you sell us off."

"I can and I do. I'm the CEO of Becks Incorporated. I make this decision."

Our guest however, inclined his head toward the couch in the corner and nodded at me. "Why don't you join us, Gwen?"

For someone giving Arctic vibes, there was a sizzling heat to his voice. Something to scorch and give you an ice burn all at the same time. My father clearly hadn't intended for me to join their meeting, but Atticus didn't budge and then gestured an arm out for me to take a seat on the couch before he would sit. As if this was *his* office. I watched my father's eyes go wide, and I had to bite back a smile. Well, well, wasn't Atticus Price interesting? If he could ruin Dad's day, then I wanted to watch.

I took the corner by the window, which put me between the two of them as they took their seats. When Atticus sat, his gaze anchored my father and then swung onto me. "So you're the one behind the algorithm."

It was a statement, not a question. "Yes, why?"

If I was expecting an answer, I'd be waiting a long damn time because all he did was give me a curt nod as his intense stare drank me in. That was the only way to describe it. He watched me like I was the answer to a question he was trying to figure out. His brow lifted ever so slightly, and because I was a masochist and had become a connoisseur of his mouth, I watched as he pressed his lips ever so slightly together. "That is interesting."

My father's harsh voice snapped the cord of tension tightening between us. "There is no need for Gwen to be here."

I clamped my jaw tight. We needed an out. Just not this out. Maybe I needed to pray to the tech gods of rich and ethical investors. "We're not for sale."

My father let out a harsh chuckle. "Sorry to break it to you, Gwen, but everything is on the table providing the deal is good. Because let's face it, Bronson Jacobson is the other option."

My gut twisted. I would put the algorithm up on an open source website before I'd let Jacobson have it. I didn't care if he alone could save my father's company from his excesses. "There is no way in hell I'm letting you sell off all my work to Jacobson."

My unlikely ally spoke up. "Look, Jacobson perhaps is a better fit in some regards, but Pendragon is moving into new technologies, and your software has many applications. The base code allows for raid AI learning, and those models, if applied in the right way, could be extraordinarily useful in the energy space. And before Gwen interjects, because I can see it on her face right now."

"Look, I hear you, but the only way this works for me is if you keep my whole tram and they keep their salaries."

Cocking his head, he studied me. "That's open to negotiation."

"Negotiation? That's not enough. I need to take care of them."

"Like I said, everything is on the table. There's opportunity for movement and growth for those we retain. It's a generous offer. But we need to access the division. But don't worry. For those we keep, they will get the full benefit of everything Pendragon has to offer, retention bonuses as well as the standard benefits, of course."

My blood ran cold. That *was* a good deal...for those he retained. But how many would that be? Not to mention, he sounded like it was a forgone conclusion. I hadn't agreed to anything. That was not the deal my father and I had made when I came to work with him four years ago.

Four years ago, there was money.

Four years ago, I signed on the dotted line.

I had, but I hadn't expected this. I hadn't anticipated my father pulling the rug from under me. I wasn't ready to give up yet. I just needed more time. "You can't be serious, Dad." I could feel my blood pressure rising. "You keep saying how this is a family company. Well, he is not family."

My father's cold anger whipped out like icicles toward me. "Gwen, that is enough!"

His shout was the splash of cold water I'd needed. Shit. I was fucking losing it.

Of course, I was fucking losing it. I was watching my life's work filter through my fingers like water. "Dad—"

"You are done here."

Ice-cold bricks of shame pelted my skin as I grabbed my laptop and stood. There was nothing left to do but stand and let my failure flow out of me as I walked away, leaving my father to make a deal with Atticus Price.

28

CHAPTER 4

ATTICUS

My skin tingled and prickled as she walked out.

Fuck me.

The other night had *not* been a fluke. Being this close to her, I just kept looking at her skin and wanting to touch it. She looked so soft. Unfortunately, judging by how bad this meeting just went down, she had not been expecting to see me. Which was bad news.

"I gather not everyone is on board with the sale?" I asked her father.

He waved me off. "My daughter is prone to hysterics. But I hope that doesn't influence your interest in purchasing our R&D arm."

"No, of course. Pendragon is serious. The terms are favorable. I have already sent them over."

He lifted a brow. "There's just one thing. The other night, we spoke of partnership and how important it is."

"Of course."

"Well, I was serious about that. Becks has been a family business for two generations now. I don't intend for that to change."

"Well, of course we would leave your daughter in place. And give you access to her software as needed. It's not like we're acquiring all of Becks."

"No, you don't understand. I don't just want an investment. I want a *true* partnership. While we could sell off the R&D arm, it's more like a merger of sorts."

I lifted a brow and sat back. My gut tried to warn me. Becker was slippery. And he thought he was slick enough to get one over on me.

"Why don't you tell me what you're thinking," I said through clenched teeth.

"Since Becks Inc. has always been a family business, we need to keep it that way. And so, I'd like to make you a proposition."

"If you want to negotiate more for favorable terms, like how much longer we'll keep the employees, we can discuss that. I, however, want *all* of the technology. No negotiating behind my back with Jacobson. It's a nonstarter. No games."

"Absolutely. No games. I'm a man of my word. And I think you're a man of yours."

He was up to something. Something I knew I wasn't going to like.

"I'm so glad we're in agreement, because the only way I'm going to let any part of Becks go is if we keep it in the family."

A tingle of alarm on my scalp had me lifting my brow and watching him closely. "Exactly what do you mean by that?"

"What I mean is, in order for me to let R&D go, you're going to marry my daughter. And of course, fulfill all of the terms you set forth. Obviously, you would also provide her with a generous prenuptial agreement for a ten-year term."

I did the only thing I could. I laughed. "Not happening."

He sat back again. "In that case, I think I'll go and see what kind of deal I can make with Jacobson."

The fucker. I knew the powerplay he was trying to make. And considering the man was up against the wall, he had no bargaining power other than the threat of making a deal with my nemesis. However, I did remember something my father had always said. *Always be warier of a caged man than a free one. There's no telling what they'll do for their freedom.* And it seemed that James Becker was willing to bargain with his daughter.

I thought back to the way Gwen had walked out. Then I remembered our first meeting on the balcony, the softness of her skin and the slice of her tongue.

You don't want to fucking get married. There is no goddamn way.

A bitter scent lingered in the air. Maybe this was why Micah hadn't wanted to come along.

"I'm not getting married."

"Then no deal. Jacobson is giving me the same offer. It's the only way we're going to sell. I would rather go bankrupt and lose everything than to let someone who is not family have any part of Becks. I care about the family legacy continuing, and this is how it happens. If you want my company, you marry my daughter. It's as easy as that."

My initial flash of fury morphed. It would be that easy, and she would be mine. I'd never wanted to be married, knowing what kind of trap marriage was. A kind of death sentence to your soul.

But this way you can have her.

I narrowed my eyes. "You have a deal."

Becker flashed a grin at me. "Excellent. Why don't you come by the house tonight? We'll have drinks and have this conversation with my daughter, civilized-like. Then you can get to know her better. See if a union suits."

James Becker thought he was getting the better end of this deal. But I hadn't even known that she came with it. He had no idea what he had, and he was willing to give it all away.

And I was just ruthless enough to take it.

CHAPTER 5
GWEN

I'D STEWED ALL DAY, AND I STILL HADN'T FOUND A WAY TO AVOID A SALE. Not to mention my father had been conveniently busy and couldn't find a time to meet with me. Despite things being strained between us, I could sometimes get him to listen.

Well, I had a chance to make him listen tonight. Family night. Friday night tradition. I hoped that tonight, maybe I could get my point across. I had to try. I couldn't let him sell to Jacobson. Not Atticus Price either. If he'd just give me more time, I could find a way out of this.

I used my key and stepped in. The aroma of baking hit my nostrils quickly. Had Clarissa actually cooked today? Ariella had been my parents' housekeeper and cook since I was little. She'd really been crushed when Mom died and had kept looking after Dad, me, and Morgan. She continued with Dad and Morgan when I left for school and stayed on when Clarissa married my father. But Fridays were her day off. Dad figured Clarissa could manage.

The soft click of my shoes on the marble made me smile. As a kid, I used to put on Mom's heels and clomp all the way down the stairs just to hit the marble so I could make that *click-clack* sound that she always made when she was getting ready to go out with my father. The only thing that had really changed at my childhood home was some of the artwork. Most of the paintings Mom had used to decorate were still up, but Clarissa had replaced a few of them. There were more family photos with Clarissa in them these days, but there were still some with my mom as well.

I'd never stopped to think about how that might affect Clarissa. She had to squeeze herself into a home that was already so established. But I knew Dad. He was never leaving this house. And in some ways, I was happy about that. After all, this was my home.

It was one of the townhouses nestled in the Upper East Side, and it had been one of those idyllic childhoods.

It was always bittersweet coming home. Memories of my mother were everywhere.

Dad and Clarissa were married when Morgan was still in high school, so that had been my main concern. But she loved my sister. To be fair, *everyone* loved Morgan. But then again, Morgan was sweet and always had a smile for everyone, so she was easy to love.

And then there was me. "I'm here. Anyone around?" I called out.

"I'm in here," came a voice from the dining room.

I followed the sound to where my stepmother set places for dinner.

I did a brief count. "Is someone joining us?" I asked as I brought the utensils to help. Normally, Friday nights were drinks and appetizers, then we headed out to our own plans. After I set the table, I went over to the bar to make drinks.

I would have a spritzer of some sort. Morgan would have something non-alcoholic, and my father would grill us about our lives.

And honestly, you had better have something interesting to say about some new development you'd made, or there would be judgment.

I could still remember when Mom was alive. I'd been so proud of myself one day, having just seen my grades on our school software platform. I'd gotten straight A's. Four A pluses, and one A in History. A ninety-eight. And when I'd proudly announced to my parents that I'd gotten straight A's, my father had insisted I recount my actual scores.

There was no point in lying because he would see it eventually. And so, I sat there and told him about the four A pluses and one A. He asked me what my numerical score was, and I told him.

My hands still got slick at the memory. He'd put his scotch down and glowered at me. "What happened to the two points?"

That one question encapsulated our whole relationship. In a world where I was winning, I was also failing.

He'd spent the rest of that evening lecturing me about how I had to work twice as hard to be seen as half as good. And a ninety-eight wouldn't cut it. I had cried, of course, which made it worse. And then he said no child of his was mediocre.

Naturally, I had spent my whole life trying to prove him right. And now he was selling me off. I tried to shake it off and returned Clarissa's smile. Apparently, she'd been speaking and I had gotten lost in memories. "Yes, your father invited someone."

"So, we are stuck for dinner then?"

Her smile was soft and held the weight of understanding. "I know. Knowing you, you'll probably be going back to the office, eager to get out of here. Honestly, hon, you work too hard. You need to make room in your life for other things like you used to." I knew she cared. I did. But I really hated being told to get a life.

"I hear you, and I appreciate it. I'm not sure how you stay married to him. And I mean that in the best possible way."

The subject change was automatic and deliberate. She gave me an understanding nod, then squeezed my hand. I glanced at her tanned skin as she squeezed. Her ring blinked again in the light of the chandelier, and my gut twisted. Her ring. It was so similar to my mother's. And in so many ways, Clarissa was similar to her too. Just a less vibrant version.

"Who's coming to dinner besides Morgan?"

"You know your father. He didn't tell me anything except that I needed to prepare."

Just as I finished helping Clarissa set the table my phone rang, and I excused myself to take it in the sunroom.

"Hello, this is Gwen."

"Hi Gwen, it's Dr. Hamann from Hearts and Hope."

"Oh, how are you? I saw the initial donation numbers from the benefit. They were good. We were up from the last two events by three percent."

"Yeah, about that. There's been a development."

My stomach sank. It was bad enough that Becks could no longer put on the benefit. I couldn't take it if the organization struggled as a result. "Oh no."

"No, no, it's good. I mean you did it, so you would know. I just never imagined."

I frowned, confusion edging out concern for dominance. "Doctor Hamann, I'm sorry, but I have no idea what you're talking about."

There was a long pregnant pause. "What? Are you sure? We have a five million dollar donation made in your name."

My breath caught in my throat. For precious seconds no air made it in or out. "What? From who?"

"It looks like the payment came from Pendragon Charities. They made it in your name. The funds cleared this morning. I thought you knew."

Fucking Atticus Price.

"I don't know what to say."

The doctor laughed. "Honestly, neither do I. Except, thank you. A donation like this will allow us to continue the work we do for years. It's a little overwhelming. But we're grateful."

Fuck me. Why would he do that? Especially after I'd insulted him.

Do you want him to take it back?

No. Of course not. But hell, five million dollars? That was... That was mind blowing and reckless.

"Well, I'm glad the money can do some good. I will find Mr. Price and thank him."

After I hung up with her, I stared at my phone. How the hell did one even go about finding a billionaire to say thank you for something like this? I didn't ask for this, but like hell was I going to turn it down. Hearts and Hope could use it.

A nearly hysterical laugh escaped my lips. Holy shit. Maybe I needed to insult billionaires more often. Maybe I could save my company that way.

The doorbell rang, and Clarissa called out, "Gwen, darling, do you mind getting that?"

"Sure." I stuffed a canapé into my mouth and started toward the door. I wished I had dressed better. Dad would likely have something to say about my outfit. I had gone to my apartment and changed into slim-fit, dark-washed jeans and a mustard-colored crop-top sweater, and had gone casual. I still had on perfume and earrings, because if I didn't, Dad would be on my back.

How do you expect anyone to respect you if you don't respect yourself and dress accordingly?

I rolled my eyes as I strode for the door. Our butler, Marcus, was also headed that way, and I gave him a shake of my head. "I got it."

"Yes, miss." The short, pudgy man had been with my family long before Mom died. He looked exactly the same. Maybe his middle was getting just a little bit wider, but he was still ruddy-faced with a patch of wiry white hair on his head that was slightly unkempt. I jogged up the three steps to the vestibule and swung the door open, freezing stock-still when I saw who stood on the other side.

Nepo baby himself.

A prickle of alarm chirped over my skin with a tingle and a hint of bite. "What are you doing here?"

"Aren't you hospitable?" Atticus Price proffered a bottle of wine. "Your father invited me."

I ignored the bottle. "We don't have anything to discuss."

There was that uptilt of his lips again. "You might want to speak with your father about that."

I crossed my arms and lifted my chin. "What's that supposed to mean?"

He lifted a brow, assessing me. "I suppose it means you will find out soon enough."

"You know I'll fight this sale, right?"

You're supposed to be saying thank you, remember?

"Somehow, I expect nothing less."

"Also, thank you for the Hearts and Hope donation. I'm not going to fight that one because they need the money. But you shouldn't have done that. It's not going to make me any more amenable to a sale."

His eyes darkened and the right corner of his lips tipped up. "I would expect nothing less."

I stepped back to allow him in, and this time he managed to hand off the wine.

The way his intense green gaze met mine, I felt stripped. Like he could truly see me deep down, and heat suffused my body.

"About this morning..." my voice trailed.

He lifted an insolent brow. "It would be a disappointment if you offered an apology or explanation for it."

I snapped my jaw shut. I wasn't sure what was worse; that he was letting me off without having to explain myself or that he chided me for attempting to apologize.

"Fine. Follow me then."

As his gaze flicked over my body once more, leaving scorch marks wherever it landed, I stopped and lifted my brow, letting him look his fill. When his eyes lifted back up to mine, he smiled at me. Unabashedly. And it was worse than the other night.

This one was a real smile. Not willful. Not sardonic. Not a half-smile. It was a full-on grin, and he was beautiful. Devastatingly beautiful.

Like this man smiling could cause an international incident. If there was a Helen of Troy of dudes, it was him. And like a fool, all I could do was stand there and gawk.

"Are you looking your fill too?"

And that snapped me right out of it. "No, of course not. I'm just making sure you're done. Let's get this over with."

I could have sworn I heard him chuckle behind me as I led him into the dining room and introduced him to Clarissa, who was a gracious hostess as always. She had a way of making everyone feel welcome, and it was always odd having her try and make me feel welcome in my own home, especially when I held so many memories of my mother here.

Heading to the bar, I asked Atticus, "What are you drinking?"

"Whatever you're having."

"Oh, I barely drink at these things. Best to have my wits about me with Dad. You should feel free."

He cocked his head ever so slightly as if asking a question he didn't know he needed to formulate yet. "Surprise me."

I stood back, assessing him. "There's something about you that screams old-fashioned. But I feel like you wouldn't want to be quite so trite. You would want to spin it. Maybe something that's a little more elegant and unique, right? Let me guess, Vieux Carré?"

His eyes widened ever so slightly in surprise, and I shrugged. "Let's just say I can read people. I have a lot of experience with my father's business associates and the drinks they order."

"And what does the Vieux Carré say about me?" His voice was like mellow smoke.

I could have been biting and eviscerating, but I chose diplomacy. "It says you're discerning. You want to be a little different, yet still traditional. Or you want to be a pain in the ass and have somebody dare to question you. Or maybe you just like Cognac."

And there it was again, a quick smile, sending my stomach into flips.

Get yourself together. He's buying out your company. You will not find this man attractive. This is not what we need today or any day, because we do not lust after toxic men. That's not what we do. We know better.

While I made his drink, Morgan came skipping in. "Hey, Clarissa, do you think we—" My sister stopped short. "Oh, who do we have here?"

I turned to her and wrapped an arm around her waist as she gave me a smothering kiss on my cheek. "Morgan, this is Atticus Price. He's Dad's guest tonight."

My sister groaned, throwing her head back, almost tilting her whole body into a back bend. Morgan was petite. Just barely over five-foot-two. Light brown skin that usually had people asking if she was Dominican. She looked every bit the cheerleader she'd been. Glossy dark hair, silk-pressed to the gods and styled in elegant curls and soft waves down her back. Her makeup was flawless, and she looked like she belonged in some kind of wealthy TV reality show for the cute, young, and adorable. Basically, she was tiny Black Barbie.

She went over and shook Atticus's hand and gave him a dazzling grin. "Welcome, Mr. Price. I hope my sister has been a charming hostess."

He took her hand into his. "I think you and I both know your sister better than that. It's a pleasure to meet you." His voice was low, mellow. And his eyes softened when he looked at her.

I gritted my teeth and continued making his drink. And yes, I may have slammed in an ice cube or two as I made it, but honestly, it's not that I was jealous of Morgan. I wasn't. I loved my sister. She was my favorite person on earth. There were days when just her laughter could brighten everything. She had Mom's laugh. But somehow, seeing Atticus looking at her with doe eyes made me want to hurl his glass across the room. Instead, I turned and handed him his drink.

He raised the glass to me and my spritzer, then took a sip. He closed his eyes and gave a small hum of appreciation.

And yes, I was ashamed to admit it. My pussy clenched.

But again, not my fault. Apparently, I did like toxic men, but because I was a fool, I didn't seem to know better.

"You did something odd to the Vieux Carré."

"You'll never know," I taunted.

He eyed the contents of his glass dubiously. "You don't hate me enough to poison me, right?"

I winked. "Again, you'll never know until it's too late."

He shrugged. "Well, beautiful company and a good drink. There are worse ways to die."

I rolled my eyes and noticed Morgan's gaze skipping between the two of us, and then back to Clarissa, who was also staring at me like I'd grown a third head. Luckily, the doorbell rang again and relieved some of the tension. Morgan ran to get it just as Clarissa started chatting with Atticus about the history of the house. I took a long gulp of my spritzer while silently wishing for something stronger. There was no way I was going to make it through tonight.

Though, when I heard a familiar bickering, I calmed down a little bit.

At least the night wasn't a total wash. Morgan's voice piped up. "It's Friday night. Shouldn't you be out with one of your super-model girlfriends?"

"If you're jealous, Morgan, just say that. You could go out with me, but then, I like my balls attached to me when I wake up in the morning, not in your hands. So that's a no-thank-you for me."

My sister snorted a laugh. "You wish I would get close enough to grab your balls."

Clarissa gasped. "Children."

Both Morgan and Lance straightened up immediately as they rounded the corner, casting sheepish looks at Clarissa.

I grinned at Lance. "Hey, I was just going to text you. Looks like dinner might go long tonight. I think we're eating here."

He gave me a wide grin. "No worries. I can adjust plans for my favorite person in the world. I will always give you a rain check. Unless it's Szechuan, because my poor tastebuds can't handle it."

"Your inability to handle spice is not my fault."

He rolled his eyes and then caught sight of Atticus and suddenly straightened. "Oh, you're Atticus Price."

Atticus cocked his head. His gaze slid to me again and then back to Lance. "You'll forgive me, please. I'm at a disadvantage. Who are you?"

Lance stepped forward while I turned to make his old-fashioned. "I'm Lance. Lance Lakewood."

"Lakewood?"

Lance shrugged with a sigh. "Yes. *Those* Lakewoods, unfortunately."

I always found it interesting how he went ahead and acknowledged the Lakewood name but still put distance between them and himself. His father and grandfather were business legends.

They were horrified when Lance chose my startup instead of the family business.

The two of them shook hands for what looked like a second too long. But then Lance grinned and Atticus clapped him on the shoulder. That was Lance though. Forever good-natured. Except when it came to my sister. I swear to God, I wished the two people I loved the most in the world would figure out how on earth to get along better.

Morgan purposely bumped into him as she walked by, then the two of them were squabbling again as usual. When I handed Lance his drink, he gave Atticus's drink a nod. "Old Fashioned too? Great taste, I see."

Atticus's smile wasn't a real one. I knew immediately. He was assessing him. Like Lance was somehow prey. It didn't escape me that Atticus didn't correct him about his drink either.

Lance tried to make conversation with Atticus, but Atticus wasn't having it. "Did Mr. Becker invite you?"

When Atticus just swirled his glass around, I jumped in to answer. "Yes, apparently Dad invited him. But I hoped he wouldn't be staying."

Atticus laughed. "So you keep saying."

I had to look away before he liquefied my insides with those wintergreen eyes. I was so focused on Atticus that I didn't even hear my father come in.

"Oh, everyone's here."

Clarissa sidled up to him. "Yes, love. Would you like to sit in here or head out to the living room for a moment?"

CHAPTER 5

My dad inclined his head toward the living room. "Let's take our drinks into the sitting room. Clarissa, darling, if you can check on our dinner and let me know when we're ready?"

Her smile was soft, and she nodded as she trailed off into the kitchen as if he hadn't just dismissed her. I scowled after her and turned my gaze to my father. "Dad, she's not the housekeeper. She's your wife. Maybe she wanted to have a drink and sit down too."

Dad just waved his hand. "You know Clarissa. She's fine. She doesn't need a drink."

How did he not see the way he treated her?

Dad directed Atticus toward one of the leather chairs as Clarissa handed him a drink. Lance remained standing, lounging in the door frame. Dad took his position in the center of the high-backed chair, and Morgan and I chose the couch. Dad took a sip of his drink and then spoke. "Well, I'm sure everyone is wondering why I invited Atticus here. Obviously, Morgan and Gwen have to be here every Friday. Lance, you're here for a specific reason."

"Sir?"

I could see Lance had no idea why he was here. Sure, he accompanied me to Friday night cocktails sometimes, but he wasn't usually in the picture unless we were going out and I dragged him along as a buffer. Dad actually really liked Lance, so he was a great buffer when I needed him. "Lance, you're here from a contract perspective. You'll need to work with our lawyers to work out the details."

"Okay. Why don't you go ahead and give me some framing for what we need contracts for?"

"Well, Mr. Price and I met this morning to discuss the possibility of selling a portion of Becks Incorporated."

I shook my head. "Dad—"

My father shook his head. "I've already made my decision. But there's one more caveat for me agreeing to sell."

The train is here.

It had been barreling down for weeks, months, years. I had been hoping against hope that I'd be able to do something. "Dad, you can't possibly—"

My father, much like he'd done in our meeting that morning, held up a hand and cut me off. "I can, and I will. The caveat is, I'm not looking for an outright sell. I'm loath to break up my company, however, I'd be far more comfortable if we kept things in the family."

What the hell did he mean by that?

He continued. "Because of that, we're going to have R&D become a subsidiary of Pendragon. As part of the package, Atticus is going to marry my daughter, Morgan."

Holy shit. My stomach bottomed out.

Pan-de-mo-ne-um.

Atticus cursed. Lance choked out a laugh. The color leached out of Morgan's face. She opened her mouth to speak, but all that came out was a stuttering, "I-I-I—" and then silence. Her hand fluttered to her throat as she tried to talk, but nothing more came out.

No! Not again. I'd worked for a year and then some to bring Morgan back to herself after Mom's death. I wasn't letting him sell her off to the highest bidder. I shoved to my feet. "What? You cannot do this. Morgan is too young. And she can't get married to him. He's a pompous ass."

Atticus lifted a brow. "There you go, complimenting me again."

Morgan's voice was timid and pleading. "Dad, I'm only eighteen. It's one thing that you're trying to get me to date someone, but marry? I'm not ready to get married."

My father ignored her. "Nonsense. You can marry him just as easily as you can marry anyone else. You'll obviously have a period of getting to know each other as we finalize the details, and after, you can go on a vacation or something."

I couldn't let him do this. "Dad, you can't be serious. That's not how it works. Morgan deserves better than that."

My sister stood next to me. "Thank you." She turned her attention to Atticus. "No offense, but I don't want to marry you."

Atticus choked out a laugh. "None taken. I don't want to marry you either."

Dad frowned. "You were open to it this morning."

Atticus placed his drink on the table in front of him and then sat back, sprawling as much as he could in the club chair. "There's been a misunderstanding."

My father pushed to his feet. "Then what the hell are we doing here? You know I'll just go to Jacobson."

Fuck. Pendragon was bad, but Jacobson was a million times worse. I would die if I went to Jacobson. I couldn't let him do that. I couldn't let Atticus marry my sister either. Morgan was only eighteen. She had her whole life in front of her. And I didn't want to chain her in a loveless marriage. Jesus Christ. I stepped in front of my father. "No, wait. I'll do it. I'll marry him. Just not Morgan."

My father stared at me. "What? That is not the deal. You're no bargaining chip. Morgan—"

"That is enough!" Atticus's deep timbre was enough to settle the room in a blanket of tension. He sat forward and drained his drink then stood. "If Gwen wants to get to take her sister's place, I'm amenable."

Amenable? I mean thank God he agreed. I guess. But still.

A hush fell over the room. Nervously, I shifted on my feet and cleared my throat. "Fine. But we're keeping my entire team. And I mean *every* last person. No salary or benefit cuts. And yearly retention bonuses commiserate with their salaries." This was insane. I was flying by the seat of my pants. But if I could protect everyone and keep Morgan free, then I would. "These are the terms for our fake marriage. Name only. We can do that. That way we keep our lives separate, and our relationships, and my team doesn't split."

And God, I loved Lance down to the fiber of my bones because he jumped right in there. "Yes, because Gwen and I—"

Atticus glanced at him and said evenly, "No."

"Excuse me?" I breathed.

Atticus eyed Lance up and down before he turned his attention to me. "I agree to your terms with one caveat. And let me be clear so there is no misunderstanding. This union will be more than just on paper. It is *very* much real."

I laughed nervously. "You must be insane."

Morgan, supposedly now off the chopping block, stared at my father. "Dad, you cannot do this. You can't make her marry him."

Dad laughed. "Of course, he's not going to marry her. He's going to marry *you*."

This was like a game of Who's on First. Atticus just shook his head. "You heard the woman. It's Gwen, or we have no deal."

CHAPTER 6
GWEN

"I didn't need you to do that," Morgan said.

I laid back on her plush Yves Delorme comforter and stared up at her coffered ceiling with its neutral muted color and recessed lighting. I could have been in a hotel bed for all I knew.

"I know I didn't need to do that. I just opened my mouth and was desperate for *you* not to have to do it. That's why I said the only thing I could think of."

The outburst in the living room had gone over with a dead weight. Dinner had been a stilted, awkward affair. The whole time, Atticus Price seemed perfectly comfortable. He didn't seem to notice at all. He sat right next to me, and every now and then his knee would graze mine. Like he knew what he was doing. Purposely driving me insane.

Focus.

Morgan was saying something that I only caught the end of. "Obviously, you're not going to marry him."

"Trust me, I'm looking for other ways out. Maybe if I can buy some time, I won't have to marry him. But honestly, yes, it was impulsive, and I just said the next best thing so that you didn't have to do it."

My sister sighed and then plopped on the bed next to me. "Gwen, I love you. You are my big sister and my protector. I know it sucks that Mom passed away, but Jesus, you do not have to protect me all the time."

I turned my head to face her. "I saw you Morgan. And I'm sorry, but just hearing you stutter and trying to talk. I don't want you to regress."

She threw up her hands. "I was shocked. And angry. And yes a little scared and panicked. But you hear me, right? I'm talking just fine. I'm strong now. Mostly due to you. You didn't have to do this."

"Do you *want* to marry Atticus Price?"

I didn't know why, but my stomach knotted as I asked the question. What if she said yes?

But Morgan pulled a face, squinching her lips and nose and squeezing her eyes tight. "No, fuck no. I don't even know the guy. I mean, look, he's hot in that kind of cold, frigid way. He may have all the requisite equipment for fun, but the man is giving me robot vibes. I don't think he even knows where the clit is."

I coughed a laugh. "Oh my God, Morgan. To me, he's giving Kama Sutra vibes." How could she not see it? The roiling heat beneath the icy surface. The man practically steamed.

"What?" Her brows rose to her hairline. "You've got to be kidding. I'm telling you, after Jason last year, I need someone who knows where it is. My friends helped with sex toys, but I want a man who knows how to go down and deliver an orgasm."

I sighed. "First of all, come to your sister for that. I've been at this longer. I have better sex toys. And second, ugh, I'm so sad for you. He wasn't into taking directions?"

"No. Every time I said, 'Hey, why don't we take this slow,' he would proceed to jackhammer my poor vag into submission."

I winced. "Shit. Sorry."

"It's fine. What those girls on social media are talking about, the cinnamon rolls who know how to go down, I weep with jealousy. And Atticus Price does not look like he's even heard of oral. So what the hell are you going to do about sex?"

I tried not to think about it. "Well, I'm certainly not going to fuck him, okay?"

Lies.

"You better not. He probably goes at it like a robot."

And then Morgan made robot arms and proceeded to wave them around and use a monotone voice. "I shall fuck you now."

Despite myself, I laughed. "Oh my God, Morgan."

She giggled. "What? You know I'm right. That's probably what it's like."

"I mean, the man is good looking and has models following him around. He must have *some* ability. Right?"

"Do you even want to risk finding out by marrying the guy? Because he's doing that whole 'this is not just a marriage-on-paper thing,' and that is concerning."

I really wished he hadn't said that, because that part had been rattling around my brain ever since. No way he meant that.

My sister watched me closely then softened her tone. "You didn't have to jump in and save me. I would have been okay."

I shook my head. "No, you wouldn't have been."

Morgan bit her lip. "Sooner or later, I'm going to have to learn to save myself."

I reached over and palmed her cheek. "I'm your big sister. If I don't save you, who will?"

"Yeah well, sometimes I think the price is too great." She grabbed my hand. "I didn't ask you to do this."

"You didn't need to. What Dad is trying to do is wrong. You and I both know that, okay? If this buys you a little time, then great. We'll get you back in school, and in less than a year, you'll have your trust fund and you won't depend on Dad anymore. I just have to keep him from trying to marry you off until then."

"I swear, he thinks it's the 1800s or something."

"Dad wants what he wants when he wants it. To hell if any of us care."

"You're really going to do this? You're going to marry him? You don't even know him."

I bit my lip. She was right. I didn't know anything about Atticus Price other than he made me unsettled and mildly irritated.

And oh yeah, he was rich enough to buy my company and me with it. It just didn't bode well for me.

"Look, my only concern is you and my employees. My whole Rebel Tech team. When Dad insisted on folding us in and developing us, letting us be the R&D arm of the company, I thought that was the best thing on earth. But I was wrong, obviously."

"I can't believe he's doing this to you."

"He's been making shit decision after shit decision for years now. I just didn't think he would bargain with me. But don't worry about it, Morgan. The most important thing is that *you* don't have to marry someone random."

"Yeah, but *you* do."

"Don't worry about me. I have my ways. Besides, a few weeks working with me and my company, and he will be running for the hills. I have been told that I am quite the handful."

My sister narrowed her gaze on me. "You've been told that by pricks. You are loyal, beautiful, wickedly smart, and funny. Anyone who doesn't see that doesn't deserve you. *He* doesn't deserve you."

"Relax, Morgan. This will be on paper only. I have it under control."

"If you say so. I just don't want you hurt again after what happened two years ago."

I forced the bile down at the memory. "I do say so. I am never, ever going to fall for a man like that again."

CHAPTER 7
GWEN

It didn't take five minutes for Lance to call me after leaving my parents' house.

My apartment was on 57th Street, technically Midtown East, even though my stepmother still insisted on telling everyone that I lived on the Upper East Side. I had opted to walk the fifteen blocks home to clear my head.

What the fuck was that? One moment I'd been standing there, with my drink in my hand, ready and willing to pitch a new venture capital firm, and the next, my father was telling me that he was marrying Morgan off to Atticus fucking Price. The Ice King of New York.

And then I pulled a Katniss Everdeen and volunteered as tribute. What the fuck was I thinking?

I narrowly avoided a puddle as I passed a gelato shop on the corner just as my phone rang. "Hey, Lance."

"What the fuck, Gwen?"

Leave it to my bestie to get to the point. "I fucking know."

"Your father has lost it. There is no way you can marry this guy. I think your best bet is finding another relationship to be in, posthaste."

I jumped back to avoid a drunk guy who was clamoring out of a restaurant and then only narrowly avoided the spray from a yellow cab splashing brown water onto the sidewalk as I crossed.

"You heard him. I don't think that's possible. Besides, if I were in another relationship, that would mean Morgan was back on the table. She can't do this. Not with a guy like that."

"And you can? I mean, what's wrong with the guy that he needs a setup anyway?"

"You know how it is better than most. New York social life. Families do business together for so long that it's completely normal for them to try and set each other up."

"Uh, yeah. A century ago maybe," he scoffed.

"Given how all this has happened, it makes me really wonder about my father and my mother. They were complete opposites."

"It doesn't matter. And I think you don't give Morgan enough credit. She can give that man a run for his money. Your sister is mean. She's tougher than she looks. She finds a way to take a piece of me every time she sees me."

"Honestly, how the two people I love most in my life cannot get along is beyond me. The two of you are like oil and water."

"Your sister hates me. The feeling is mutual. She's not my favorite person. But that's okay, because I love you. And let's get back to the more important thing; you are falling on your sword right now. And you can't do that. You can't marry him. He's cold. Clearly ruthless. And I wasn't going to say anything about it in front of him, but there are rumors. Some say Pendragon is unethical. There have been rumblings and murmurs about Pendragon Tech for years. And his father... Well, he most certainly is a shady fucker. His own board ousted him, but no one has been able to pin anything specific on him while he was CEO."

God, I was so screwed. Lance was right. But I needed options, not more problems. "What am I supposed to do? If I wiggle out of this, everyone suffers. My sister, my team, *everyone*."

Lance was quiet for a beat. "There has to be a way to avoid a marriage."

I could almost see him tugging at his hair. He was probably at home in Soho, pacing back and forth over the parquet floors, attempting to wear a path in them.

"Look, Lance, I'm going to stall as best I can. With any luck, we wouldn't even be able to do a proper New York society wedding for months. I may have a solution by then. And that will give me time to get Morgan somewhere far away. Grad school in London for example. And it buys me time to come up with a different deal. Right now, however, Atticus Price is the devil we know, and I have to play along with this plan. At least it's not Jacobson."

Lance was silent for a long breath, but then he finally spoke. "Maybe if your Dad knew—"

My stomach cramped painfully, and I had to stop and use a post on the corner for support as a knot of anxiety and quick flash of fear dissipated. Lance and Morgan only knew some of what had happened with Jacobson. Lance would have jumped off the deep end and ruined his whole career if I'd told him everything. But Bronson Jacobson was the devil. That one stupid date. I had never regretted anything more. I walked away unscathed, but God knows Morgan wouldn't have.

"Unlike my sister, I don't need saving, Lance. I've got this."

Lance sighed. "But what about love? He's not going to make you happy."

I chewed on my bottom lip. "It doesn't matter. My sister and my team are what matters. For them, I can do this. People agree to arranged marriages all the time. Besides, it's unlikely that I'll see him very much in advance of the nuptials, and like I said, it will buy me some time to figure a way out of this. In the meantime, I guess I'm engaged to the coldest man in New York. The saving grace is that I know he works nonstop. I'll never see him. We'll be like ships in the night. It'll probably be a month before he realizes that he's got a fiancée in the city somewhere."

"How are you going to take this guy touching you? I mean, you don't even know him."

Lance's question was soft, and there was a gentle tone to his voice, which clued me in to just how worried he was. I passed a gaggle of tipsy bridesmaids peeling out of a bar and winced as one held her friend's hair back as she vomited on the sidewalk.

"Lance, you need to stop worrying about me. I'll figure this out. And like I said, I'm never going to see the guy. I'll be in my apartment, and he'll be in his. This will all be very civilized. In the meantime, I'm just going to find a different solution to the money issue."

He was silent again. "I'm just saying, you haven't had a serious relationship since Michael. And then that shit with Bronson Jacobson went down, and I worry."

"Have a little faith, would you? I can handle Price."

"Can you? When was your last date?"

"I might not date a lot, but I do things. I have hobbies. Interests. Besides, I don't need love."

"Name one interest. Just one. From the last year."

Low blow. "I don't know... I-I..." Fuck. I had things that I liked to do. And I used to do them all the time. And then everything changed. "I dance."

He laughed. "When was the last time you went to a class? If you tell me it was this week, I will leave you alone. Hell, if you tell me it was anytime this month, I'll stop harassing you right now."

When the hell was it? Maybe it was six months ago. I'd told myself I'd feel better if I just went. But then instead, I just felt worse because my body didn't work the same way, so I didn't go back again. "Don't be a dick, Lance."

"I'm just saying, you're going to need help with Price. You need to convince him to go slow, or wait, or something."

"I love you, Lance. But I'm not discussing my theoretical sex life with you. Besides, it's not going to be like that. This is an arranged marriage. He'll have his affairs, and I'll do whatever I normally do."

Lance sighed. "Look, I'm just saying this guy might have a red room of pain or something. I've heard rumors."

"Rumors that he's into pain?"

"Rumors that he's into sex. Kinky sex. No holds barred sex. Make women line up at his door sex. You're out of your depth."

Maybe he had a point. "Look, I'm not planning to sleep with him. And honestly, it might not even come to that. You need to trust me."

"I'm just looking out for you."

"I know, and I appreciate it. It's going to be fine." I really hoped it would be. But I didn't have a choice. I'd made this bed, and now it was time to lie on it.

"I hope you know what you're doing," he said with more than a little doubt in his voice.

"Me too, but it's me or Morgan, so I will figure it out."

"Would it be so bad if Morgan had to be the one to fall on the sword for once?"

Something bitter twisted on my tongue. "Yes, it would."

CHAPTER 8
ATTICUS

"So, you're getting married."

I eyed Micah over the rim of my scotch glass as he leaned against the window in the living room overlooking Central Park.

"Do you have any advice to offer?"

"Other than this is madness?" he laughed. "No. I'm good."

I shrugged. "Ever helpful."

His chuckle was soft. "Do you have a plan? Because last I checked, you walked into Becks Incorporated with a plan, and then you disregarded it. Which again, is fine. But tell me you know what you're doing."

I nodded. "Yes, I'm in control here."

That was a lie.

Tonight's dinner had been a shit show. Becker had thought I would marry his younger daughter. Which was horrifying enough. But what I'd expected even less was for Gwen to offer herself up instead.

Which you're not upset about.

I pushed to my feet to pour myself another drink, because if drinking wasn't on the table, then I had a bleak outlook indeed.

"How the fuck was I supposed to know she would volunteer? How was I supposed to know Becker would bargain one sister for the other?"

"I did try to warn you he wouldn't let it go," Micah reminded me. "When you told me what happened in his office, I tried to tell you to be careful with that. So now we're stuck. If you say no, he goes to Jacobson."

"You think I don't fucking know that?"

All this was made worse by the fact that Micah *had* tried to warn me. I didn't usually miscalculate. I'd been going for the tidiest deal possible. And if it meant Becker wanted to tie his daughter to me, I would do that. And I would bury his legal team in so much paperwork they'd never find the loopholes I'd slide in there. Like a one-year marriage, leaving her with enough money that she would go away quietly afterward.

Liar. You want her.

Fucking hell. I did want her. But that was not the point.

I needed to be married before my thirtieth birthday thanks to a little clause in my grandfather's will. It had been buried under a mountain of legalese. And our family lawyer had neglected to highlight that little point. If I didn't, my voting shares would be distributed amongst voting members of the board.

"I got the job done, didn't I? We have what we want."

Micah stared at me. "And you're telling me this has nothing to do with the sparks between you and Gwen Becker on the balcony at the Hearts and Hope benefit?"

I shrugged. "I admire her fire." The lie tumbled easily off my tongue.

"Her fire. Is that what we're calling it?" he asked with a smirk.

I turned to scowl at him before taking a large sip of my drink. "Don't be a dick."

Micah just shrugged. "I'm a Price. Dick is an explicit part of the job description. You're not supposed to make this shit more complicated."

I drained my glass, letting the amber liquid burn all the way down. "You think I don't know that?"

My brother frowned at me, watching me closely. "If you're sure you know what you're doing, then I'll follow your lead. But if you don't, you will burn and we'll all go down with you. Everything you built and everyone you love. That includes your Mum."

I glared at him. "That's a low blow."

He shrugged.

"You know exactly what would happen if I didn't make a deal."

"Yes, I do. But is this marriage worth the fight with Jacobson and Dad? You were supposed to be laying low. This is going to be like waving a giant red flag in front of their faces."

Just thinking about the way Gwen had pressed her lips together and refused to let me have her sister... I still didn't understand why it made me want to grin. She had basically called me a thieving monkey dick, and I'd actually found it damn hilarious. "I have it under control, Micah. This way, I can keep her close. Keep her off Dad's radar. Simple."

"Um-hm." He didn't look like he believed me. "It doesn't hurt that she's completely bangable though, right?" he asked with a sly grin.

My lips twitched. "Don't talk about your sister-in-law that way."

Micah rolled his eyes. "It's actually relevant that she's bangable. You know this has to look real. That pesky little provision from Grandad. The board has no choice but to uphold it. If the board gets one whiff things are fake, we'll have problems. You will lose your voting shares to Dad. And there are those who sided with him who are still on the board. They'd love any reason to bring him back. So they'll be looking for any whiff of impropriety. You have to make it look real."

And that was the kicker. As far as I was concerned, this *was* going to be real. It was going to be more difficult reminding her that her future depended on this. "It will be real."

My brother lifted his brow. "Okay, if you say so. As long as you keep the goal in mind, we won't have problems. I'll do my best to keep the board off your ass."

"That would be appreciated."

"What is it about her, anyway?" he asked.

I drained my third glass of scotch and slammed it back down. "I have no fucking idea. She's a fighter. She absolutely will not say die even when it's in her own goddamn best interest. She's the most mule-headedly stubborn woman I have ever met. It doesn't make any sense."

He watched me closely, his green eyes narrowing. "But keep your wits about you. Don't fall for her. We don't need complicated."

"That's never going to happen," I denied firmly.

"If you say so."

"I do say so."

He nodded slowly. "I'll get the paperwork to you. Get her to sign the contract and the NDA. We have secrets to protect."

"I already have Pierce working on that and a full brief."

"At least you haven't completely lost it." He paused and rubbed his chin. "Are you going to tell her about the clause."

The invisible elephant.

I could feel my throat closing. "No. It won't matter to her anyway."

"Everything matters. Watch yourself, Atticus."

I watched my brother stroll out of my living room down the hall toward his room. And I could feel the tethers of control start to roughen around the edges, like someone was gently pulling the strings that kept it all together. I dragged in a deep breath. I knew what I was doing. I was in control. Total fucking control of the situation. This would be easy. All I had to do was get her to follow the fucking script.

CHAPTER 9

GWEN

You agreed to marry a perfect stranger. One you're not even sure you like.

After I arrived home last night, I'd really sat with the weight of what I had agreed to. I was going to marry Atticus Price, and I didn't even know the man.

I woke to a text from him, or at least I assumed it was him.

Unknown: *Lunch at La Table Ronde at twelve.*

Me: *Who is this?*

Unknown: *Your husband.*

I spent the rest of the morning focused on those two words. *Your husband.* And now that I was walking through La Table Ronde on my way to meet him, I felt like I was walking the plank, praying for some fairy godmother or Tinkerbell to come along, sprinkle dust on me, and tell me I didn't have to jump off.

But there was no way out. This. Was. Happening.

As soon as he saw me approach, he slid out of the booth, looking like sex on a stick had just been delivered to my doorstep.

Three-piece suit with a vest. He'd taken off the suit jacket though. Leaving himself in a vest and a crisp white shirt with rolled-up sleeves. He looked young and casual. But there was something so elegantly aloof about him. God, why couldn't I look away?

When I reached him, he leaned down for a kiss on the cheek, and I realized just how tall he was. I had worn heels, nothing too outrageous, but I wanted to really give myself as much power as possible. I'd put on vermilion red Manolo sling backs, paired with a Chloé pencil skirt that went below my knees but hugged every curve, and a petal-pink pixel top tucked in.

"Thank you for meeting me," he said, his voice a mix of gravel and smoke.

"I didn't know I had a choice."

When he brushed his lips over my cheek, I caught a whiff of his cologne, and the hint of citrus, musk, and spice hit me straight in my core.

And I could have sworn he might have sniffed my neck, like he was scenting me or something.

Holy shit.

Once I was seated, he took the seat next to me and signaled to the waiter to take my order. I, unfortunately, was too distracted with the decor of La Table Ronde.

The Round Table. Exclusive, French, expensive. The average person couldn't reserve a table here, so I'd never been inside. And it was a stunner. Like something out of Gatsby. Opulent all at once with its chandeliers and its architecture. It was gorgeous.

After the waiter came and took my order, I finally lifted my gaze to meet Atticus's. He was watching me intently. "What are you doing?" I asked.

"Besides looking at my wife-to-be?"

Just hearing those words sent a shiver through me. "Yes, I know that, but why?"

"You're going to have to get used to me looking at you."

Dear God. There was no getting used to that. I pressed my thighs together, hoping to alleviate the ache. "Am I?"

"Yes, we're about to get married shortly," he reminded me. As if that was necessary. "You should act like you're used to it."

I frowned at that. "What do you mean, shortly?"

"Weren't you the one who proposed to me? I assumed you had a timeline in mind."

My mouth fell open. "I did *not* propose."

He sat back and gave me an insolent smile. "I seem to recall you proposing. You stood up and said, 'I'll do it. I'll marry him.' I didn't ask you."

I sputtered. "M-My father was about to marry off my little sister. She's only *eighteen*. What was I supposed to do?"

He chuckled softly, making the butterflies in my belly dance. "You're so easy to rattle."

"I am not," I muttered through clenched teeth.

"If you say so," he said with a wink and a grin.

I had work to do, and I needed to get back to it. It was better if we got this over with. "You requested my presence, so what am I doing here? Look, I get that you want to back out, but I don't see another way. Not with my sister on the line and—"

He sat back and crossed his arms. "For starters, I don't want to back out. I made the deal. The software comes with you attached. Second, since we need to convince the world we're madly in love, it's probably important for people to see us out and about together so they'll believe it."

I frowned at that. "What does it matter what people believe?"

"Not people. The Pendragon board. Let's call it a family dispute. My father wants back at the helm of Pendragon. It was a tough vote to get him out and wrestle my company from him. Part of the reason he was ousted, were dirty deals, deceiving shareholders, and allegations of sexual misconduct. Even then, it was a fight and he still has friends on the board. Friends who can push for a vote of no confidence if they get even a whiff something is off, which would leave him a window to return."

"This sort of arrangement is not that uncommon," I said. "It is humiliating to be the second choice, but it's a business merger, so it's not that surprising."

His eyes narrowed ever so slightly. "Who said you were the second choice?"

What was he talking about? "I was there. Dad planned to pair you with Morgan."

"Just because that was his plan doesn't mean that was *my* plan. Your father has been putting out feelers for over a year of a partnership with Becks. With one small caveat. Any part of Becks had to be kept in the family. I knew what his price was. When your father suggested a partnership, I assumed he meant you. Which was the only reason I agreed."

"Me? Why?"

He lifted a brow. "Other than you have something I want and I was willing to do anything to get it?"

I knew why but to hear him say it burned. "So romantic."

"I never claimed to be romantic. You have something I want. I can provide you with something you need. I wasn't going to let anyone else have the opportunity."

This is for your employees. For Morgan.

"Right. Fine, we're here. We're having lunch. People can see us. What is it going to cost me personally?"

The smile he gave me was all teeth. "Oh, I probably should have warned you. This isn't the sort of situation where you will be able to see me every third week or so publicly for about thirty minutes and then escape from it. This is *real* in every sense of the word. You and I are getting married, but before that we'll have a big splashy engagement party to celebrate our union."

I squared my shoulders. "Exactly what do you mean by *every sense of the word*? And is an engagement party really necessary?"

He *tsked* at me. "For *my* bride, it's necessary. Like I said, this is what your father requires for me to get what I want. I agreed. I stick to my commitments. If I'm to do this, I'm doing it all the way. So get used to it. We're going to move this along as quickly as we can. Given that I shun the spotlight, it'll be easy enough for the public to believe that we've been seeing each other for a while and no one knew."

Every sense of the word? Like a real marriage? Like *real*, real? I tried to shut down the immediate fluttering in my belly and commiserate throb between my legs. "You really have thought this through."

He leaned forward, pinning me with his wintergreen gaze. "You have no idea." Sitting back, he added, "First thing's first. We'll do an announcement. My team is already on it. I'll send it over today so you can approve it. It'll be basic yet tasteful. Not a lot of flair." He reached for his jacket then pulled a box out before sliding it over to me. "Of course you'll need this."

I stared at the box. *Holy hell*. "You really have thought of everything." My heart skipped beats, but not in a fun, happy way. More like in a terrified running-too-fast-being-chased-by-a-lion kind of way.

I reached for the box and stopped breathing as I opened it.

The ring was a four carat stunner of a brilliant cut diamond in a pavé band. Simple, elegant, classic, beautiful... and cold. *Impersonal*. Like looking at a magazine cut out.

"So this is for me then, is it?"

He nodded. "Yes. If you prefer something else, I can have it replaced."

I stared at the glittering diamond, unable to eat a bite of the salad in front of me. "It's beautiful."

"Of course it is. Put it on, please."

"You don't want to do that part?" I asked cheekily.

He lifted a brow, gaze intense on mine. "Do you want me to?"

Goddamn. Being the subject of all that intensity was... discomfiting. All I could do was stare, but he was deadly serious.

"No, I've got it." He only marginally relaxed his shoulders when I picked up the ring and placed it on my finger.

It felt like it weighed two tons, and I could barely lift my finger.

"I emailed the contract. Did you look over it?"

God, my head was spinning. This was moving too fast. I just needed to pause for a moment. I dragged in a deep breath. "You mean the email I received three hours ago? I've been a little busy. I haven't had the chance to go over it fully."

"Okay, well then allow me to enlighten you, *wife*. Our marriage comes with a very distinct nondisclosure agreement."

"*Future* wife. And that's probably pretty standard. I don't want the world knowing." I added with a whisper, "It's humiliating enough."

"Right. Among other things, there's a prenuptial agreement in there."

As if I wanted to take him for his money.

Isn't that what your father is doing?

"Of course, there is. But remember, I didn't volunteer to marry you for my own personal gain."

"Still, it's better that way," he said. "The settlement will be substantial, of course."

"Right, being a true romantic again."

He shrugged. "It's practical. I'm getting the distinct impression you think that this is temporary and transient, or fake in some way, and I want to assure you it's not. This is very real. Whether we have a contract or I had met you in one of your local bars."

I stiffened at that, thinking about the night we met and the raw visceral attraction. But I couldn't come right out and ask about us sleeping together. "What's that supposed to mean?"

"It means that we will live together and attend events together, and well, for all intents and purposes, we will be married in every way."

"Wait a minute, you expect me to move in with you?" I asked incredulously.

"Yes," he smirked. "Where did you think you were going to live?"

I swallowed hard. "My apartment. Alone. Like I do now."

"No, you'll be moving into my penthouse."

"But that's not what I agreed to. I said I'd marry you, but I thought it would just be on paper. You know, one of those be-seen-publicly-once-a-month type of deals."

He pressed his lips together. "I know this isn't what you wanted, but this meeting with us is a formality. Primarily to get you to sign off on the NDA and the prenuptial agreement. All other arrangements have already been made with your father."

"Wow." I watched as the muscle in his jaw ticked. And bile rose in my throat as the waiter arrived with my shrimp étouffée. "Oh God, you are deadly serious."

"I am."

"Then why did you even bother meeting with me since you and my father have already signed off on a lot of the paperwork? Am I just expected to turn up to honor and obey?"

He ground his teeth at that. "There was something magical about you on the balcony that night."

"Oh sure. It was probably the glitter."

"Yeah, the fucking glitter. I'm *still* finding glitter in places I certainly didn't expect."

I laughed. "Well, if that's all you wanted, your average stripper would suffice."

"Got something against strippers?"

"Nothing, actually," I said. "Dancers are incredibly strong. And to hang upside down on a pole while gyrating and dancing is a skill that's difficult to master."

"It sounds like you know a lot about strippers."

"Yes, I do, actually. I take a pole dance class. At least I used to."

He choked on a sip of water. "Fuck."

"What? For fitness."

"It has to stop."

"The hell it does." I wasn't great at pole dancing. Hell, I didn't even love it, and I hadn't done it in at least six months, but just the sheer idea that he would tell me that I *couldn't* do it, made me want to rage. "You can't stop me."

"Then I guess we don't have a deal."

"All right, if I don't do this, what happens?"

"Perhaps I marry Morgan. That's what your father would prefer."

Another roll of queasiness made me push my plate aside, which was a damn shame because I loved shrimp étouffée. And I was starving.

"No," I said emphatically. "That's not happening. So when we leave here, we are the real deal."

"Yes," he agreed. "From the moment we walk away from this table, we are together. So if what you said last night was true and there's someone else lurking around, get rid of him. You have until tonight. If you don't get rid of him, then I will. And I promise you, the way that I get rid of him will be unpleasant to both of you. So do it now."

"Is that a threat?" The words tore out of my throat.

Atticus cocked his head. And in that moment, I sensed a lethal edge to him. It was just under the surface. And unfortunately, instead of repelling me like it should, it made something pull in my core again.

"There isn't anyone."

"Excellent. So Lakewood isn't going to be a problem?"

I frowned. "Lance? He's my best friend. There's never been anything romantic between us, and I'm not getting rid of my best friend. You'll have to just work around that."

He pursed his lips then. "If you say so. Friendships are fine. I'm not bothered."

"And you said I was supposed to live with you?"

His brow furrowed. "Yes. The Park Tower. Upper West Side."

"And what about my apartment?"

"You can keep it if you like," he said. "Or sublet it. But you won't be sleeping there."

All my tightly held reins of control that had kept me going for the last year were slipping between my fingers like they were water. I sighed. "Why are you doing this? You don't want this. You can get a wife any way you want."

His wintergreen eyes searched mine for a long moment before he spoke. "I'm old enough that a wife brings great value. It looks good to my board and my shareholders that I am settled. Happy."

He was going to make me ask. Shit. "You still haven't been clear, so I have to ask. What about sex?"

His gaze dipped to my lips instantly, and I licked them nervously once I had his attention. "What about it?" he asked.

"Well, I assume you're going to want it. You want me to have no one, but does that stipulation extend to you, or is it one sided?"

His teeth grazed his bottom lip as he leaned forward. When he spoke, his voice was low. "I won't be fucking anyone else."

Holy Sheeeeit. I tried to calm the pulsing between my thighs by pressing them together. I swallowed then cleared my throat. "I—I need to like someone at the very least to sleep with them. Right now I'm hovering at barely tolerating."

"Interesting," he murmured. His gaze swept over me then, his slow perusal making me hyperaware of every inch of my skin. "I'll only kiss you in public while we get to know each other. I won't touch you until you beg me to."

"Until I—" I narrowed my gaze at his arrogant smirk. "Did you say beg?"

He shrugged. "That I did."

The laugh whipped out of my throat before I could pull it back. "You will have an epic case of blue balls long before I beg."

"We'll see. I should probably mention that you'll only be getting your orgasms from me for the foreseeable future."

"You scared a toy can do it better?"

"No, Ness. Toys are tools. But I'm the one you'll be using them with. Not as a replacement."

His arrogance was truly next level. "My name isn't Ness."

He gave me his secret smile. The one I noted he only seemed to use with me. "It's a fitting nickname."

"How? My name is Gw—"

"Gwen, is that you?"

I froze, a tingle of ice slipping down my back, coiling itself around my spine, and holding me in place.

Don't be him. Don't be him. Don't be him.

I turned my head slightly to the right, and there he was, Bronson Jacobson, and I forced myself to swallow down the bile that immediately crawled up my throat. Across the table, Atticus frowned at me. And then he did the most interesting thing. He took my hand in his and stroked his thumb over my knuckles. What the fuck?

But I couldn't think, because there Bronson was, staring at me, when all I wanted to do was poke out his eyeballs. "Oh, it's you."

"Yeah." He leaned in to give me a kiss on the cheek, but Atticus stood, forcing him to stop what he was doing.

"Jacobson. It's been a long time." Atticus didn't let go of my hand, but he shook Bronson's hand with the other one. "You caught us on a lunch date."

Bronson's eyes went wide. "A lunch date? You two? How the hell did that happen?"

I couldn't answer. I could not respond. If I tried, I knew I was going to throw up everywhere. But Atticus took the reins. "We met at a charity benefit. I couldn't take my eyes off of her. Especially after she glitter bombed me."

"It was an accident." A warm flush crept up my neck as I realized his teasing had calmed the anxiety enough for me to speak. "What do you want, Bronson?"

Bronson slashed a dark gaze to me, and there it was again, the rolling nausea. "I saw you and I wanted to say hi. If you weren't such a—"

Atticus jumped in before he could finish that sentence. "Jacobson, if you don't mind, I'd like to finish lunch with my fiancé."

Bronson whipped his eyes to Atticus and back to me, finally noticing Atticus was holding my hand. I could see it then. The hatred was clear from the scowl on his face. I tried to warn Atticus with a shake of my head, but he didn't pay me any heed.

"You're serious?"

Atticus smiled, but it was cold, sending goosebumps up my arms. "I am very serious. We were hashing out wedding plans. Do you mind?"

Bronson nodded curtly, shook hands with Atticus again, and said he'd be seeing him soon. And then he was gone.

When Atticus sat down again, he released my hand. "So, are you going to tell me what that was about?"

I shook my head. "No. I just can't stand him."

"Which I understand, but do you want to tell me why?"

"No, I do not."

He nodded once then turned his attention back to his food. Somehow along the way, ginger ale appeared at my side, and he nodded at me. "Drink it slowly. It'll settle your stomach."

I shook my head. "Why?"

"You need it. You were looking a little piqued."

As I sipped the ginger ale, he continued. "Okay. We have talked a lot about what I need from you and this marriage. Do you have anything you need from me?"

I thought about it for a moment. He'd already signed the deal with my father. What more could I ask for? Then it hit me, and I realized it was time to negotiate.

"Okay, protect Morgan."

His brows knitted. "What do you mean?"

"Morgan, my sister, protect her. If I do this, you make sure my father doesn't sell her off to the next highest bidder because he doesn't know how to manage his company and he is once again in a hard spot."

"Do you think he would?"

I leveled a gaze on him, and he nodded solemnly. "Of course, he would. Consider it done."

"I need one more thing, actually."

He cocked his head, and I could see a spark of gentleness in there. It was fleeting, but I had seen it for a moment.

I swallowed and continued. "You leave Morgan alone too."

He stiffened and jerked back an inch, and confusion was written all over his face. "What do you mean, leave Morgan alone?"

"You don't touch her. You don't talk to her. You don't intimidate her. She deserves to be left alone."

"Is that who you think I am?"

"Well, I heard my father. He indicated that she was the original bargain."

"She wasn't, or at least he didn't spell that out. And when your father said he wanted to keep the business in the family, I didn't quite see what he meant."

"Okay, but Morgan is the only thing I care about. That and my employees. You were willing to marry her as of yesterday afternoon. If I'm taking her place, pretending for the world, I can't have you sniffing after my sister."

He looked affronted. "That would never happen."

I looked at the document he'd sent me on my tablet and stared at it for a long moment. I'd told Lance I could handle this. But if I signed this, that would be it, wouldn't it?

But if you sign this, you have protection for Morgan.

I grabbed the stylus and scrawled my signature.

When I showed him the tablet, he smirked. "Let's get out of here."

I nodded. Somehow during our exchange, our food had already been boxed up, and I was given a discreet bag to take with me.

"What's this?"

"I noticed you didn't eat. Obviously, you're anxious. I just wanted to make sure you ate something."

"Oh, that's thoughtful. Thank you."

He led me through the restaurant as several guests stood to give him a nod or speak a small greeting. When we reached the sidewalk, there was a car waiting. "That's my driver, Gavin. He'll take you anywhere you need to go."

"So that's it? Do we shake or something?"

He laughed, but then he quickly sobered. "I do want to make one thing clear."

"What's that?" I asked warily.

"Morgan was never an option. I'll protect her, like I said. And I'm not interested in her. I like my women to be actual women. She's still a kid."

"Okay." The word came out strained, and some of the tightness in my chest eased. "In that case, I guess I'm going to be your wife."

Then he wrapped his arms around me, and I froze. "What are you doing?"

"Rule number one," he whispered in my ear. "This has to look real. I'm going to kiss you now."

CHAPTER 10
ATTICUS

Fucking Christ, she smelled good. Like lemons and something sweet.

I wrapped my hands around her waist, more than aware that we were being watched and that Gavin was grinning at me like an idiot from the car.

When I eased my hand along her neck, sliding my fingertips into the base of her hair, the soft tresses tempted me into sinking my hand in further. When I pressed my fingertips gently against the spinal column in her neck, she relaxed, her lips parting ever so slightly.

And those deep dark eyes of hers were glued to my lips. When her tongue peeked out to moisten her bottom lip, I couldn't help the little groan of need that escaped.

Dipping my head, I brushed her lips with mine ever so gently at first. But one taste and my tenuous control snapped.

I deepened the kiss, devouring her mouth as if I had been starved for days. My hands roamed down her back, pressing her closer to me. I could feel her curves against my body, the softness of her breasts pushing against my chest.

I slid my hands down her back and over her ass, pulling her closer to me as my dick pulsed with aching need. And all I could think about was how to prolong this. How to make this moment last forever.

I couldn't stop myself even if I tried. The feel of her pressed up against me was like the headiest aphrodisiac I had ever known. I groaned as her tongue swept against mine, and I knew I was falling into the abyss.

The need to taste her, to have her, rose up like a tidal wave. I tried to fight it, to wrangle it, but I couldn't. I had to have more, had to make her mine.

Only Gwen. Only Gwen.

She made these sexy little mewling sounds at the back of her throat, and my hand automatically tightened in her hair, fisting the soft tresses.

I was in trouble.

Back off before you maul the woman on the street. You've made your point.

I wanted to be inside her, to feel her body tense and convulse around me. I wanted to be buried deep in her sweet heat, to feel those soft velvet walls clenching around my hardened cock. I wanted to be balls deep in her and see the shock in her eyes when she found out how deep I could go.

I wanted to stretch her open and watch as her eyes rolled into the back of her head as she howled with pleasure. I wanted to watch her lips part and her breasts heave as I filled her with my cock. I wanted to watch as she arched her body and called out my name. I wanted it all.

Fuck me.

I dragged my lips from hers, fighting for breath.

She looked up at me and I could see the lust and shock reflected in her gaze.

She took a step back. "What the hell was that?" she asked in a harsh whisper.

"The kind of kiss that seals a deal."

CHAPTER 11
GWEN

The morning post kissmageddon, I could *still* feel every slide of his tongue through my entire body. I was still freaking tingling.

You cannot think about that kiss when you see him. This is business. That's all.

I shifted on my feet as I stared up at the sunlight glinting on the glass at the Park Tower.

The whole neighborhood screamed wealth and opulence. All around me, women sashayed by in their red-soled shoes, while others pushed ten-thousand-dollar strollers. I knew I'd had a privileged life. I'd been educated at Dalton, then Columbia, rubbed elbows with the Hamptons summer kids, but this, this was something else.

I couldn't do this. I'd never fit in. I tried to turn around and drag my roller bag behind me. But then I saw Atticus's car across the street, and Gavin grinned at me and nodded his head from the driver's side window. I gave him a little wave and then turned right back around.

There was no way I was going to let him see me run away. The building was gorgeous. It was one of Hank Goodwin's green buildings, and it even had some multipurpose uses. There were portions that were open to the public, like a park for children. It was a stunning piece of architecture, and I was going to live in it.

Don't be a chicken shit.

Tightening my grip on my suitcase, I gave Gavin a smile and charged forward. It was going to be hard enough managing my life outside of this marriage. The acquisition, making sure my father didn't have any more shenanigans in mind for Morgan. Although, I did trust Atticus when he said he would manage that. I just hoped he would keep his word.

My whole team would be freaking out. Four years ago, before I joined my father's company, I had a ragtag team of engineers, a couple of product managers, and an idea for the multipurpose algorithm that could be built, not just with facial recognition, but to actually do medical imaging, help with missing persons, teaching applications, etcetera. And surprisingly, we'd done well. But we had run out of money and needed a big investor. Cue my father to act like he was actually being helpful.

We'd been absorbed into Becks Incorporated with all kinds of promises about how we would get to grow and develop.

And we had. We'd also grown a lot larger than I wanted, and there was a lot of bureaucracy. And now to get bought out like this... It was a wound none of us needed.

But that was a problem for another day. Today, my problem was getting to know my new husband-to-be. When I walked into the slick terrazzo entry, the doorman smiled at me. He had warm brown skin, a gap between his two front teeth, and the broadest, sunniest smile I had ever seen. "Hello, Miss Becker. I'm Manny. I'm your daytime doorman. Anything you need, just call me and I'll make sure you get it."

I tried to return his smile. "You know who I am?"

His smile deepened and that popped a dimple. "Yes ma'am. You're the future Mrs. Price."

Why did that make my stomach twist? I had already agreed to this. "Oh, um, how did you recognize me?"

"Oh, Mr. Price already sent down your photo."

"My photo?" Where the hell had Atticus gotten a picture of me?

"Don't you worry," Manny added with a smile. "You look great."

How I looked in a photo was hardly the problem. The problem was, somehow Atticus had a photo of me?

I'd been in a good deal of shock when I left my parents' house on Friday. Had I failed to notice Clarissa slip him a picture of me? Also, what the hell?

Manny took my roller bag from me. "Right this way, miss."

He led me past the front desk and past the security station that required a key fob. "I suppose I need one of those?"

"Yes, there's already one upstairs for you. Your key fob gives you access to the private penthouse and to the pool after hours, as well."

"Great, there's a pool?"

"Oh yes, there is. When we drop your bags, I'll give you a map of the whole building so you can't get lost. And if you ever do, or if you're in the elevator and you don't know where you're supposed to be going, just call down to the desk."

"It looks like everything is taken care of."

"Well, we try. And just so you know, there are two night doormen as well, Emilio and Derrick. Anything you need at night, they can handle. The Park Tower is very secure. You will notice blue lights everywhere. Those are safety and security lights. If anything goes wrong or you feel odd about anything, just press one of those, and it'll ring straight down to security. And in your case, if you use your keypad to access it, you'll get patched straight to Mr. Price's personal security.

"I didn't know I would need security."

"You won't, ma'am. This is just to make you feel more comfortable."

"And I do." I gave him a warm smile. "Thank you, Manny. You've been very helpful."

The ride up to the penthouse took forever. The whole time, my stomach just turned over and over again as I contemplated exactly how I ended up here. Friday night dinner had been normal and unremarkable. Right up until my father dropped the bombshell.

Christ. I had been irritated with Atticus one hundred percent. But what my father had done, the way he'd just handed me over, or rather, the way he'd tried to hand Morgan over, I just couldn't even believe it.

I could still see Atticus with his too-knowing eyes, and his hint of a smile. I was constantly trying to figure out what on earth he was thinking, what he was going to say, what he was going to do. He was just infuriating. Why on earth did he want to marry?

Once the dust had settled yesterday, I'd taken a look at the original contract he sent my father. While it made me sad that I would lose control of most of my hard work, it had been fair.

When the elevator finally slowed, I wiped my sweaty palms on my dark jeans, wrapped my hand around the handle of my suitcase, and waited for the door to open. The door into my new life. I expected to find Atticus waiting for me on the other side, but he wasn't there.

Great, because when your new wife to be is moving in, why on earth would you be there?

I tried not to balk at the bite of rejection. I was used to it. It sucked, but I was a big girl.

Someone came around the corner as I stepped into the foyer, looking around. What was I supposed to do, just casually walk in?

"Oh, you're early."

I turned at the sound of his voice, and he smiled at me. He was handsome. Lean and tall, but not quite as tall as Atticus. "Oh, sorry," I said. "You're not who I expected."

"You would not be the first person to say that to me. I'm Micah, your brother-in-law-to-be." Then he gave me another broad smile that immediately put me at ease.

Where Atticus was cold, Micah was warm. He seemed fun. "Why do I get the impression that you're trouble?"

"Because you seem like a smart one. Come on in. Atticus is on a call. I'll show you in."

"I did text him to let him know I was coming."

He shrugged. "My brother is a bit of an ass. Sorry, but you should probably know that."

"Yeah, you know what? So is my father. I'm an asshole expert."

"Excellent," he laughed. "Glad I'm not alone here."

He led me from the foyer to the expansive living room. I'd been in beautiful penthouses before. That part wasn't new, but the view of Central Park was unparalleled.

On a clear day like today, with the sun shining bright, I could see right down into the horses and carriages giving tours. And of course, the rest of the city view was magnificent as well. It was stunning. Awe-inspiring, honestly.

Micah grinned. "It doesn't suck, does it?"

"No, it doesn't suck."

"Are you hungry? Magda can make you something to eat."

"I'm not hungry, but who's Magda?" I asked.

"She's our housekeeper, but let me show you where everything is. The kitchen is right this way."

When I walked in, I realized there was no way this was *just* a kitchen. It looked like it belonged in the best restaurant. Marble and glass intermixed with stone, which actually gave just a hint of Tuscan influence, and all commercial grade appliances.

"God, please tell me that Magda is some kind of professional chef, because if she's not, that would be a sad, sad waste of a beautiful kitchen."

"It is a masterpiece, isn't it?"

"Please tell me you cook. Or maybe Atticus? Because I'd hate for you to have this kitchen and not use it."

"Oh, you know Atticus," he said with a grin. "He's not really a *stand in the kitchen and make something* kind of person. But Magda can make anything from all over the world. You name a cuisine, and she can probably make it for you or at least figure out how it's done. She's pretty incredible."

I smiled at him. "I like you very much, Micah."

"I like you too, Gwen. I think you'll be good for him," he said, his voice sobering. He slowed as we approached what I thought was a study, but it turned out to be the library.

"Oh my God," I squealed. "This is freaking fantastic."

"It was meant to be a second or third office, but I convinced Atticus that we needed to make this the library. Then when either of our mothers is visiting, they can have some solace and read."

"Oh, different mothers, same father?"

He nodded. "Yes, our moms actually get along, and they're both likely to visit on occasion if you don't mind."

"That's nice. I'm glad you and Atticus are close. You've probably had some fun along the way."

Micah shrugged at that. "Only a little."

I gestured toward a set of shelves that housed nothing but romance novels. "Please tell me these get read."

"You got me. I discovered a whole world of Sci-Fi and alien romance, and I can't stay away."

"Oh my God, are you serious?" The revelation made me giggle. "You aren't just kidding me, right?"

He shook his head. "No. There was an article in the *New Yorker* about romance novels and how there were all kinds of subgenres. So I was curious and thought I would check out a few and maybe have a laugh about it. But now here I am, caring about the blue alien who was trying to help a woman whose human spaceship crash-landed on his planet."

"Wow, this is a conversation I never thought I'd be having."

"Oh, Gwen, you have to read them. I'll make you a list of my favorite ones."

"Now I'm *certain* I like you a lot."

He shrugged. "You're not the first person to tell me that. I am pretty brilliant."

I chuckled. "We are going to start a book club. I feel like Atticus would hate that."

"I don't really care what my brother hates," he said with a wink.

He led me through the rest of the house, showing me the powder rooms, where his room was down the hall in case I needed anything, and finally to my room.

I gasped. "It's huge!"

"That's because it's the master bedroom."

My scalp prickled with awareness, and I automatically turned to see Atticus coming down the hall from the room we had skipped. "I can take it from here, Micah," he said.

Micah darted his gaze between me and Atticus. "Right. Manny will let you know when the rest of your belongings have arrived. Do you have any other things you need help with?"

"No. I've just got a few boxes arriving later today."

"Right. I'll just get it organized with Magda to help you unpack everything. And Clyde should be here later as well, He's our butler. He does nightly turndown and that sort of thing."

"Um, I think I can manage."

The entire time Micah spoke, Atticus glowered at him, though Micah seemed not to notice. "Gwen, I have to say, it's been a pleasure. Our book club starts next week. I'll be a gracious host and let you pick the first book."

"Okay, I'll try and think of something."

"I'm counting on you. Oh, and the spicier, the better." He winked as he headed back down the hallway. "Just so you know, I'm no prude."

I snorted a laugh because I couldn't help it. He was a little bit outrageous, and I adored him already.

Atticus growled though. "There won't be a book club."

I whipped around to meet his gaze. "Excuse me?"

"A book club with my brother? That's not happening."

"I'm sorry, I must have misunderstood. I didn't realize that when you bargained for my company that also meant that you could tell me what to do with my personal time." I glanced into the enormous bedroom. "So, where do you sleep?"

And then he flashed me that grin again. That knee-buckling, pulse-pounding, make-you-burn-your-panties grin. "This is *our* room."

The way he emphasized *our* made my head spin. "It's not necessary that we stay together, right? A big penthouse like this, I'm sure you have another room. Or I'll happily sleep in the library. It's fine."

"What did I tell you yesterday?" he asked.

His words came rushing back to me. *This is real.*

"You signed on the dotted line, Gwen. We are doing this. We will be married in a few weeks. Just pick the day, and I'll get you a wedding planner." He was so matter-of-fact, as if this wasn't my life.

"I thought we'd have more time before..." I let my voice trail off.

"Servants gossip, Gwen. Even mine. We must keep up appearances. We are both in this, so until further notice, we both sleep here, in that bed."

I swallowed hard. "Well, technically we're not married yet, so I thought maybe..."

He grinned at me, stepping into my space. And Jesus Christ, that smile was feral and probably meant to intimidate, but there was something so unbelievably delicious about it. "You can relax, Gwen. I have no intention of touching you unless you ask me to."

There was a hint of gravel to his voice, which had me thinking about all the ways I wanted him to. And then I shuddered and steeled my resolve. *Get it together.*

"I know I signed on the dotted line. I was just surprised, is all." Something else caught my eye. "What's with the satin pillowcases?"

He shifted on his feet uncomfortably. "I know this is an unusual situation so I wanted to stock the house with things you need. Your step-mother said you'd need satin pillow cases for your hair. Oh and a shower that wasn't a rainwater shower I had mine converted earlier this week."

He'd spoken to Clarissa? He'd changed the shower for me? I started at the pillowcases with no idea what to say or do. My nose grew suspiciously tingly and I had to drag in a deep breath. Why was he being so nice? Hadn't he browbeat me into being here? "Why would you go to all this trouble?"

"It's not trouble if it's something you need. Welcome home, *wife*."

"*Future* wife. Are you going to kiss me again?"

His gaze dipped to my lips, and I automatically licked them to moisten them. "You know what? I don't think so. Unless, of course, you're asking me to."

And because I was a stubborn fool and knew how complicated this was going to get, I looked the man dead in his eyes and said, "I'd only ask you to kiss me over my dead body."

CHAPTER 12
GWEN

BLISSFUL WARMTH SURROUNDED ME LIKE A COCOON, AND THE SCENT OF sandalwood and pine lulled me into relaxation like a spa aromatherapy treatment, and I let myself sink into softness.

Somewhere in the deep recesses of my mind, I knew it was close to morning. I knew I had to get up and get to the office and figure out the logistics of keeping my company together.

But I couldn't.

Or you don't want to.

Just five more minutes. Even as I reached for the thread of the conscious world, it slipped through my fingers and I was dragged back into dreamland.

A dreamland where Atticus was the star. His full lips brushed my temple, and I moaned into the caress.

He chuckled softly, his warm breath tickling my skin. His hand slid down my arm as his fingers traced lazy circles on my skin. I shivered, my body responding to his touch even in my dreams.

Atticus leaned down, his lips ghosting over my jawline and down my neck. My breath hitched as he nipped at the sensitive skin just below my earlobe.

"I just knew you'd be soft," he murmured against my skin.

My heart raced as Atticus's lips continued down my neck, leaving a trail of fire in their wake. His hand found its way to my breast, and he palmed it gently before pinching my nipple. I gasped, arching into his touch.

Atticus's mouth closed around my nipple, sucking gently before switching to the other breast. My hands tangled in his hair, tugging the soft strands as he pleasured me.

His big body covered me, his cock pressing insistently against my thigh, begging for access.

Something jostled me, and my eyes fluttered open, the remnants of the dream still lingering in my mind.

I couldn't believe the intensity of the dream, the way Atticus had touched me, his mouth sucking on my nipples, sending a pulsing electric zap straight to my clit.

It felt real, almost as if I could still feel his lips on my skin.

I ran a hand over my hair and realized my satin bonnet had made a run for it in the middle of the night and my hair was tousled now.

I needed to shake off the remnants of the dream and get ready for the day ahead.

But when I tried to sit up, I couldn't. A heavy arm was wrapped around my waist and held me anchored against a hard, muscular body.

Atticus.

The heat that had enveloped me in my dream was very real.

It was far too hot. Furnace-like, and I tried to shift and adjust and realized I was imprisoned. An arm was wrapped around my waist, and I was atop a very hard body.

And right between my legs, was... Oh my God, his pulsing dick was *right there.*

When I tried to shift my hips away, the length of his cock followed me. I realized I had been rubbing against him, and sometime in the middle of the night, his dick had started to jut out of the top of the pajama pants he'd worn to bed.

Heat suffused my face, and my gaze darted up to his.

Did he know? Was he awake?

I stared at him for a long moment, holding my breath, assessing.

It wasn't my fault. I was asleep. I could hardly be held responsible for what I did in my sleep. I'd gone to bed wearing pajama shorts and a silk camisole. The strap of my camisole had fallen down somewhere in the shift of me apparently climbing Atticus like a tree. And my shorts had bunched up, making room for his dick to shift under the opening and stroke my panty-clad clit.

Also, the man was gorgeous and stunning, even while sleeping, and his arm was not only wrapped around me, but it was cupping my ass, holding me firmly against him.

His hand squeezed my ass, rocking me ever so slightly over the length of him, and my gaze snapped back up to his face. There was no tension around his mouth, no frown that I was used to seeing. He was asleep. He looked completely at ease and relaxed. The little motion happened again, and I bit back a moan.

Fuck. I couldn't do this. I needed to get out of there. I tried to shift and adjust myself, but there he was again, and this time, he rolled. His hands on my ass again, rolling me to the side, pressing me tight against him. His massive hand palmed me easily, holding me in place and then rocking me against him.

A zing of electricity started to snake up my spine.

Fuck. Oh God. My eyes fluttered shut as he rolled again.

"Mmmm," Atticus murmured in his sleep. "That's it. Just like that, Gwen." And he rocked me against him again.

Gwen. He was dreaming of me?

No.

Another moan slipped out.

Oh God, this was wrong.

I didn't want to like this. I wanted to hate him.

But fuck me, he was hard, and big, and felt amazing, and the little thrusts happening now against me were making my brain swim, making my thoughts fuzzy as the little motions sparked zings of lightning that poured through my blood.

I bit my lip to stop the soft moans and needy sounds that kept sliding from my throat.

He rubbed, and stroked, and rolled, and moaned, damn him. And the sound did something to me, swirling in my belly and making me twist a little over him.

With his other arm, he tucked me even closer to him, dropping his head to kiss my shoulder. "Feels... good. Come all over... you. Throat. Pussy... in your ass."

I froze. He wanted to what?

And why did heat spike my blood at the thought.

My mouth dropped open in a silent cry when his hand found my breast, his touch even more intimate and arousing than it had been in the dream.

I was so turned on my panties were soaked as he slid his cock over the fabric, and I whimpered in protest when he stopped brushing his lips over my shoulder.

But then he moved to my neck and then my chest. He paused at my breast, and his tongue flicked out, licking at the peak, circling it before sucking it gently.

"Atticus," I murmured, my head falling back, my eyes drifting closed as he moved, his hand tightening on my ass.

"Atticus," I said, this time trying to shove him away, but he didn't move. He just kept rolling that big cock over my pussy.

He made a small noise of protest, his hips rolling slightly, stroking deeper with his cock.

I froze.

He was still asleep. Definitely still asleep. I shifted a little, trying to get away from him, stifling a gasp of alarm as his cock found a new and more exciting way to rub against my clit.

I closed my eyes, trying to hold myself still.

"Please wake up," I whispered, my eyes flying open to see if he was awake. He was going to regret this.

And this wasn't good for me. But considering everything I'd been through, it wasn't fear tearing through my veins. I was... excited. And horny, and needy. This was so bad.

I lifted my head, trying to shake him a little. He had to be awake. His brow furrowed slightly, but his lips were slack.

He wasn't awake. He was still asleep, and he was thrusting against me, fucking my clit and enjoying it.

I sucked in a sharp breath, my arms coming up to press on his chest.

His grunt of protest had me gasping. Oh my God.

"Oh, God, God, God..." I whispered. When I started to come, I bit back a groan, struggling to stay quiet as I arched my back and ground my clit against the ridge of his cock just as a gush of his semen soaked my panties.

His hands tightened around me as he made me come. "Yes, Gwen. Fuck... So beautiful."

Our breath came out in ragged pants, filling the silence.

And then the sound of our breathing was replaced by his snoring.

Son of a bitch was still asleep.

CHAPTER 13
ATTICUS

I woke up with aching bones. Fucking hell. I'd had the world's most fucking vivid dream. All night, I'd been surrounded by the smell of lemons and cream.

Automatically, I reach for Gwen, only to find her side of the bed empty and cool. Cranking open an eye, I searched for her, but she was gone.

The vivid dreams I'd had last night featuring her came back in a fiery jolt of need and pulsing electricity. It had felt so real. As if I'd had her ass in my hands, and she was riding my dick.

"Gwen? Where are you?"

I heard something out in the living room, and I forced myself to sit up then glowered at my now rock-hard cock that was working hard at trying to escape the confines of my pajama bottoms. "Down boy, she's not here. There's nothing we can do about it."

He didn't seem to care.

It had been hard to fall asleep at first, but then so easy. Once she settled in a little and stopped moving around, it was the best night's sleep I'd had in a year. Maybe more.

And then came those dreams. The ones where she was begging for me. I imagined I could hear her whispered, breathy, 'Atticus.'

My cock bobbed, and I growled. "I said, fucking down."

I threw the rest of the covers off and climbed out of bed. When I heard one of the timers in the kitchen, I checked the clock. It wasn't even six yet. What the hell was she doing in there?

I found Gwen in the kitchen, packing her lunch. "You're up early."

She whipped around, her eyes roaming over my bare chest before she answered. "Making my lunch for work."

"Running away from me, Ness? Not that I blame you."

"What do you mean?" she asked, nervously licking her lips, but her gaze didn't meet mine.

"Did something happen last night?" I asked.

Her eyes went wide. "Like what?"

I ground my teeth. "You ran out of bed this morning. What happened? Did I snore or intrude on your side of the bed?"

She shook her head, but I could tell she was holding something back.

"Why are you running? Why are you up this early?"

"I'm not running. I just need to get to work. In case you haven't heard, my company is being acquired. I need to figure out how to tell my people and deal with what happens next."

"At five thirty in the morning?"

"Yes. This acquisition is going to be a blow to the team. There's a lot to do, and Lance will be here in a minute."

My flair of rage whipped out. "Fucking Lakewood. Remember what I said about being your only one? I meant it."

"Oh, for fuck's sake. Jesus, I need to go. Who is my point of contact for the acquisition? I have lots of questions, forms, paperwork."

I scowled at her. "First of all, you work with me, directly. You don't work with anyone else." Fuck, something was wrong here.

"Correct me if I'm wrong, but aren't you the CEO? Aren't there, you know, *people* I can talk to? *Anyone* but you?"

I lifted my brow and crossed my arms. "You know, I'm starting to get the impression you're trying to avoid me."

"I'm not trying to avoid you. I just assume that you are very busy."

The muscle in my jaw ticked. "I am busy. But as a new acquisition, you are very important to Pendragon Tech. Plus, you are going to be my wife. So I'll see to it personally. Anything you need."

The security buzzer went off, and she checked her watch. Then she muttered a curse. She hit the button on the panel next to the fridge and spoke quickly. "Sorry, Manny, please send him up. I'm not quite ready."

She was going to go without finishing our conversation? "We aren't done, Gwen."

"Sorry, I have to go."

"Okay, fine. Lunch today. You come to my office, or I'll come to you. We have an engagement party to plan."

She pursed her lips. "I'll be meeting with my team and probably won't have time for lunch. We might have to talk when I get home."

"Oh, we're having lunch," I insisted.

"Like I said, I'll see. " She sashayed toward the door, grabbing her canvas bag.

"Just so we're clear, Gwen, Pendragon has a whole communications package for you. Someone from my office will be there to assist you and handle it however you want."

"Can I go now?"

I leveled her with a glare that held hers for a long moment. "By all means."

But I followed her down the hall into the living area. As she shouldered her bag, she frowned at me. "What are you doing?"

"Well, since Lance is picking you up, I might as well say hello."

Like I was letting her walk away without being clear to him where she belonged.

"Just like that?" She lifted a brow, watching me warily.

"Is there a problem?"

The sunlight streaming in hit the auburn streaks in her hair, highlighting them like she had spun copper into it. "No, no problem."

The elevator door dinged, and Gwen grabbed her handbag. When I rounded the corner, there was Lakewood, handing a to go cup to my fiancée. I scowled at him, but he took no notice as he said, "Holy shit, you've moved in with Jay-Z?"

Gwen laughed. "You're ridiculous. Not Jay-Z, just my overbearing fiancé."

"This place is—" He stopped speaking abruptly when he finally noticed me.

"Lakewood," I said through my teeth.

He gave me a nod. "Oh, hey man, nice digs."

"I didn't expect you this morning, especially this early."

His smirk told me everything I needed to know. He thought we were in a competition for Gwen. He was going to find out otherwise.

"We have a tradition, Gwen and I," he said with a grin. "I bring her morning hot chocolate and walk her to work. It doesn't change now that she lives here."

I saw the sweep of his gaze over my shirtless form, and then his gaze over Gwen in her rose-colored silk blouse, a black pencil skirt that tapered just below her knees, and the red-soled Louboutins. "Right." I turned my gaze to Gwen. "Like I said, lunch. We need to talk. I'll meet you at noon." I frowned when my gaze reached her finger. "Where is your ring?"

With a pursed lip, she tugged on her necklace to show me her engagement ring. "Right here. I'm clumsy with my hands and it weighs a ton, not to mention it's too big."

"You should have said. We'll have it resized."

"Fine. I've got to go."

"Lunch today."

She swallowed. "I'll see. I might be really busy."

The fuck she would be. Either she came to me, or I'd go to her. "Okay, whatever you need."

Without a glance to Lakewood, I tucked my arm around her waist, pulling her close, and kissed her. I poured every ounce of desire and desperate clawing need into the kiss. I wanted her to remember who she was sleeping next to before I let her walk out the door with Lakewood.

Even as I coaxed her into a response, a thought danced at the edge of my consciousness. I was letting her walk out the door with Lakewood, who had brought her fucking hot chocolate.

Did she not like coffee? If she did, why didn't I know her coffee order? More importantly, why the hell wasn't it in Pierce's dossier? He was usually more thorough than that. Her lips parted in a surprised gasp, and I took advantage, sliding my tongue into her mouth.

There was nothing more satisfying than hearing that little moaning whimper she made at the back of her throat. As the kiss deepened, I tugged her closer, my body pressing against hers. I could feel the heat emanating from her, and it only fueled my desire. I wanted to consume her, to make her forget about Lake-wood and everything else in the world. I could feel her body respond to my touch. Her hands made their way into my hair, pulling me close.

Reluctantly, I tore my lips from hers, my heartbeat racing too fast. And I whispered, "I'll see you at lunch, Ness."

CHAPTER 14
GWEN

HE HAD NO IDEA.

That's all I could think about the entire walk to work with Lance. Atticus had gotten me off this morning and he had no idea.

Did you want him to have an idea?

Yes.

No.

Maybe.

Ugh. It had just felt so... intense and visceral and real. And he really had been asleep and horny.

I knew what this was, but why was I disappointed that he had no idea how he'd touched me in his sleep?

Lance prattled on about communication strategies for the team and how we had to try some new sake bar around the corner, and how maybe now I could actually take a goddamn break.

But I was too busy, too focused on the horror show of my life

My husband-to-be had gotten me off this morning. Spectacularly. Worse, he'd been asleep when he'd done it.

Imagine how good he'd be fully awake?

Oh my God. And then he'd come out walking around in those thin gray pajama pants, and I could fucking see everything. And he'd still been hard. Very, very hard. Honestly, he needed to be careful, because that thing could club somebody on the head and knock them clean out.

"Are you okay?"

"Sure. I'm fine," I muttered as I played with my cup of hot cocoa. The warmth soothed me, but I hadn't taken a sip.

"I know you better than that. You look stressed the hell out, Gwen. I know you think you have to do this thing, but you don't."

"Yes, I do. It's done anyway. The engagement party is in a couple of weeks."

He pressed his lips together. "I guess the view can't be ignored."

I didn't like the subtle dig, but I let it slide, knowing he was just worried about me. "The penthouse, yeah, it's a stunner. And if I'm being fair, at least Micah is nice. I can't read Atticus at all. He's like a granite wall."

A granite wall with a very big—

"So what, he's kissing you now?" he asked.

A wash of heat hit my face so hard I was surprised it wasn't sand-blasted. "Um, what?"

"That kiss, is that a thing now?" he asked through clenched teeth.

Hell. "Look, this thing is happening, so I'm trying. And he is doing... I don't know, doing a reasonable facsimile of trying. Your anger is at the wrong person. Dad is the one who used me. Dad is the one who put me there."

"While I'm pissed off at the old man, it looked like Pendragon was doing a whole hell of a lot more than trying."

"Well, we have to make it look real, okay? I'm trying to make the best out of a shitty situation. You were there. I was blindsided. It's already hard enough without your judgment. We are stuck, so we might as well try to get to know each other." Utter bullshit. I didn't want to lie to Lance, but he wasn't going to let it go.

"But I thought—"

I tugged him to a stop. "You thought what?"

"I thought that you weren't going to do it."

"We covered this, Lance. If I don't do it, Morgan has to. And while Atticus Price might be cold-hearted and not particularly gregarious or chatty, he met the terms. Someone else might have pushed for more. It's a good deal. And even better, it's not Bronson Jacobson."

"And what about you? I care about you, Gwen. You're just going to suffer in silence?"

"Yeah, if it means my employees have what they need and aren't carved up for parts. If it means my sister doesn't have to get tied to somebody at the age of eighteen, yeah. I can do anything."

He sighed, his shoulders slumping. "It's just... I don't know. I'm used to you fighting."

"Well, I am plum out of fight right now, Lance. I am exhausted, trying to hold everything and myself together. So I need some help."

"I told you, I can go to my family. I—"

"No, when I said help, I didn't mean *you* falling on a fucking sword. Only one of us gets to do that, and I have already fallen. When I say I need help, I need you to assist me in making this transition as smooth for my people as possible. You running in to rescue me doesn't save Morgan."

He sighed at that. "Fuck. You really are between a rock and a hard place."

He had no idea. I squeezed my eyes shut, trying not to think of just how hard Atticus was last night. "I have come to terms with it. So, right now, I just need your support, Lance."

"You have it, always, Gwen. And I'll get with Morgan about your engagement party."

"I appreciate that, but there's a party planner," I said. "Neither one of you has to do it."

"But as your man of honor, presumptuous, I know, but—"

I shook my head. "You really think Atticus Price is going to let you be the man of honor?"

Lance tipped up his chin. "I'd love to see him try to stop me."

I could see it, Lance and Atticus were going to be a problem. Because there was absolutely, positively no way Atticus was going to let another man stand up next to me at our wedding.

Over his dead body.

Or mine.

CHAPTER 15
ATTICUS

"You're here early."

I scowled when I found my brother and Pierce in my office going through our financial report. "Well, what the fuck are you two doing in here?"

Pierce just shrugged. "Micah said you had a better display board."

He was right. I did have a better display board. For reasons I couldn't quite fathom, Micah hadn't wanted a massive corner office. He'd kept his smaller one. It didn't matter how much I tried to force him into taking one of the executive offices, he still didn't want it.

"Okay, what are we looking at?"

Micah rolled his shoulders. "I'm looking at the due diligence from Becks. Something is not adding up."

I ran my hand through my hair. "We vetted them. So what's the problem?"

Pierce just shrugged, somehow managing to balance his chair just so without tipping over one way or the other. He was a graceful motherfucker, and he was annoying. He moved with the stealth of the training he'd no doubt had in Special Forces. "It's not so much the bottom line. R&D divisions are always a money pit. That's not even my main issue. My issue and why I'm here is the security aspect of it. See that client list? Sixteen clients. All having purchased, or so we think, specific access levels to this new software. A new push and release are expected in the next month. So on paper, R&D should be flush with cash, but it's not. Where is that money going?"

I frowned as I looked at the balances. "Okay, do we have any other companies for comparison?"

Micah held up a folder. "Check your iPad. I'm having a sneaky look at their books, but none of it makes sense."

"Why do you always come to my office when you want to hack something?"

"What?" he asked innocently. "You said I couldn't hack the NSA anymore, but you didn't say I couldn't hack at all."

I slid my gaze to Pierce. "You're not going to say anything?"

"No. If I can't ask you about your afternoon delight, I'm not going to ask him about his hacking activities. I like my bank accounts the way they look."

I rolled my eyes. "Both of you are assholes."

Both my brother and Pierce grinned at me.

I reviewed the findings on my iPad after I removed my jacket. My frown deepened the more I read. Gwen was right. They didn't have any money. Her father had, in essence, set R&D adrift, knowing she hadn't signed off yet. And we hadn't ratified our contract. So, how the hell was she going to pay her employees in the next few weeks while we sorted out the nitty-gritty details?

No wonder she was fucking stressed.

Fuck.

"There should be customer funds in here. Do you think someone is pinching it? Is it Lakewood?"

Pierce glanced at Micah. Micah glanced back at Pierce and then to me. "Um, no. Lakewood is clean. We looked."

I ground my teeth. "Define clean."

Pierce just shrugged. "He's clean on paper. No nasty drug habits. No wife or child support to worry about. Nothing anyone can really blackmail him with. And he's good at his job. Actually, I think we have a skillset opening for him in London."

I smiled then. "London, you say?"

"Well, he's been tech operations here, but he can be more useful somewhere else while we work out how all the employees fit in."

"Pierce, sometimes, I want to kiss you fully on the mouth."

"I think my last girlfriend read a lot of romance novels like that."

I grinned at him. "I'm sure you read some too."

He shrugged. "I cannot confirm or deny. The point is, I can get rid of him if you want."

"And by rid of him, I know you just mean to London, right?"

Pierce just rolled his eyes. "Okay, if you say so."

Micah shook his head. "You let him casually talk about murder, but I can't talk about hacking?"

I scrubbed a hand over my face. "I swear to God, I need better friends. One of you, tell me something useful."

Micah hit a couple of keys and then used his laser pointer. "Right there. That's the one we should dig into."

I glanced at the numbers, the deposits, and the receivables. "What company is that?"

"AKC Consulting," said Micah. "It's a small tech firm. From the amount of receivables in there, they're not doing enough business to be able to afford access to this kind of software. Not to mention, what are they going to use it for? They're a small house. As far as I can tell, they just pump out apps."

"Right, so what's their story?"

"Well, the issue is more like, who are they owned by?"

A prickle of alarm danced at the base of my spine. "Fuck."

"That's precisely the right sentiment. Jacobson. Not the younger. The senior. The senior is a lawyer who executes a trust."

"Fuck. Let me guess, a trust that benefits Bronson Jacobson. What is his hard-on for this software?"

Pierce, still bouncing on two feet of his chair, shrugged. "It could be about the girl."

"They know each other, but have they dated?" Micah asked.

Pierce shook his head. "It didn't come up. I've got nothing on them. They've been in the same circles for a long time, but her movements indicate nothing about knowing him on a personal level."

"Okay, then. Unlikely his interest is about her. If it's not her, then it's fucking me."

Micah scrolled through the data. "What do you want to do?"

"For now? Float the money to cover their salaries and operations until we hit the final on this deal. I'll send a new contract to Gwen that covers what she'll need for salaries and to continue running until we take over fully."

"Right, done." My brother studied me closely. "What's wrong with you?"

"She didn't tell me she needed help."

Pierce just chuckled, and Micah just shrugged. "Why would she?"

"Because I'm going to be her husband. We are going to be married. She could have asked me for thirty million dollars, knowing I would feel obligated to give it to her."

"Maybe she isn't the kind of woman who wants your help," Pierce suggested.

"Everyone wants something from me."

Micah shrugged. "I don't. Pierce doesn't."

"You know what I mean. Women. Women always want something."

"Well," Micah said, "it looks like Gwen might be one of the few who doesn't. And maybe you need to treat her accordingly. Besides, brother, you made that choice."

"I made that choice because it came with the software."

Micah cocked his head and gave me a sarcastic smirk. "Okay, if you say so. But the moment you found out that the woman from the balcony was Becker's daughter, you were all in."

That itchy, too-tight feeling on my skin was almost too much to bear. "What's your point?"

"My point is you finally met a woman who doesn't actually want anything from you, and she's tied to you at no-fault of her own. You're going to have to find a way to navigate around it. You can't just buy your way out. If you want her, you're going to have to do a little work and maybe chill out just a little."

"I am chill."

That statement was the only thing capable of making Pierce tip over in laughter.

CHAPTER 16
ATTICUS

LA TABLE RONDE WAS BUSIER THAN USUAL WHEN I WENT TO MEET MICAH after my morning meeting. I found him in our usual corner, a waitress flirting with him shamelessly. As usual, he didn't seem to notice. Just pushed his glasses up and gave her a bland smile.

When I met him, I just shook my head lightly. "Poor thing has no idea that you're not even noticing."

Micah shrugged. "Oh, I noticed. I'm just looking for something different."

"Well, brother, what was it that society mag called you? Oh yes, filthy rich and nerdy hot. I feel like you can find a woman easily." I shrugged. "Or man."

He shook his head. "Sorry, I'm more discerning than that. I'll know it when I see it."

"If you say so."

Neither one of us was particularly enthused about this meeting, but Richard Lions was an old family friend. He'd just chosen the wrong side of the board vote to oust my father. "Where is Lions?"

Micah shrugged and dug into his light salad. My brother, who was even more regimented than I was about things like food and exercise, indulged himself often because he'd eat a salad at eleven o'clock in the morning, then small meals every few hours or so. And then he'd eat a whole fucking cake about once a month or so. Made no sense to me, but it was none of my business. "Your guess is as good as mine. He claimed that this was an urgent meeting."

Lions was a wild card. One who made it clear that we couldn't trust him. But ignoring him could have dire consequences.

I lifted my brow. "I have more important things to do." Namely, deal with my soon-to-be wife. I'd cleared my lunch calendar to meet with her, but she hadn't accepted the meeting.

My brother put down his fork. "Someone is eager to see his new bride. How'd it go last night?"

"You mean besides her hating me and being pissed off that her father essentially sold off her and her company?"

He laughed. "So it went well then."

I kept thinking about her scent. All morning it had clung to me, even after I showered. It was enough to make my balls ache. "As well as I expected."

"Are you still sure this is the best call, Atticus?"

"She's signed the contract, so yeah."

"You know how dangerous it is having someone that close. We could be exposed."

"I'm not worried about it. She's my wife. Besides, Gwen protects her people. Once we're married, I'm included in that. We can trust her."

Micah cocked his head. "You're serious? You really intend for this to last? No other women?"

"Are we seriously talking about my sex life?"

"Sorry, but you opened your sex life up for discussion. You've written it into the clause. So, do you intend to shag her then?" Micah's British accent was mostly gone these days except for the occasional slang word or two unless he was talking to one of his friends back in London.

"Not up for discussion."

His quick bark of laughter was unabashed. It was almost like the old days of us playing Knights of the Round Table. Micah was always Merlin. We'd been fighting an imaginary dragon with our paper towel roll swords and broken a Ming Vase.

Micah still bore the scar just under his chin from the beating our father gave us. My scar was on my soul from him forcing me to watch.

The memory of Micah and me playing on the estate grounds a few weeks after his arrival in New York was vivid and sharp.

At first, I hadn't wanted a brother, but it had been nice to have someone to talk to. I mostly avoided my father, and my mother was always busy. Outside of school, I had some friends, but I was a loner. Having Micha around helped me come out of my shell.

We used cardboard rolls as swords, and he tied a pillowcase to the back of his T-shirt to act like a cape, as he was playing Merlin, of course.

He was supposedly training me to become a great king, but I needed a lot of training. Despite being smaller than me, he was surprisingly quick on his feet.

We laughed, played, and made noise like children. When Micah began to whine for a snack, we went up the back stairs to the kitchen.

After getting us both snacks, I accidentally threw a pretzel at my little brother. Micah, not one to back down, retaliated with his cardboard sword.

While playing, we moved into the sunroom where I knocked Micah's sword out of his hand. As he chased after it, he skidded on the floor and bumped into the sideboard, causing a vase to fall and shatter.

The resulting clatter and crash of the vase happened in slow motion.

Even through the hazy fog of memory, my palms began to sweat as I remembered trying to push Micah out of the sunroom, but it was too late. Next, came the choreographed dance of Dad running in, me stepping in front of my brother, and my father shoving me out of the way.

It was at that moment that Micah realized he had not been drawn into a fairy tale, but into a nightmare.

I shook my head to clear the stinging memory. "Shut up, Micah."

"Sorry. Sorry. It's just... You know that's not going to work, right?"

"Forget it. Let's circle back to Lakewood. He has to be dealt with."

"What's the urgency?" Micah asked.

"For starters, he's far too close to Gwen. He's going to jeopardize everything about this deal."

He drained his smoothie. "She doesn't know why you agreed to the marriage, does she? She really thinks it's about the software?"

Gwen thought I was bailing her company out, but I needed her as much as she needed me. She had no idea why though. And if she ever found out, she wouldn't like it. Matter of fact, she'd raise hell. "I told you before, I want the predictive algorithm. She serves our purpose in this case, so it works."

"Yes, of course, the algorithm. I just didn't know a predictive software algorithm had such nice assets. And that little clause about your thirtieth birthday has nothing to do with it."

"Shut your mouth," I growled.

He inclined his head toward the door. "Look alive."

"Showtime," I muttered under my breath.

Richard Lions had been my father's VP of Operations. He'd known what my father was up to all that time, and he'd chosen to cover his own ass.

Micah stood, but I didn't bother. As he approached, Lions seemed unfazed. "Micah, Atticus, thanks for seeing me."

I ignored his outstretched hand and leaned back in the leather high-back chair. With my fingers steepled in front of my chest, I asked, "What is it you want, Lions? I've got plans. If you hurry up, I can still make it to lunch to see my fiancée."

"Congratulations on the nuptials, by the way." Lions shook Micah's hand, took a seat across from us, and cleared his throat. "You've got every right to be pissed off. I chose wrong. Not much I can do about it now."

I eyed him and narrowed my gaze. "You chose wrong? Is that how you're going to play it?"

Five years ago I discovered my father had been slowly siphoning my company out from under me. My grandfather had left Pendragon Tech to me, *not* my father, and I'd had to wrestle control from him and take the appropriate steps to protect my mother after he'd spent years gaslighting her. And Lions wanted to tell me he had 'chosen wrong'?

Micah tried to diffuse the building tension. "I think what Atticus means is that you need to tell us why you're here."

I scowled at my brother. He had more diplomacy than I did, but in this case, it wasn't deserved.

Lions nodded. "Yes, of course. I just want you to know, Atticus, back then you were known more for your playboy ways than your business acumen. I had to make a call about what I felt was best for Pendragon Tech at the time."

I leaned forward then, fixing my gaze on him, staring him down. Everyone thought I was cold and calculating because they never saw the heated rage that lived right under the surface of my skin. "And you chose that psychotic geezer. But it's just business, right? Still, it makes me wonder why the fuck we're even meeting with you."

It would be so easy to eviscerate him, to tear him to shreds, and energy pulsed through my body because I wanted to do it. I wanted to lay bare every sin that I knew he'd committed, the ones he didn't have a clue I knew about, and the ones the public certainly didn't know about. I wanted to do it right there in the middle of the restaurant. To lay them at his feet as I pummeled him.

Micah, already reading my mood, leaned forward as well and plopped a hand on my chest. "Speak, Lions. You don't have long."

Lions sputtered. "Your father and I don't speak anymore. Not since I realized what he'd done to your mother. Those of us who supported him didn't know. At least I didn't."

"I don't give a fuck," I growled.

Lions used a napkin to dab sweat from his brow. "He's coming for you. He's got a plan. He's been working with Jacobson for nearly a year. They have a partnership."

I chuckled then. "That's not news. We knew that already."

"Okay, then do you know he sent spies into Pendragon? I don't know who they are, but you've got a leak, and you need to plug it. He knows all about the Becks deal, and Jacobson is doing everything he can to get in on it, so you'll be stuck with him anyway."

Micah shook his head. "He can't come back. The board themselves ousted him."

Lions shrugged. "All I know is that he's making his moves. He's already got several board members on his side. Not me, though. My vote is still in play, and I won't vote for him. Not this time. But he has gotten some support, so you need to watch yourselves."

Micah sighed and adjusted his tie. "You've wasted our time, Lions."

The older man sat forward, pinning me with a direct stare. "I fucked up, okay? I backed the wrong horse, and that's on me. But it's in good faith that I come to you now. Your mother and my wife were very good friends. And after my wife died, your mother was there for me. She was kind. I didn't know what your father was doing to her. Maybe I've come to you out of loyalty or revenge, I don't know. But you have my vote. I suggest you gather others. It's going to be a fight."

"Is that all?" I asked through clenched teeth.

"All I know for certain is that he knows about the Becks deal, and that's not public knowledge yet. He's got something planned about your mother. You need something to fight back with. Something good. If she's not hidden and safe, make sure."

He pushed away from the table and stood, striding out without a backward glance.

Micah turned to me. "Well, what do you think?"

"I think Lions is a disloyal fool. And I think he deserves whatever happens to him."

When I glanced over at my brother, he was pinching the bridge of his nose.

"But I think he's right," I conceded. "Dad is coming for us. But I say, let him come."

CHAPTER 17
GWEN

IF THERE'D BEEN A WAY TO AVOID THIS CONVERSATION AND MAKE SURE that I didn't have to go through with this, I would have done it.

But the die was cast. I had to talk to my father.

I went to my office to drop off my bags first, and Carrie, my assistant, gave me my messages. I gave her a warm smile and said, "Hey, can you get an all-hands meeting on the books for today? Whatever time is the least harrowing for most people."

"Okay, I'll see what I can do."

"Thanks."

She gave me a nod, and I took the elevator to the top floor to see my father.

His assistant, Teresa, wasn't at her desk, so I let myself in, much to his surprise.

"Gwenyth, what are you doing here?"

"We need to talk, dad."

"I thought I was clear about my expectations Friday night."

"Dad, you can't decree something as insane as this and expect me not to have questions, or thoughts, or problems."

"I can. R&D has been a drain on us. This solves the problem. I don't have to sell off Becks. I don't have to cover up for the company. I just have to parcel you off."

"The point is I have a whole team I need to address. What do I tell them?"

"Tell them the truth. Honestly, Gwenyth, do I have to explain how to run a business to you?"

"As if I would take advice from you. It's your over expansion that got us into this mess. When I came on board four years ago, you swore to me you wouldn't do this. So why? Do you hate me that much?"

"I do not hate you. I'm trying to teach you something, Gwen. The world is not all sunshine and roses. Sometimes you'd have to make tough decisions. If you don't know that by now, then you don't deserve to run your own company. I made the best decision that got me what I needed for my people."

"I'm one of your people, Dad."

"Not entirely. You are part of Pendragon now. And I got the best of both worlds. That's called a compromise. Now, I have a meeting this morning. You're dismissed."

"Absolutely not."

My father's brows popped. I never argued with him. "I beg your pardon?"

"Yes, you should beg my pardon. I could make this messy and loud. I could make myself a giant pain in the ass. I do not have to go quietly into the night."

"Didn't you sign off that you would?"

I swallowed hard. "Fine. But until Pendragon takes over fully, you still have the little business of running the company and getting us ready for the merger. Payroll sent me frantic emails that we are off their books, but we're not on Pendragon's yet. So how am I supposed to get anyone paid?"

My father looked me straight in the eye. "Well, Gwen, that sounds like your problem, not mine."

CHAPTER 18
ATTICUS

A‌FTER LEAVING THE RESTAURANT, I CLIMBED IN THE CAR, AND G‌AVIN flicked his gaze to mine in the rearview mirror. "Are you all right, boss?"

I ignored the sarcasm dripping from his words. I wasn't taking any shit right now. "Yep, I'm fine. Let's head to Becks Incorporated. I just found out that my fiancée is not where I told her to be, so I guess I have a lunch date at Becks."

He studied me in the mirror. "So you're really doing this?"

"You know, I like it better when you just drive."

He chuckled softly. "Who did you piss off now?"

"I didn't piss anyone off. Richard Lions did the pissing off."

Gavin navigated in the traffic easily. I swear to God, the man knew no fear. He'd probably honed that skill during his years driving Formula One, but he'd had a nasty crash, and it had almost killed him. He had gotten into private security after that.

"What did Lions want?"

"Apparently, to warn me that the old man was coming for me. But I knew that."

"Did he give you anything actionable?" he asked. "We can get Pierce on it."

"Micah is already on it."

"Good. Since he's got your flank covered, are we going to talk about the wife thing?"

I rubbed at my jaw. "Don't you start, too." The bunch of them were the worst gossips.

"I like her. I'm just saying it's complicated. And right now, do we really need complicated?"

"I have it under control."

Liar.

"Sure you do, boss."

Once we arrived at Becks, I signed myself in like some kind of visitor. But this time, instead of getting off on the top floor, I got off on the sixth. Corporate R&D, previously known as Rebel Tech, it had been rolled into Becks Incorporated four years ago. And that was the beginning of James Becker's expansion plans.

Those plans had not gone so well for him. Too much too fast. Story of his life.

The woman at the desk pushed to her feet when she saw me. "Can I help you?"

"Yes. I'm Atticus Price. I'm here to see my fiancée."

Her eyes went wide. "Um, who-who is your fiancée?"

I lifted a brow. The announcement had gone out to all media outlets today. Either she hadn't seen it, or Gwen had instructed her staff to pretend it wasn't happening. For now, I'd assume the former. "That's our Gwen. Always keeping secrets. Can you let her know I'm here for our lunch date?"

She nervously tugged on her bottom lip with her teeth. "Um, I-I'm not sure she's still able to meet. She's got the whole team in an all-hands meeting at the moment. I'm the executive assistant for the finance team. I'm just helping out. I'll, uh... I'll let someone know you're here."

"No, don't bother. Just point me in the direction of the meeting."

The phone rang and she sighed. "Okay, down that hall to the right, and then all the way down. It's the largest conference room we have."

"Thank you."

I strolled down the halls, taking in all the bright puffs of color and the little alcoves with comfy seating. Hell, were those napping pods? Their whole R&D department looked and felt like a startup. I followed the assistant's directions and found the conference room just in time to see Gwen finishing up. I let myself into the back of the room, watching her as she presented to her team.

"In closing, I'll say that this move to Pendragon is exciting. We'll have the funds and the support. Everyone keeps their jobs and their salaries. I know that's always a point of contention and worry, and Pendragon has been so kind as to offer retention bonuses and their standard benefits. It's a good deal, and I hope that you all trust that I fought for you. So why don't we let this news settle for a bit. Think about it overnight. If you have any questions or concerns, I will do my best to clear my calendar and make time for each of you for the rest of the week."

And then she dismissed her team. Some people stayed, looking dazed in their seats as they turned to stare and whisper at each other quietly. Others ran out immediately, calling people on their phones. Probably their spouses. And all through it, there was Lakewood, right by Gwen's side.

He ushered her out the rear entrance, and I had to fight against the crowd in order to follow. When I caught up to them, Lakewood's hand was on the small of her back, ushering her down a hall into a corner office. I reached them just before Lakewood could close the door, and I said, "I hope I'm not interrupting you two."

Lakewood's expression fell, and his genial mask slipped just a little. "Price, why are you here?"

From inside the office, Gwen's soft voice came through. "Atticus?"

She peered around the corner, and I could see the tension lines around her mouth and the worry in her eyes.

"I came to meet you for lunch, remember?"

She blinked once and then stuttered, "We don't... I don't have a lunch on the calendar."

"We made a plan this morning, love."

The moment I said *love*, Lakewood looked like he wanted to hit me. And for that matter, so did Gwen. "Well, I can't right now. We need to meet and—"

"Do you mind if we have this conversation privately?" I turned to Lakewood. "You'll give us a few, won't you?"

Lakewood's gaze slid from me to her and back again, and he looked like he was going to dig in his heels. But Gwen sighed as she walked over. "Lance, give me ten. I'll meet you in your office, okay?"

He nodded and gave me a sharp nod before sauntering out. As he walked, I watched several of the women, and a couple of the men, look after him. That was interesting. He obviously had no problem garnering attention. So why was he sniffing around Gwen?

For the same reason you are.

"Atticus, I'm sorry," Gwen said as she closed her office door. "I am swamped. I thought I told you that this morning."

"And I told you I would see you at noon. It's twelve on the dot. So, are you ready?"

She ran a hand through her curls, and I realized that her hair was straighter and sleeker than yesterday but with big, bouncy curls added in. I wanted to touch the softness, but I kept my hands to myself.

"Atticus, I get it. The announcement has been all over the media. Half the team asked me about it before we had our meeting. Now I'm being called by media outlets and society pages. For fuck's sake, Atticus, I cannot deal with you, or this wedding, or anything else right now. I have employees to take care of."

"I understand that, but you still need to eat."

"So you think that I'm just going to drop everything?" she asked, clearly frustrated.

"To be fair, I told you to be ready on time. And you aren't. When we plan to be somewhere, I expect you to be there."

Her brows furrowed for just a moment. And then she gave me a stunningly sweet smile. One I should have recognized as the warning it was. She sat on the edge of her desk, and all I wanted to do was tug up that pencil skirt and run my hand over her ass.

Fucking hell. The blood drained straight to my cock, and it was hard trying to get my brain back online to focus.

"I'm sorry, Atticus, but I'm baffled. Did you just essentially tell me to be where you say when you want me to be there?"

"That's harsher than I said it, but I just like things a certain way."

"Well, prepare to be disappointed. Because I do not heed instructions. I do not do as I'm told, and contrary to your belief, I do not work for you."

"Don't you?"

"No, I don't. I did read that contract that you sent over. We, as far as this new arm of Pendragon goes, are partners. My entire team reports to me, and I do not report to you. Do you understand what that means, Atticus Price?"

A warning skipped up my spine, telling me to back off. But instead, I only stepped forward, drawn in like a moth to a very, very bright flame.

"I have a feeling you're about to tell me."

"Oh yes, I am about to tell you."

She planted her hands to the side of her desk, shoving up her tits and arching her back. *Fuuuck.* My gaze drifted to the rigid tips of her nipples enticing me through silk.

All I wanted to do was bury my face between them. Would she come if I just sucked on them? Jesus. I shook my head to try and clear it.

"While this is a partnership, Gwen, I still run Pendragon. And that algorithm will be available to all teams as we see necessary and fit."

"Yes, but sometimes that algorithm just doesn't work the way you want it to. It needs to be customized to each use. Constantly improved upon, and that is *my* team. You'll notice, if you bother checking your email, that I had some changes and addenda added to the contract."

Fuck. I'd been with Micah half the morning, and I hadn't seen that the contract had been returned.

"So one of the clauses you put in there was that you will not stay where I put you?" I asked.

Her chuckle was soft and sweet. "One of those addenda was that you not be a prick."

I flashed a grin at her, and her gaze skittered to my lips.

Yeah, she was just as attracted as I was.

I stood in front of her, planting my hands just shy of hers so I could lean over her body.

"What is it you want, my little Lioness?" I smiled down at her.

She lifted her chin, and my gaze was on her lips again, thinking about the kiss this morning and the dream last night. The one that had seemed so real, like she was close enough to touch. Like if I had just put my hand on her ass a certain way, she would have ridden me, just the way that I liked.

"Is there something else you need, Atticus? Because if not, I have a job to do. Employees who are wondering where the hell their next paychecks are coming from."

I couldn't take my eyes off her mouth. Her lips were expressive, transforming her whole face. She was saying something. Something important. And then it clicked, and I pulled back several inches.

"What do you mean your employees are worried about where their next paycheck is coming from?"

"The moment you and my father made that deal, we are in limbo until the final takeover."

"Correct me if I'm wrong, but since you're tied to me now, shouldn't you have asked me for help? That's the kind of thing you come and ask your husband for help with."

"As far as I'm concerned, I'm not married yet. And I solve my own problems."

I frowned at that. *I'm essentially a blank check waiting to be written.* "Why don't you just ask? We're about to be married, and I have a vested interest in this team."

Tell her you already solved the problem.

Actually, no, I wouldn't tell her just yet. I wanted to see just how stubborn she would be.

"I know all too well how these things fall through and promises get forgotten." She pushed to her feet, bringing her body in full contact with mine, and fucking Christ, the full body shiver that ran through me wasn't something that could be controlled.

She stepped around me, opening the door. "Now, if you don't mind, Atticus, I have actual work to do. Please look at the contract changes and sign it so I can pay my fucking employees. Employees like Carla over there, who's going through chemo treatments. And Michael, who just had a brand-new baby. Oh, and there's also Paul, who is desperately saving for a house. I don't have five million to throw at the problem to prove a point, but they are my responsibility and I made them a promise. They are counting on me. So I am the one that needs to fix this for them. I can at least do that much."

Shit. "I get it."

And for the first time in my adult life, I had been summarily dismissed.

CHAPTER 19
GWEN

"Dude, you are on the cover of every society page in the city."

I groaned as I slipped off my shoes and my sister strolled into my office. "Hey, Morgan, what are you doing here?"

She snorted a laugh. "My sister is on the fucking society pages. Where else would I be? We need to discuss."

"What about school?"

"School schmool. I just turned in a design project," Morgan said as she threw a copy of the *Times* on my desk then pulled up her phone showing me the gossip sites.

"You know I didn't intend to be on the society pages, right?"

"Well, that's one way to say that you weren't trying, because would you look at that? That is... my God. Was it terrible? Because it doesn't look terrible."

"I'm not going to tell you how my kiss was." Besides what could I say? I still think about it, but for him it was all business?

"Oh, come on. Give your sister a thrill. The man could play the Ice King in your favorite fantasy movie, but the pictures of him kissing you are hot, hot, hot."

I sighed. "It was fine."

"Please, be fucking for real."

Rolling my eyes, I muttered. "Okay, it was better than *fine*. It was one of those kisses that your body tingles about for days." We'd kissed yesterday, and I could still feel the after-effects of it. Hell, my lips still tingled.

Macy West, one of my lead developers, poked her head in. "Sorry, boss, but I could have sworn I heard Morgan."

"Oh, for fuck's sake, Macy, stop calling me boss. We were room-mates for how fucking long?"

Macy plopped herself on my couch next to Morgan. "Calling you boss gives me such a fucking thrill, mostly because you hate it. I always told you that you were a badass, so in a way, it's like telling myself I was right all the time."

"Would you two please stop?"

The two of them were exact opposites. Macy, with her paler-than-pale skin and light blond hair, dark lipstick, black sweater, and black, skintight jeans, was in complete contrast to Morgan's caramel coloring, dark silk-pressed waves, and solid white fashion sweat suit. "You guys would make a great *Town & Country* cover," Macy said.

"If you say so. Now please, you guys, I have work to do."

Morgan shook her head. "No, ma'am. We need to talk about this kiss."

Macy hoisted herself up and went to the closet where I kept my secret stash of gummy bears and pulled out a bag, opening it before offering Morgan a handful and then me. When she was settled back on my couch, Macy popped a gummy bear in her mouth. "Okay, spill. I don't have much time. The QA guys are going to call me in a second as soon as they find the next round of bugs."

I groaned. "We have customers waiting on this release."

Macy shrugged. "I know that. The team are working their asses off on it, but there are still bugs. Or more features, as I like to call them."

I rolled my eyes. "Do you want me to take a look at it?"

She shook her head. "Nah, we've got it covered. Now spill."

"There's nothing to spill, Macy."

"Lies. Because right now, I can see the look that you two are exchanging, and I know something is going on. You have to tell me. It's like friend-code."

I rolled my neck, trying to ease the tension. Seeing Atticus today had only made it worse. Since meeting him a little over a week ago, it was like there was an electric crackle all over my skin that I just needed to release like a giant lightning bolt or a really big orgasm. "It's nothing. We met, hit it off, he asked me out."

"I'm not buying it. You've been keeping secrets, boss. I want them. Show me the gorgeous ring I see in the photo."

"Mace, I can't tell you."

Morgan nudged her with an elbow. "Okay, Macy, she can't *tell* you. But if you guessed, she could probably confirm."

I rolled my eyes. "Jesus Christ, Morgan."

"What? Macy and I are basically your only friends and people in your life that you make time for. She needs to know because I need someone to talk to about it. I can't call you because you're too busy."

"You forgot Lance. You can also talk to him."

Morgan ignored me. "Like I said, Macy is the only other person in your life that *I* can connect with."

I sighed. "I'm not going to tell you, but if you guess in the ballpark, I wouldn't deny it."

Macy clapped her hands together and laid the bag of gummy bears aside. "Okay, um, I saw you wearing a massive rock in that picture, and you can't tell me that was costume jewelry. That shit was real. The kind of elegance those Park Avenue princesses wear. Was that really an engagement ring?"

I sighed and nodded, then pulled my chain out to show her the ring.

She and Morgan both whistled low when they saw it.

Her eyes went wide. "But you just met the guy. You don't even know him. I would have known if you were dating. You never leave this place."

I shrug. "Sometimes things move fast."

"No... You never leave this place, and you've been chasing down money because Becks is a shit show. Your father hasn't been able to manage all his acquisitions. He spent more money than he had, and now the piper has come for payment and he doesn't have it. Which means he needs to sell off parts of the company."

I rubbed the back of my neck. Sometimes, I hated having smart friends.

"Okay, so I'm in the ballpark. So... Oh my God, is this an arranged-marriage kind of thing?"

I sighed. "Morgan, I feel like you prepped her."

"I did not!" my sister said indignantly.

Macy shook her head. "Well, the moment I saw the ring and the gossip rags, I assumed something was going on. At first I thought maybe they were exaggerating. Because you know how they immediately love to put two sets of rich people together. But let's face it, you're not the usual demographic. And while people don't know it, you're no longer as rich as you used to be."

"Yeah, thanks for pointing that out."

"I still want you to have everything you have ever wanted. So rich is good, but you're not the usual type of socialite. You actually work for a living, for one thing. And you're hella smart. I'm guessing Pendragon wants a partnership, and your father is pushing for marriage."

"Well, that's that, I guess."

Macy shrugged. "So, how big is his dick?"

I choked on a gummy bear, and half of it went down the wrong pipe. Morgan and Macy both jumped up and came over to pat me on the back until we dislodged it. "Oh my God, I don't know," I sputtered.

Macy laughed. "I'm so sorry I almost killed you, but how was I supposed to know you were going to clutch your pearls at the mention of his dick size?"

"I have *not* seen his dick yet. We have agreed to take it slow. At least that part of the relationship. Everything else is moving at warp speed."

I eased back in my chair and hoped Macy would forgive my lies.

I slanted Morgan a glance as she dug through the gummy bear bag for the green apple ones and said, "I knew something was going on with you two. The way you jumped up to volunteer and the way he watched you at dinner... I mean, I know I thought the guy was cold, but there's something about you that thaws his frigid exterior a little. It's so hot."

"Wasn't that you calling him the Ice King just yesterday?"

"That was before you said you were going to try and work on things. So, how big is his dick?"

I rolled my eyes. "I wouldn't know. I told you I haven't seen it."

Morgan and Macy both shook their heads at me, and my sister said, "Well, that's something you are going to have to rectify soon because you don't want to be tied to someone forever if you don't know what you're working with."

"Will both of you relax? It's not going to be a problem."

My sister watched me as Macy finished off the bag of gummy bears. I was going to have to be careful. There was no hiding anything from her. One little slip and she'd see exactly how I felt about Atticus Price and his kisses.

CHAPTER 20
ATTICUS

I'd been so focused on her and the big picture that I didn't see what her father was up to. She was fighting for her people and hadn't asked for help. The fight was a trait I admired. But goddamn it, I wanted to help. It was hard not to be impressed by her, but she was far from being impressed by me. I needed to do something about that.

When I got home that night at nine-thirty, I knew where I'd find her. Not that I was having her followed, I was just having someone keep an eye on her. After all, if Lions was right about my father and Jacobson, it was better to keep an eye on her than not. But if she knew, she'd be irritated. So I didn't tell her.

I knocked on the slightly ajar library door. "It's late, you should go to bed."

She barely lifted her head. "As you can imagine, it was a long day for me."

"Of course, it was. Did you eat anything?"

She frowned. "What time is it?"

"Nine-thirty."

She gave me a sheepish half-smile. "Then other than my gummy bears, no."

"You need to eat. I'll get Magda to warm you a plate."

She frowned at that and then sat back and crossed her arms. She still wore her silk shirt from earlier, but she'd swapped that fuck-me skirt for sweatpants. "What are you doing?"

"What do you mean, what am I doing?" I asked, leaning against the doorframe. Her gaze swept over me, leaving little licks of heat everywhere it touched me.

"This act. Being nice. You have already made it clear in public that we are the real deal. But it's not like you talk to me other than to bark orders. Why are you being nice?"

I sighed. I had said that. And I had been an ass. "I'm just trying to make sure you've eaten and that you get some sleep. That's all."

She frowned, working her bottom lip with her teeth. "I still don't trust you."

"I'm well the fuck aware of that. Now eat something. Go to bed. We're tied together for the foreseeable future, and you're going to be my wife, which makes it my job to take care of you. So fucking eat, would you? And not gummy bears, for the love of God."

She looked adorable with her pursed lips and narrowed gaze. "I don't remember the last time someone took care of me. I promise you, I'm not a damsel in distress. You don't need to ride in on a horse to save me."

I cocked my head at that. The way she'd bit out the words. When was the last time someone had taken care of her? "Okay. But I'll have Magda warm something up for both of us. I know if I didn't have a chance to eat, you certainly didn't either."

"I'll eat later." She inclined her head toward the bowl of gummy bears.

I shook my head. "You can't be serious."

"Have you ever had a gummy bear?" She cocked her head and studied me, her gaze doing a slow perusal of my body, turning those little fires into furnaces as she went along.

"Not since I was twelve."

"Well, you're missing out. Gummy bears are my favorite. And they're surprisingly filling."

I shuddered. "You know they're nothing but sugar, right?"

"And sugar is delicious."

"You need to eat proper food." I pressed my case. "You know, protein. A vegetable or two."

"And I will. I'm just busy. So right now, I'll stick to empty calories. Tomorrow I'll guzzle down a smoothie. Get lots of protein and veggies."

I sighed, turning when I saw Magda coming down the hall with a tray. I took it from her with a smile and a nod of thanks and then turned to my wife-to-be. "No, you're going to eat real food now."

Gwen pierced me with a narrow-eyed pout that only made me want to kiss her as I placed the tray on the coffee table.

"You can eat with me," I said. "How's that?"

Magda had piled the plates high with enough for two and had included two spoons and napkins.

"Christ, Atticus, are you going to follow me around and make sure I eat?"

"If I have to." I sat down on the couch and patted the seat next to me as I lifted the silver plate covers. Scents from the rich stew wafted into the room, and I could see her nose twitch. Just knowing that she considered gummy bears an acceptable meal irritated me. Why wasn't she taking better care of herself? "You're going to eat. Then you're going to put away the laptop and get ready for bed."

She squared her shoulders. "I'm still not—"

I put up a hand. "Yes, I know. You're still not sleeping with me. Got it. Noted. And maybe you'll remember that I promised I wouldn't touch you until you begged me to. Your only job is to sleep there."

She pushed to her feet and came to join me on the couch. When I handed her a spoon, she took it reluctantly. "Only because I'm being forced to sleep there."

"Do you have to sleep there? Yes. Am I going to make you do anything you don't want to do? No. Except for the eating thing. So tuck in."

I didn't start to eat until I watched her spoon the first bite of stew into her mouth. And when she gave a delicate moan and her stomach grumbled, I nodded appreciatively and started to eat as well. "See? Not so bad, is it?" I asked.

She rolled her eyes. "Fine, it's delicious. But still, I'm not done working for the night, so I'm not going to bed yet."

"I'll give you a couple of hours. But you're not going to be of help to your team if you run ragged and don't feed yourself anything better than gummy bears."

She opened her mouth to argue, but instead, I tore off a piece of the dinner roll and shoved it in her mouth before she could talk.

She made this adorable little growling sound at the back of her throat, but then she moaned. Fuck, I was hard. There was something about feeding the woman that oddly also made me want to fuck her. Jesus, I needed help.

"What would the world think if they saw you feeding me?" she mumbled around the bite of bread.

I shrugged. "If I concerned myself with the opinions of others, I'd never get anything done."

She ate three more bites hurriedly. "Can we be done now so I can finish?"

"With the pace you keep, you're burning yourself out. Take it from someone who knows."

She grinned at me and then took one of the rolls back to the desk. "Question for you."

"What's that?"

"Does anyone ever insist that *you're* going to burn out?"

I wet my mouth before answering. "Sometimes. Mostly Micah, but yes."

"But do most people ask you that? Or is the assumption that you should work hard?"

I pressed my lips together. "What are you getting at?"

"You know exactly what I mean."

I shook my head. "No, I don't."

"What I mean is, you're a man. Nobody questions how much you work. Matter of fact, people question your commitment if you don't work hard. But as a woman, I'm not supposed to work like that. But if I don't, they question my work ethic. I just care about my job, and about my team, and—"

"You think you have something to prove?"

"Don't I?"

"You tell me."

She swallowed hard. "For years, I have worked to make this company something I could be proud of. Something my father could be proud of. I don't know, to honor my mother's legacy or something. Everything she gave up so my father could build Becks. I have my team, the software, the job. It's all I have."

"I doubt that. You have a sister you clearly love."

She coughed a laugh. "Morgan, yeah. You're probably wishing you'd taken the other sister now, aren't you?"

Fury flashed hot over my skin as I cocked my head, assessing her. "Why do you do that?"

"Do what?" she asked around another bite of bread.

"I'm not sure what it is exactly, but it's almost like you deliberately mark yourself as less than Morgan. Just because your father does it, that doesn't mean it's true."

Her brow furrowed. "First of all, I do no such thing. I love my sister."

"That's apparent. You were willing to fall on the sword for her."

"Well, I wouldn't need to fall on the sword if you didn't want to carve out part of my father's company."

"That's what Bronson Jacobson wants, and he doesn't care about your software. He just wants to make sure I don't have it. But I'm a businessman. Your father is the one who dangled you out like a carrot."

She sighed. "Whatever little pissing contest you have with Jacobson is not my business."

"It's your business now. You are marrying a Price."

She swallowed hard. "By force."

"Look, there are benefits to being married to me, and you're not taking advantage of it."

She shrugged. "Aren't you counting your lucky stars though? You got me for a bargain."

"For the record, just so it's crystal clear, I got you because *you* were the one I wanted. Morgan isn't the one who glitter-bombed me and called me a nepo baby. She's not the one with the eyes that see straight to my soul. She's not the woman with the lips that tempt or the one who cracked shards of ice off my personality."

A soft gasp was her only response.

"Now that I have some food in you, though I wish you'd eat more, I was serious about wanting you in bed in two hours. If not, I'll come back, and I won't ask as nicely."

Then I left her sitting in the study before I did something stupid like kiss her again.

CHAPTER 21
GWEN

I DIDN'T SLEEP WELL.

And no, it wasn't because my brand-new fiancé was hogging the bed or because he'd somehow managed to maneuver me on top of him. *Again.*

Hell, it wasn't even because he'd woken me up, hard and pressing against my clit. How the hell did he manage to make me come while sleeping? *Again.*

All night, I'd been thinking about what Atticus said about me not asking for help. That my pride would get in the way of helping my people. He'd said I needed to trust him. Could I?

Not a good idea. You were sold to him. Letting your guard down is dangerous.

Dangerous, yes. But I had bargaining power. Maybe I needed to exercise that.

It had taken me all morning to work out the proposal for him. When I turned up at Pendragon Tech though, I wondered if I'd made a mistake.

The pretty brunette in the front room of his office eyed me up and down.

I'd worn lavender wide-leg pants and a white cap-sleeve top. I looked fine. So why was she looking at me like I was yesterday's garbage? Her gaze was the same as one of those girls in high school, and boy oh boy, had they found me lacking.

She has nothing to do with you.

I forced a broad smile at her. "Hi, I'm—"

"I know who you are," she said in a clipped tone.

Well then. "All right, is my fiancé in his office then?"

I saw the muscle in her jaw tick as she kept typing, not bothering to meet my gaze. "He's very busy."

"Okay, but he told me anytime I needed anything, I was to come directly to him. So I'll just pop in really quick."

She shoved to her feet and yelled, "I said he's occupied."

But I still managed to bypass her. I might not be a Price yet, but if Atticus told me to come to him directly with problems, and last night was a test, I planned to take him up on it.

I knocked on his door, knowing he could see it was me through the glass, but I could also see that he wasn't alone.

Bronson.

The cold sweat that popped up on my skin made me swallow hard.

Fuck. Fuck. Fuck.

I forced a smile on my face and opened the door as he gestured for me to come in.

"Well, this is a surprise," he said as he walked around the desk, and all I could do was force that tight-lipped smile. Bronson was glowering at me from the couch.

He can't hurt you. He cannot hurt you. Your company is not in his hands.

Atticus made a show of brushing his lips over mine. I could also feel the heated stare from the doorway behind me, which meant bitchy-face was pissed.

"Mr. Price, I'm so sorry, she just—"

Still tucking me against him, he shifted to the side to look at her. "Gwen is about to be Mrs. Price, which means that she has access to me whenever she wants it."

I could almost hear her sputtering, and I wanted to turn to look and relish it, but I couldn't. I had bigger fish to fry. What the hell was Bronson doing here?

"I'm so sorry to interrupt. You said to come by whenever, and I just..."

"You're fine," Atticus said. "Jacobson was just leaving, actually."

Bronson stood then, adjusted his suit, and rebuttoned his jacket. "How could I interrupt the lovebirds?" He shook Atticus's hand. "I guess we'll be talking more."

Atticus just cocked his head. I couldn't read that expression, but it felt icy. "We'll see how things go."

Bronson turned to me and spread his arms as if he expected me to walk into them.

Get fucked, asshole.

When I didn't step forward, Bronson stepped toward me.

But right before he could touch me, Atticus wrapped his hand around my middle and turned me aside so that all Bronson managed to do was tap me on the shoulder. His gaze narrowed at Atticus then swung to me just for a second. "Well, I guess I'll leave you two alone for whatever you'll be getting up to in here."

I pursed my lips together. "That, delightfully, is none of your business." And then I turned my back on him.

I knew to never turn my back on a wounded animal, ever. But I had to. Because I had to gather myself like nothing was wrong.

The door closed behind us, and the warmth from Atticus was gone.

"I'm surprised to see you, Gwen."

"I-I didn't know you had a meeting."

"Jacobson? He was in here trying to make a deal to license your tech. He knows with the acquisition that he no longer has a route except through Pendragon. Why?"

"No reason," I said. "I just didn't expect to see your competition in here."

He cocked his head and studied me as I tried to force my face into an emotionless mask. "Right," he said warily. "Let me get you a drink. What would you like? Pellegrino? Coffee? Tea?"

"Oh, tea, please." I needed to do something with my hands. I hated coffee with a passion. I loved the smell of it, but ugh, the taste... yuck. It didn't matter how much sugar I added or dilute it with milk, I still hated it. Lance always made a point of bringing me hot chocolate in the morning so I could look like one of the cool kids.

"Right. Tea it is then. Here you go."

But I'd turned to stare out the window, and his voice right behind me startled me. When I whipped around, my hand knocked against the mug, sending the contents splashing onto his shirt. "Oh my God, I'm so sorry. Fuck. Fuck, fuck, fuck. I'm so sorry."

I immediately reached into my bag and pulled out tissues, trying to soak it up, but his hands stilled mine. "Hey, it's okay. It's just a little spilled tea. I have another shirt in there. I'll change real quick. Don't move."

"Is this you telling me where to be again?"

"Maybe," he grinned. "But I do want to know why you're here, so give me two seconds."

He disappeared into the bathroom, giving me a second to take several deep breaths. His office wasn't what I'd expected. I'd expected another version of the penthouse. Cold. Bare. But there was oak paneling, dark and masculine. Leather couches and chairs. And there were photos here. A couple of him and Micah, one from what looked like a beach trip. Then I noticed one of him and another woman. I could see immediately that they had the same eyes. Probably his mother. And there was another photo of him with an older woman and Micah, also grinning. He looked happy.

I turned around to find him coming out of the bathroom. He didn't seem irritated at all that I was snooping. And he came out of the bathroom shirtless. My God.

For fuck's sake. I'd seen him shirtless the other day, but this was shirtless in suit pants. Jesus Christ.

I dragged my fingers along the corners of my mouth to make sure I wasn't drooling and also to make sure my lipstick was all right. Then I forced my gaze off his chest as he reached into his closet to pull out a clean dry shirt.

I deliberately tore my gaze away to his desk, and my heart stuttered when I saw a photo of myself. It was from the gala. The lighting was superb, and I was laughing. I remembered the moment. It was something Morgan had said. I looked happy. Where did he get this?

Suddenly, I felt his shadow next to me, and I turned to find him watching me. "Where did you get this photo?"

"I called the photographer from the event."

"Okay, it's weird that you have it."

"How is it weird that I have a photo of my fiancée on my desk? After all, shouldn't I? And since you brought it up, we need more pictures together. I'll have Leah organize an engagement photoshoot."

Oh, right. Engagement. We were getting married. I was his fiancée. He *should* have a photo of me, and I *should* have one of him.

No. Fuck that. There was no way I was going to have his sardonic face on my desk all day. Absolutely not.

"Um, you know what? We'd better have Morgan organize that. There may be a photographer she knows who's great at photographing bronze skin. We want the pictures to look good, don't we? I'm sure Morgan has contacts, and she can ask Clarissa to help."

He frowned. "Sorry, I didn't even consider that."

I shrugged. "Well, why would you?"

"I just... I never thought about involving your family. If there is anything else I'm not thinking about, please tell me."

He seemed to mean it. "Right. Listen, about last night..."

"What about last night?"

155

The way his voice went low and throaty made me clutch my thighs together, trying to stave off the melting of my core.

"I have been thinking about what you said. About me not asking for help and just fighting for my team. I'm just used to doing everything on my own. The one time I accepted help, it turned out badly."

That was the understatement of the century.

"Tell me, what do you need, Gwen?"

Morgan had told me that when I was dealing with him, I needed to use my assets. The problem was I wasn't charming like her. But I did have other assets. So I sat on the corner of his desk, angling my body to face him.

Immediately, his gaze dipped to the sliver of skin that appeared when I turned my body.

He eyed me up and down, his wintergreen gaze scanning me very slowly as he sat down in his desk chair, stroking his chin, watching me. While I was the one who had walked in here to bargain, he looked every bit the predator who was waiting for lunch.

Come clean. Tell him a little about Bronson.

"Okay, you're right. I need help and support. I know that you want the software. And obviously, it's yours, as am I. But I need to pay my employees. I need money to do that. We have client deliverables to finish."

"I see that. And what, you're here to negotiate that?"

"Yes. I propose that maybe our arrangement not only be for public consumption. The way you watch me sometimes, I think you want me. And you're obviously not hard on the eyes. Maybe this should be less an on-paper thing and a more real thing?"

He lifted a brow. "So, you walked here to negotiate with your tits and ass?"

"I'm just saying, we could—" I expelled a long breath and tried again. "Look, I'm not good at this, so let me just put it all on the line. I think you want me. And I would be lying if I said I didn't feel some kind of spark with us at the gala and when you've kissed me. It's just gotten all convoluted. And then you were throwing prenups at me and telling me I'd be in your bed. Anyway, if it means that my team gets what they need and that maybe things are less contentious between us and you will help me, then maybe I'm proposing a real marriage."

He watched me with narrowed eyes, his gaze hooded. "Do you have any idea why I kissed you the other day?"

"At the restaurant or the penthouse?"

'Well both, but mostly at the penthouse."

"No."

"I was jealous."

I frowned at that. "Of what?"

"Let's see, you left my bed at five thirty in the morning, not to go for a workout or anything, not because you're hungry, but to meet Lakewood."

Was he serious? "So? Lance had been my best friend and my right hand for years."

"Exactly. I don't like it because I want you to be mine. Only mine."

I swallowed hard. What was I supposed to say?

"And you were wearing that fucking pink silk blouse. It pebbled your nipples, and all I wanted to do was get my hands on them."

My mouth just formed a small *O* as I stared at him.

"I was irritated because Lakewood noticed as well. And I'm sure you walked with him all the way to work with your ass swishing back and forth in that skirt."

I swallowed hard.

He pushed to his feet, bracketing me on the edge of his desk, his breath warm on my neck, and I flushed deep.

"Take me at my word, Gwen. I've already taken care of the payroll problem. I handled it yesterday after we talked. You don't need to offer yourself up for sacrifice. You've done enough of that."

"But I—" I licked my lips and tried again. "I don't understand."

"When you come to me, I want it to be because you are so desperate you can't be anywhere but in my arms. I want to know that you're pressing your thighs together to try and calm that ache you have for me. And it doesn't matter, but I could swear that I know exactly how your ass feels in my hands while you're riding me. That's how vivid my fucking dreams of you are. But I want you because you *want* to be here. Not because you're trying to bargain or because your father is a prick who has given you to me. So, Ness, you're going to come to me because you want to. And I was serious when I said that you *will* be a Price. Which means you'll have everything you need."

"I—thank you. But I don't like uneven scales."

He pursed his lips, but his eyes stayed soft. "We're not keeping track, Ness."

"Why are you calling me Ness? My name is Gwen."

He chuckled softly, his breath against my neck. "You'll figure it out."

I turned and tried to twist out of his barricade, but he didn't budge. "Atticus, are you going to let me go?"

"No, I don't think I will."

"What?"

"I'm sure you haven't eaten today, so I'm going to feed you. And then I'm going to send you back to your office, fully fed and satisfied."

And why, oh why, did my traitorous pussy shudder at the sound of the word satisfied?

CHAPTER 22
GWEN

I SHOULD HAVE KNOWN I WOULDN'T ESCAPE THE DAY UNSCATHED.

I hadn't even gotten my usual sprawled-all-over-my-fiancé wake up call for my birthday. Which was bullshit. If I was going to have to sleep next to a gorgeous billionaire every night, the least he could do was warm a girl up.

Warm you up. Sure.

Whatever. I was almost getting used to the cuddles.

The point was this morning I'd woken up alone to a cold bed. Atticus was just coming back from the gym as I was leaving to meet Lance to walk to work. He hadn't even given me a performative kiss for Lance. Just kissed my forehead and told me to have a good day.

Even Lance hadn't said anything this morning, so I thought I'd escaped. My assistant, Carrie, had gotten the team to sign a card since that was the level of fanfare I was allowing.

However, no one told my sister.

The off-key singing down the hallway was my first clue. The raucous laughter was the second.

Maybe I could hide and she would just go away.

Alas, as the singing drew nearer, I knew it was too late.

I wasn't even embarrassed about it as I slid down my chair and hid under my desk. Maybe if she didn't see me, she would just go away and leave me to work in bliss.

Suddenly, a low baritone that *could* sing joined my sister.

Lance. The traitor.

He knew how I felt about my birthday these days. I used to love my birthday. It used to be my favorite day.

Not anymore though. One year older. Twenty-five.

Ugh, there had to be a way out of this.

The door to my office opened without the courtesy of a knock. I sat as quiet and as still as I could under my desk. Morgan and Lance still sang at the top of their lungs, though, Morgan purposely going even higher and more off-pitch.

God.

Mom had taken her to voice classes when we were kids because Morgan was convinced she was born to be a Broadway actress. Obviously, that never worked out, given my bleeding ears.

Finally, they stopped, and I held my breath, thinking they might just go away.

"Where the hell is she?"

Lance laughed. "You know Gwen. If she could avoid the whole day, she would."

"She can't keep avoiding her birthday."

"That's why we make it a point to celebrate even if she doesn't want to," Lance said. "I thought this year we were going to take her on a trip."

"Have you seen her schedule?" Morgan said shrilly. "As if I haven't already tried."

He sighed. "I guess we'll have to sit in here until she comes back. Even if it's all night."

Damn it, Lance.

Morgan laughed. "So while we wait, why don't you tell me what the penthouse is like? I keep trying to visit, but she's always here."

"I've never been further inside than the foyer," he muttered.

"Come on, you have to have *some* intel. I hear the Park Tower has a waterfall inside going down the center from the sixteenth floor to the second."

They stepped closer, and I could see their feet as one of them placed something on my desk. "Aren't you worried about her?" Lance asked. "I mean, she's your sister. You should be worried. Especially since she dove into this for you."

I could hear the irritation creeping into Morgan's voice when she spoke. "Do you dare to judge me? I didn't make her jump off a cliff for me. I didn't ask to be married. I don't even know the guy. How is that my fault?"

"You could have handled it better. At least I tried to do something."

I could almost hear Morgan rolling her eyes. "Oh, right, because you sat there and said, 'Oh no, I'll fall on the sword for my beloved Gwen.'"

"She's my friend. It's what you do."

"Yeah, I get that's what you do, but I know *why* you do it."

Lance's comeback was weak. "Ugh, shut up. You're the worst."

"No, *you're* the worst."

"Oh, Jesus fucking Christ, you're both the worst," I called from under the desk.

Lance laughed. "I told you she was here."

I climbed out from under the desk and turned to glower at the two of them. "How did you know?"

"Don't you remember that epic game of hide and seek all over campus?" Morgan turned to Lance. "Gwen hid under the headmaster's desk. We couldn't find her for hours."

"Fine," I said, dusting myself off. "Are you both happy now?"

Neither one of them was fazed by my lack of enthusiasm one bit. Morgan skipped from foot to foot, and Lance just grinned like an idiot.

"I hate you both."

My sister just laughed. "It's your birthday. You should celebrate it. You know how I feel about this."

"Why do people do this to me? I swear, it's like you don't know me."

In one of the few shows of solidarity between them, they both said in a singsong voice, "Because we love you."

"You know I don't like celebrating."

Lance sighed. "I know. But it's important. This is a big deal. Twenty-five."

"Yeah, just that much closer to thirty. Woohoo."

Morgan did a flourishing gesture toward the cake. Chocolate cake with white frosting had been our favorite cake to bake with Mom. But this looked like a super birthday version. There were strawberries and other fruits piled on top, as well as rose petals. "Oh, you dressed this one up."

"Of course. It's a special occasion. Oh, and I added a little rose water infusion to the cake, and I added a strawberry layer."

"Okay, now you're just showing off."

My sister gave a happy little twirl. "Well, cake is my love language. I don't like to bake anything else, but there's something about making someone a very specific cake that makes me happy."

"I do appreciate you."

"Oh, and there's a gummy bear surprise."

I lifted a brow. "What?"

"Yeah. I had to cut out the middle after the cakes were cooled then ice them and plug the middle back up again. I'm pretty proud of that feature."

"Wow, this cake is perfect for me. Thanks, Morgan."

She leaned her slender body into mine, squeezing me tight. "You were avoiding me. Sisters don't avoid sisters."

"I'm not avoiding you," I lied. "I'm just busy. But we shall celebrate this weekend. It's not ideal, but we've got this merger to deal with right now. But we're doing brunch with Clarissa, right? And then we'll do some shopping after. A little retail therapy. I deserve to buy myself something fabulous."

"Yes. And I deserve to watch you buy something fabulous."

"Is this you asking for a present too?"

She shook her head. "Nah, I want to watch you enjoy it."

I squeezed my sister's hand. "I will. I promise."

"Now, if you don't mind, I need to go get ready for a date. I just wanted to make sure you had cake first."

"Thanks, Morgan. I appreciate you making it specially for me."

"What are sisters for?"

She punched Lance on the shoulder and blew me an air kiss and was gone. Like a little cake fairy godmother.

When my sister left, Lance caught the full brunt of my ire. "Lance, you really should know better."

He gave me an impish grin. "What? I tried to help with the singing. And she twisted my arm. She's surprisingly strong."

"Right. For someone who claims not to like my little sister, you let her talk you into a lot of shit."

"Well, she's part of the package. So sometimes, if it's going to benefit you, I need to let her talk me into stuff."

"Sure. Whatever you say."

"And look, before you try and weasel out of our birthday drinks tradition, I know you have a shit ton of work to do, so I'm willing to postpone until Sunday."

I sagged in relief. "Honestly, I don't think I deserve you."

His eyes went soft as he searched my face. "You deserve better, but you're stuck with me. How are you going to get away from your minder?"

I rolled my eyes. "He's not my minder."

"He looks like your minder. Dark, brooding, disapproving. I felt like I was trying to impress your dad."

I wrinkled my nose. "Can we please not say the D word right now?"

He pressed his lips together in irritation. "Let me guess, he didn't wish you happy birthday today."

I shook my head and toed the carpet with my stocking-clad foot, having ditched my shoes hours earlier. "It's fine. He doesn't matter."

"No, he doesn't. Because you have me."

"Thanks, Lance. That means a lot."

"Let me get a piece of cake, then I'll get out of your hair," he said. "On Sunday, we'll do drinks then we're having our marathon."

"Yes. We're starting with the Van Damme movies." During my junior year of college, my boyfriend Michael had missed my birthday because he was traveling to see his parents, so Lance had cheered me up by bringing me vodka, mixers, and really bad action movies. That had to be one of my best birthdays ever. It had become sort of a standing tradition after that.

"You are surprisingly bloodthirsty," he laughed.

I shrugged. "What can I say?"

"Your thirst for blood is probably why I fell in love with you in the first place."

He said it like a joke. Like he always did. Except this time, it didn't feel really as much like a joke. An odd tension swirled around us, and I could see the thing that I tried to never look too hard at. Lance was gorgeous with his sandy brown hair, perpetual stubble, and soulful brown eyes. I should have wanted him, except we'd always been friends. And I needed our friendship.

Maybe too much.

"That should be a Van Damme title. Hard to love."

He gave me one of his easy smiles, and suddenly that awkward discomfort was gone.

At the door, he leaned in and hugged me just like usual, squeezing me tight, wrapping me in warmth and comfort, and I squeezed him back.

"Happy birthday. Please, go home and relax, would you?"

"Oh, don't worry. I plan on making her do exactly that."

CHAPTER 23
GWEN

I released Lance automatically, but he didn't let me go.

Atticus scowled at Lance's arm that still hung around my shoulders. "Hands off my wife."

Lance apparently had a death wish, because while he let me go, he turned to face Atticus, crossing his arms in front of him, blocking Atticus from my view. "She's not your wife, *yet*."

I swallowed hard and tried to push Lance out of the way, but he wouldn't budge.

Atticus's eyes narrowed, and I could see the barely leashed control in the tension of his shoulders. I knew he was seconds away from exploding, and I didn't want to witness the aftermath.

Atticus stepped closer, his eyes on Lance, "I suggest you walk away, Lakewood." There was an edge to his voice that made me shiver.

We were not having this pissing contest on my fucking birthday. "That's enough, Atticus. Lance and Morgan just came by to wish me a happy birthday."

But neither of them was listening to me.

Lance smirked. "Is that a threat, Price?"

Atticus didn't answer. Instead, he stepped even closer to Lance, and the tension crackled around us, spitting out little spikes of electricity. It was like watching two animals circling each other, waiting to see who would make the first move.

Fuck that. I still had work to do, and it was going to be tough getting blood out of this carpet.

"Lance, it's okay. I'm fine. I'll see you later."

Atticus's voice was low and menacing. "That's right. Off you go, *Lance*."

Lance smirked, looking back at me. "I'll see you Sunday," he said as he brushed past Atticus and sauntered lazily down the hallway.

I only let out a shaky breath when he reached the elevators. But as I turned to face Atticus, I froze at the look in his eyes. It was a mix of anger, lust, and possessiveness that made my heart race.

"You didn't have any right to talk to him like that, Atticus."

"Didn't I? I thought I was clear, Gwen. I'm not tolerating any relationship."

I jabbed a finger in his chest. "And for the tenth time, it's not like that. He's my best friend, and he and Morgan brought me a birthday cake." I gestured at my desk, showing him the evidence of his overreaction.

His brows snapped down. "It's your birthday?"

What was that tone? There was no way he was feeling hurt.

"Yes. I don't like to celebrate it, but Lance and Morgan have no chill."

"You didn't tell me."

"Like I said, these days I don't want all the fanfare."

"But it's your birthday. There *should* be fanfare. We could throw—"

I stopped him in his tracks, seeing where this was going. "I do not want a party full of your business associates with me feeling uncomfortable and making small talk. That wouldn't be fun for me."

"Well, we should do something together."

"Remember what I said earlier about not wanting fanfare?"

"But Lakewood gets to break that rule?" he asked.

"What is your problem with him anyway?"

I didn't expect his answer or how raw and unfiltered it was when he said, "Watching him touch you and knowing you let him celebrate your birthday makes me want to rip him to pieces." Each word was punctuated with a step toward me. "Knowing you let him in at all is enough to drive me fucking batshit."

"Well, that's not my—"

His wintergreen eyes focused intently on mine. "He had his fucking hands on what's mine."

Before I knew it, Atticus had me pressed up against the wall, his hands roaming over my body. "Mine," he growled before his hand gently encased my neck and his lips crashed down on mine.

I moaned, my body responding to his touch despite the fear in my mind.

His lips moved to my jaw, nipping and biting as he kissed his way down my neck. "Mine," he repeated, his mouth on my collarbone.

His hands slipped under my skirt, and he groaned softly against my skin. He pressed his lips to my stomach, and I could feel his hands on my thighs, making their way up. His fingers hit the lace band of my panties and he growled, "Mine," as he stroked a knuckle over my panty-clad center.

I was completely at his mercy, and I hated it.

Liar.

With my blouse unbuttoned, he pushed it off my shoulders, exposing my bra. And before I knew what happened, he dragged his lips from mine and unsnapped my bra with one hand.

His gaze went hooded as he licked his bottom lip. "I fucking love these." He pushed my breasts together and wrapped them in his big hands. "I can't wait to fuck these with my cock." His voice was low and husky, and his words elicited a shudder from my body.

I whimpered, wanting him to touch me while simultaneously wanting to push him away.

"I want to taste them," he growled as fire sparked in his eyes.

When his mouth found my nipple, I gasped and dug my hands into his hair as he began to suck the hard nub. His tongue swirled around and around, gently laving the sensitive flesh.

I gasped, my back arching and my nipples hardening. I should be pushing him away. This was so far beyond any public kisses for show. This was all for me.

Atticus's hand found my other nipple, and he pinched it gently between his fingers. The feeling was exquisite, and I couldn't help but moan.

"Atticus, please," I begged, sinking one of my hands into his hair. He made his way to my other breast, and I couldn't help but whimper with need.

"Please what, Ness?" he asked, gently grazing my nipple. I cried out, the sensation overwhelming as he continued to tease my skin.

"I need you," I moaned, bucking my hips against him, hoping to relieve some of the tension.

"In what way?" he asked, softly trailing his tongue down my belly.

I couldn't even answer him as his strong hands gripped the back of my thighs and he lifted me easily off the floor. All I could do was grip his shoulders tight as he carried me over to my desk and seated me on the edge of it.

Holy shit.

He reached behind me, and when he brought his hand back, he smeared icing on my nipples.

The way he watched the rise and fall of my peaked tips with every breath I took was enough to make my knees week. But when he took the left one into his mouth, I cried out, the spear of need making me desperate.

He knew what he was doing to me, but he took his time, taking each of my nipples into his mouth, sucking them greedily.

I moaned, as my head fell back.

His mouth slowly traveled lower and lower, stopping at my belly button to lift his head and watch me.

His gaze did not leave mine as he licked his fingers. The sight of his tongue drawing his fingers into his mouth made me shiver.

"I can taste you a little. Your flavor is mixed with the frosting. You taste so sweet, Gwenyth," he murmured.

This was it. This was how I was going to die. Spontaneous combustion at the hands of Atticus Price.

CHAPTER 23

His hands drifted to the side zipper on my skirt, and he made quick work of getting it down, leaving me in my stockings, garters, and panties.

"Fuck me. Is this what you've been wearing under all your clothes?"

I nodded frantically, all semblance of resistance gone out the window. At this point, he could ask me anything, and I would give him whatever answers he wanted just to keep his mouth on me.

"Easy, baby. Not so fast." He released my nipple, and I whimpered in protest. He moved his mouth to the other one and sucked, his fingers still teasing me through my panties.

I was throbbing with need, and I knew that if he kept doing what he was doing, I would come.

"Wait, Atticus."

He released my nipple with a pop and dragged his gaze up to mine. "You want me to stop?"

My gaze searched his. His pupils were completely dilated, and his gaze was hooded and lazy. His lips were swollen too.

"I—"

The safe thing was to say yes. Run away. But I couldn't. My body just wouldn't accept the idea. "Please don't stop."

He was like a drug, and one taste was enough to get me hooked. He suddenly stopped, and I whimpered in need, my hips bucking against him. "Please, Atticus."

"What do you want me to do to you, baby?"

I panted as I tried to gather my thoughts. His hand had slipped into my panties, and I was very aware of the fact that he was teasing my clit. I had never been this turned on before.

He knelt down to the floor, holding my legs apart as he kissed my inner thigh. He was inches away from my soaked panties, and I could feel his hot breath through the fabric as I squirmed against him.

He nipped at my panties, and I let out a small cry. I felt my cheeks flush and my cunt drizzle.

He chuckled softly, "Fuck, you smell good, Gwen. You smell so fucking good." He looked up at me with a devilish smile and his fingers hooked the edge of my panties.

Atticus's lips reached my pussy, and he kissed me right above my mound. He spread my lips open, and I could feel the air touch my wet folds. He looked up at me, his eyes fiery with lust.

"Spread your legs for me, Gwenyth," Atticus growled, and I was too far gone to protest.

I whimpered at the feel of his warm breath on me. My mind protested, but my body absolutely loved it, and I whimpered again, my legs parting for him.

"You're glistening for me. Fucking soaked," he murmured, his voice deep and husky. "I can't wait to get my mouth on you."

Teasing me, he slid a finger under the elastic of my panties and stroked it through my slick heat.

"Atticus," I cried out. At this point I wasn't above begging.

"That's it, Ness. My lioness wants to give me that needy pussy?"

The wash of embarrassment had me trying to clamp my legs closed, but his damn shoulders wouldn't allow it. All I managed was to buck my hips toward him.

"Please, Atticus," I begged. Yep, we really were begging now.

"I like the sound of that. I like that you know what you want. And I want to give it to you. But not yet."

He pulled his hand from my panties, and I whimpered again. He pushed me back and quickly undid my garters and pulled my stockings down and off.

"You look so fucking sexy in your little panties."

His fingers slid back between my thighs, and I moaned loudly when he slid one under my panties and stroked through my slick folds again.

I cried out as he slid the tip of his finger into my entrance. "Fuck, you're tight," he murmured. "Please, Ness, relax for me. Let me make you feel good."

I was too far gone to hear him. His finger was doing extraordinary things to my body, and I couldn't think about anything but getting more.

"I love the way you open up for me," Atticus growled.

I moaned, rocking my hips against his hand. "Please," I begged.

But instead of giving me what I wanted, he stopped and pulled back, bringing his finger to his lips and licking it clean. "Mm, you taste so good. I can't get enough of you, Gwen."

It was only then that I realized he was still fully clothed, and I was spread open before him.

"I want to taste you," he murmured, his voice deep and husky, "I *need* to taste you."

I shivered at his words and at the loss of his finger. I was so close to coming, and I knew he knew it.

"I want to taste you," he murmured again. "Will you let me?"

I nodded quickly, and he wrapped his fingers around the delicate fabric, twisted, then ripped. "Oh my God."

The look in his eyes was pure desire, and the control I'd seen from him so far was nowhere to be found.

He slid me to the edge of the desk, and his hands found my thighs again.

"Spread your legs for me, Ness. Spread your legs and let me see you."

I whimpered as I did as I was told.

The way he looked at me, like I was the most beautiful thing he had ever seen, made me feel sexy. Powerful.

Atticus brought his mouth to my entrance, and I groaned loudly at the first swipe of his tongue.

He growled as he licked at my slick folds. "You taste like sugar, sweetness. I can't get enough of you."

He licked up my slit again, then sucked my clit into his mouth, swirling his tongue over it.

"Fuck, I knew you would be sweet," Atticus moaned, his eyes locking with mine.

I cried out as he sucked my clit into his mouth, while he pushed two fingers into me.

"Oh, God," I moaned as his mouth and fingers worked me over.

"You've been teasing me. All I can do is think about you. Coming home to you. Having you be the last thing I think about before I fall asleep and the first thing I think of when I wake up," he murmured. "Your taste. Your smell. Your touch. Your sounds. You, Gwen. You, you, you," he murmured.

He dragged his tongue over my hypersensitive bud again and again. When I started to shake, he slipped one of his fingers out of my pussy and stroked it over my back entrance.

He brushed his finger over the sensitive flesh again, and I quivered. It felt so foreign but so good. At this point I'd do anything to come.

My hands fisted his hair, and I rose up to meet his licks and thrusts. With every tilt of my hips, the tip of his finger slid a little farther into my ass until finally he was working both fingers into my pussy and ass in time with his mouth sucking on my clit.

He growled loudly when my muscles started to clamp down on his fingers, drawing them deeper inside me.

I cried out again as he continued to lick at my clit through my orgasm. He sucked it into his mouth as I came, then licked all the way up my slit until he was kissing my stomach.

I was still trembling when he pulled his fingers from my body and brought them to his lips.

He groaned loudly as he licked his fingers clean. "Fuck, you taste so good. I can't get enough of you."

I was trembling and still trying to breathe when he leaned forward and gently pressed a kiss to my lips.

"I want you, Gwen. I need to feel you wrapped around me."

My hands found the hem of his shirt, and I quickly slid it over his head. I pressed hot, open-mouth kisses to the column of his neck and chest, dragging my nails down his back.

He pulled back, pulling me to my feet. When we were standing, he gripped my chin in his fingers and kissed me desperately as he tore at his clothes.

He brought my hand to the front of his pants, and I wrapped it around his cock. Holy shit. He was huge. There was no fucking way. He fished a condom out of his wallet then stayed my hand. "While that was a good idea in theory, fuck, I can't let you touch me like that. I will come in my pants."

For once, I felt like I had the power, like I was in charge. I pumped him again, and his knees buckled. "Gwen, baby. No."

After three more very deliberate pumps of his cock, he stopped me. "Naughty, naughty."

He turned me around and bent me over my desk, sliding a hand to my thigh to bring it up on my desk, then he dipped a finger into my pussy. "Are you ready for me?"

"Yes," I groaned.

He gripped my hips, and the tip of his cock pressed against my pussy.

I gasped at his size. So damn thick.

"Fuck, you're tight. You're so tight, Gwen," he growled.

Holding himself still inside me, he kissed my back and shoulders, murmuring how beautiful I was.

"You feel so good," he groaned. "So fucking good." He slid his hand between my thighs and found my clit. He circled it with his fingers, and I arched into the caress. His other hand gripped my hip, and he started to move.

I whimpered at every push of his cock. He was moving slowly, deeper with each push until he was filling me completely.

He dragged his cock out and pushed back in.

"Fuuuuuck," he groaned.

"Harder," I demanded.

I wanted him deeper, wanted him harder. I wanted him to fuck me like he'd been dreaming about.

He fisted my hair and turned my head so he could make eye contact. "Say it, Gwen."

He throbbed inside me and had me melting as I arched my hips against his.

"What?" I gasped.

"Mine," he growled. "Say it."

"Yours," I whispered.

He pushed into me slowly again. "Good girl," he groaned as his cock buried inside me.

He pulled out and pushed in a second time. "Mine," he hissed again.

I nodded, my eyes wide as I felt him push in a third time. "Yes, yours," I gasped, and my body shook as he pushed inside of me.

"Mmm," he moaned. "Say it one more time."

"Yours," I gasped as he thrust into me.

His pace quickened, and he grunted, "Fuck, Gwen."

"Please, Atticus," I whimpered as I felt him thrust into me harder.

"Please what, baby?"

"Please, don't stop."

Gasps escaped my lips. His cock was so deep inside of me, hitting my G-spot with every thrust.

He groaned, "Fuck, I'm not gonna stop." He leaned down and kissed me, and I could taste my own arousal on his tongue.

"Yours," I panted.

"That's it," he murmured.

"Yours," I moaned again.

He slammed into me. "Say my fucking name."

"Atticus." His thrusts were getting harder and faster.

"Say it again."

"Atticus!"

I moved my hands to the desk and pushed back against him. I cried out when he thrust harder into me.

He slid his hand between my thighs and found my clit again. I groaned at the feeling of his fingers stroking over my clit. He slid his thumb over the sensitive bud, and I cried out.

"Holy fucking shit," he groaned as he rubbed my clit again and again.

My body was shaking, and my pussy muscles started to clench around him. "Oh, God, Atticus," I moaned.

"That's it, baby. Come on my cock."

I felt like I was flying as my orgasm slammed into me.

"Fuck," he groaned. "That's it, baby. Squeeze my cock."

The way he was sliding in and out of me, keeping his thumb on my clit, I started to come again.

Pushing into me hard and deep, and the way he was stroking my clit had me flying. I was still shaking with my orgasm when he groaned loudly and slammed into me once, twice, three more times.

My muscles clamped down on his cock, milking him of his cum as he filled my pussy.

A groan escaped his lips, and he collapsed against me, his cock still buried in my pussy.

I could feel his hot breath against my neck as his breathing steadied.

His lips kissed my neck, and I moaned. He pulled out of me before turning me and setting me on the desk.

Without a word, he went to the adjoining bathroom and brought me back a wet washcloth. Gently, he placed it against my sore pussy, kissing me with more gentleness than I'd thought him capable of.

He cleaned us both, then tried to reclasp my bra. But when his fingers grazed my nipples, I drew in a sharp breath. His gaze went dark again and he released me. "On second thought, you'd better do this before we spend all night here."

In ten minutes, we were both dressed and in his car on the way back to the penthouse. His hand lay in my lap, fingers tracing along my thigh. Then his phone lit up with a message.

Suddenly, his hand jerked away as he stared at the text. Then he leaned forward. "Change of plans, Gavin. Head to Mom's."

CHAPTER 24
GWEN

Atticus was quiet. He didn't say much after directing Gavin to turn the car around.

"Is everything okay?"

He slid his gaze to me as he texted someone furiously. "Um, I'm not sure. Hopefully."

And that was that. When we finally arrived after the silent forty-five-minute drive that had me basically just staring at my phone and trying to answer my emails, we stopped at what looked like an enormous English manor house. The lawn was green and sprawling, the driveway long and winding. And the house was shockingly charming despite its size. There were bright flowers outside, and it was clear that somebody took care of it. So what were we doing here?

It took me a moment to realize there was something moving near the hedge maze. Something in white.

Atticus cursed, and Gavin had barely put the car in Park, before he was out and running toward the figure in white. I realized belatedly that it was a woman. And as Atticus ran toward her, she took off running in the opposite direction. Gavin cursed under his breath and then jumped out of the car. I opened my door, not sure what to do to help.

As she darted into the maze, I saw which way she went, and I kicked off my shoes and went in after her. The grass was cool and dewy against my feet, and my skirt didn't allow much room for movement, but still, I was able to follow her into the maze. "Hi, hello." I inched toward her with my hands out, showing that I meant her no harm.

She shook her head. "No, no, no, no. I don't want it. I don't want it."

"I get it. I understand. There's a lot I don't want. Sometimes people tell me I have to accept what's happening and I always refuse. Because why do I have to accept it, right?" I could see her better now with the moonlight illuminating her face. She was a little older, maybe late fifties. But there was no mistaking those eyes. The pale green. Wintergreen. This was Atticus's mother. The resemblance was striking. Softly, I said, "Hi. I'm Gwen."

She frowned at me. "Gwen?"

I could hear quick steps behind me, and I put a hand out to stop them. "Yeah. I'm a friend of Atticus."

She shook her head. "He'll destroy you. That's what he does. He destroys things. Lucian is coming."

Behind me, Atticus's voice was low. "Dad's not coming, Mom. It's me, Atticus."

She shook her head and then slid her hands over her ears. "No, no, no, no. Lucian is coming. Lucian is coming."

I put my hand up. "Hi, what's your name?"

"Jessica." Her voice was low and timid.

"It's nice to meet you, Jessica. Like I said, I'm a friend of Atticus."

Her brows furrowed. "Atticus?"

"Yes, Atticus."

"He's a good boy, my son. But his father... He has his father in him. He'll destroy you. You have to run." She darted for me, and I almost stumbled backward as I held on to her tight. While she might be thin, she was not frail, and her hands dug into my biceps. "You have to run. He's going to get you. He's going to destroy you. You have to run. He threw me in here. Away from Atticus. Away from Micah. He never wanted me to be happy."

After recovering from the scare, I dipped my voice low. "Jessica, you're okay. And I know you think Lucian is going to do something, but Atticus would never let that happen. Atticus hasn't done anything to hurt me. Or you either. He loves you."

I managed to pull her fingers off my bicep and free one of my arms. I slowly rubbed my hand in circles on her back. "You're okay now Jessica. I think it's a little chilly out here. Maybe we should go inside?"

Her brows furrowed. "Inside?"

"Yeah, where it's warm. I think I might like a hot cocoa."

"I could use a drop of bourbon."

I gave her a tremulous smile. "Yes, I like bourbon, too."

"Atticus won't let me have a drink. He acts like I'm the child."

"Well, Atticus doesn't know everything, does he?"

I slid a glance toward him. His face was drawn tight, and his eyes were wary on me. I ignored him and led his mother toward the house. She directed me to a side door where we found a woman in a nurse's uniform looking worried. A short, round, Latin woman with curly hair stood behind her in a robe and said, "Oh my gosh, Mr. Price. I'm so sorry. She—"

Atticus spoke for the first time since we arrived. "It's okay, Dania, it's okay. We've got her inside now."

That's when I realized that Jessica had a pair of scissors in her hands.

Atticus gently took them from his mother and handed them over to Dania, and then the nurse attempted to take Jessica from me. But she let out a blood curdling scream. "No. Just Gwen. I want Gwen."

I rushed to calm her down. "Don't worry, I'm not going anywhere. If it's okay, I told Jessica we can have some hot chocolate before she goes back to bed."

The nurse and Dania looked at me curiously. Then their gazes went straight to Atticus behind them.

His voice was low. "Some hot chocolate won't hurt. Easy on the bourbon though."

I merely nodded and kept my attention on Jessica.

After I made her hot chocolate and got her settled, I poured a mug and walked over to Atticus. "Here you go. I put some bourbon in that one too."

"How much did you give her?"

I shook my head and pitched my voice low. "None. I just pretended to pour it in there."

He sighed and scrubbed a hand over his face before taking a sip of his hot chocolate. When he lifted his gaze to mine, there was raw pain, worry, and concern in his eyes, and I saw the vulnerable little boy in there. I had no idea what was going on here or why she was like this, but I knew he needed me.

When Jessica was done with her hot cocoa, I went with her and her nurse to get her teeth brushed, and then settled her back in her room. Dania shook her head when I looked at the window, which was open. "During the day, she likes the breeze. It was my fault. I forgot to lock it, and she just snuck out. Luckily, the alarm went off and alerted us."

"Is she always like this?"

"Ninety percent of the time, she's great. She just needs a companion. It's the other ten percent that's unpredictable. And she can get hurt."

Jessica took my hand then. "I know you're good Gwen. And you're good for Atticus."

I gave her what I hoped was a warm smile and then patted her hand gently. "Well, we'll see about that."

And before I knew it, she drifted off. When I turned, I found Atticus leaning in the door frame, watching us intently. His long body was tilted at an angle, and his expression was somehow warm, angry, and concerned all at once. As I left the room, he stood still enough to make sure I had to brush past him on my way out.

I looked up at him and said, "I'll wait in the car."

He gave me a nod. But before I could make my escape, his hand traveled down my arm and took my hand, squeezing it gently. "Thank you."

Those two simple words spread through my body like hot water, warming my aching muscles.

I could deal with bossy Atticus. I could deal with domineering Atticus. But this Atticus, the vulnerable one, the one who was worried about his mother... It hurt me to see that Atticus, and he was the one who seemed to crack my armor.

CHAPTER 25
GWEN

ONCE AGAIN, I WOKE UP SURROUNDED BY HEAT. ALL-ENCOMPASSING HEAT, like the perfect sizzle of a Caribbean day. That sort of warmth that chases away the winter blues. And this heat was moving. There was a hand wrapped around my waist, sliding up under my camisole, fingers playing along my rib cage, and they were accompanied by a low groan.

"Gwen, please don't leave."

I held perfectly still. I wasn't leaving. I wasn't going anywhere. I couldn't because he had me in a vice grip.

"Please, I'll do anything. Just don't go."

The pitch of his voice was so low he almost whispered.

He's sleeping.

And he was dreaming that I was going to leave. This pleading, this willing me to stay, it was breaking my heart.

My gaze swung to the clock on the nightstand. It was six-thirty. I didn't have to meet Clarissa and Morgan for several hours, but I did have some work to do before then.

There was some twist in the algorithm that our developers were trying to fix, and the team had said something was wrong with the data set, so I just wanted to look at it myself.

But that could wait, because when was the last time someone held me and whispered and moaned in their sleep?

When Atticus's hands slid further up my top, I froze.

Oh God, I had to wake him up, because if I didn't wake him up, he was very much going to be palming my breasts, and well, after the last time, it was probably better that he didn't.

Except my libido was already up and awake, and I bit back a moan.

He was so good on the desk in my office. I could only imagine what he could do on a bed.

The imagery of him holding my hands over my head as he drove into me flashed through my mind and... Oh, Jesus.

Automatically, I shifted my hips back toward him, and he groaned again. And oh, there we go. Liftoff.

He palmed my breast, his big hand nearly enveloping the left one fully. Then his thumb brushed over my nipple, and a shudder rocked my body.

"Gwen?" It sounded like a question, and I sighed, trying to bite back the moan desperately but failing miserably. When he did it again, he tucked his face into my neck, his cheek brushing my collarbone. "I thought I was dreaming."

"Atticus..."

He tested the weight of my breast again, kneading gently. "You want more of what I gave you in your office?"

"Yes, but it was—" He cut me off with a pinch to my nipple, and I gasped.

"Don't say it was a mistake." He hitched his hips, bringing his cock in direct contact with my ass.

Wait, what? When we'd gone to bed last night, he was wearing pajama bottoms.

It was his groan that had me unconsciously moving back to meet him again.

"Baby, you feel so good." And then he froze, as if he'd just realized the same thing I had. "We both went to bed with clothes on."

"Yeah, I know."

With his free hand, he adjusted the blanket and looked down. "Looks like we were grinding in the middle of the night."

He gave another hitch of his hips, and I glanced over my shoulder to watch him as his cock slid against my ass again.

"Fuuuuuck, Gwen."

I bit my lip. "I'm not doing anything."

"I could argue that your ass is. Fucking hell, I want you."

"Atticus, we don't even like each other."

"I know. But we could try."

His voice was pleading as his thumb and forefinger pinched my nipple lightly, and I arched my back into his touch. "I'll be gentle this time, I swear. I'll go slow. Fuck, just let me touch you."

His voice was breathy and coaxing, so intoxicating I couldn't think.

His hand slid down my belly to the edge of my shorts and underwear. Then he paused. "Will you let me make you feel good?"

And the moment he said those words, my pussy clenched.

He kissed my neck. "Let me make you come. Please, Gwen."

With a whispered, "Yes," I parted my thighs, shifting slightly so I was on my back to give him more room.

Into my neck, he whispered, "Fuck, yes," as he slid his fingers down below the elastic of my shorts and my panties. Then he groaned again.

And I moaned, the sound turning into a gasp when he did a full swipe of my slit.

He kissed my neck and palmed my breast again. "Fuck baby. You're so fucking wet. I'm going to make you come so hard."

Then he bit my neck, and his finger slid all the way inside of me.

I tried to keep my hips still, but I couldn't. They started to rock. "Please, Atticus, please more. I-I need more."

He bit my neck again, but this time he sucked the skin between his teeth and then soothed the bite with his tongue.

I couldn't do anything except moan his name.

He added a second finger inside me, and I tried to hold still, but again my hips started to move.

"Pretty, pretty baby," he said as he scissored his fingers. "I'm going to make you come again, over and over."

And I moaned again.

He kept up the steady rhythm, and he kept sucking my skin into his mouth. He kissed down my shoulder, and he was sucking and licking and nipping at my skin. One of his hands was pinching my nipple, and then he shifted his fingers inside of me again.

"I want you, Gwen. I want to make you come on my fingers and my cock. I want to slide deep inside of you and fuck you so hard that we wake the neighbors."

"Oh, please, Atticus, please..."

"I want to slide inside of you and feel your pussy clench around me. I want to fuck you so hard that you scream my name."

And with that, I pressed my thighs together on his hand, arching my back as I cried out.

I rocked my hips, but he kept his fingers moving steadily as he kept sucking and licking and biting my neck. And his fingers were rubbing against my clit, and I was rocking and panting and clenching. I was so close.

"Please, please..."

He bit my neck again. "I want you to come so hard for me now and then come again when I fuck you."

With that, I clenched around his fingers and screamed his name. And I heard him whisper, "Good girl."

He slowed his fingers, and I felt completely empty when he finally removed them. And then his lips were at my ear. "Do you want me to put my cock inside of you?"

I could barely make myself nod.

"Will you let me fuck you?"

I nodded again, and he kissed me softly on my neck. "I want to fuck you hard, baby. I want to make you feel good, and then I want to make you feel like you're losing your mind. And I want to watch you come again, and I want to come with you."

I felt him shifting his hips away from me, and I turned my head slightly to watch him.

He was hard, and he was long, and he was making me wetter just by looking at him. He was edging toward me, and then his hand was between my legs, touching me again.

"Please, Atticus. I need you. Please."

He nudged my legs wider, and I opened for him.

He pushed his cock inside of me, making me moan. He was big, and I was sore, but he entered me gently, and I was so wet. When he started to thrust, I clenched around him.

He muttered, "Fuck, fuck, fuck," over and over as he thrust harder, and I pushed back against him. And when he reached down to rub my clit, I quivered around him.

"Yes, oh my God, yes, Atticus!" I moaned his name, and I was watching his face as he pulled out and pushed in again and again.

I lost myself to the feeling of his cock sliding in and out, and of his hand on my clit, and to the feeling of him inside of me. Then my body started to tighten, and I felt the sensation of my orgasm start to crest.

"Atticus, yes, yes, yes, please..." I was moaning and pleading and arching my back, and his hand was still on my clit.

"Oh fuck, baby, yes. Fuck, yes."

As my orgasm crested, he bit my neck. It felt like I was spinning, and the only thing I could do was hold on.

I felt Atticus's cock jerk inside of me, and his teeth pulled at my skin as he pulsed, jetting his cum inside me.

As he relaxed and adjusted our position so that we were laying on our sides, his cock still inside me, he whispered, "Christ, Gwen. You will be the death of me."

"Same."

CHAPTER 26
GWEN

I RELUCTANTLY LEFT ATTICUS IN BED TO MEET MY SISTER AND STEPMOTHER for breakfast.

"Give the birthday girl whatever she wants," my stepmother said to the waiter as Morgan excused herself to go to the powder room.

I laughed and shook my head. "Don't let her ply me with liquor. I'll have the eggs benedict with a side of the sweet pancakes."

He nodded. "We can do that."

"You don't have to feed me like this, Clarissa." I wasn't used to being doted on.

Clarissa shook her head. "I could have made you breakfast at the house, but something told me you didn't want to celebrate with your father."

I shook my head. "I don't want to talk about him."

Clarissa sighed. "I'm so sorry, honey. I wish I could explain the man or make some kind of excuse for him, but what he's done to you is just fucked up, completely wrong, and I'm sorry."

"It's fine. I just..." I sighed. "Every time I think that he's going to be a different kind of father, a different kind of person, I get disappointed. That's okay. I should learn to stop hoping."

"Oh, honey. I don't want you to stop hoping. Your father is just a dick sometimes."

"Then why are you still married to him?"

She shrugged. "Well, I'm sort of obligated to keep loving him. I know it's messy, but I do. And well, mostly I love you girls. so there's not much I can do except sort of endure him."

"Clarissa, you could do better. You could have someone who loves you back."

"Your father loves in his own way. He's just used to being selfish."

"Can we not talk about him today," I said. "I'm just tired of him, and if we're going to celebrate my birthday, I want to do it in a fun way."

Clarissa nodded. "Fun coming right up. About your wedding, please let us help plan. Have you picked a wedding date?"

I laughed. "I love how quickly you can adjust."

Morgan came back from the bathroom. "What did I miss?"

Clarissa said, "I was just asking your sister when she's getting married."

Morgan groaned. "Are we still doing this? I thought you, of all people, would have found an answer, a way out."

"I don't think so. Especially now that I know he's helping me meet payroll for the next few weeks. I have employees to take care of, you know. Anyway, thank you for the cake on my birthday."

Morgan grinned. "The gummy bears. I know that made you happy."

I'd eaten a slice of it this morning for energy. Instead of tea, I'd chosen sugar. What? Don't judge me. I'd wrapped it up to take home before we left the office, and then he'd put it in the fridge for me when we got home from his mother's. Which was sweet.

"So, how is it going with Atticus anyway?" Morgan asked. "Is he the evil and brooding super genius that he seems to be publicly?"

I put my hand up. "We're not going to talk about it. Now where are we going shopping?"

Morgan took that opportunity to tell me about some boutique she wanted to explore, and Clarissa was saying how she needed a new coat. I knew that shopping together would make them happy, and I would try my best not to stare at my phone all day because all they wanted to do was spend time with me. Which was great. And as I watched my sister, I was happy that she was happy. I knew this whole situation just stressed her out.

Then I started to wonder... Would Atticus have fingered Morgan like that if the roles were reversed?

I coughed as I took a sip of water. Both my stepmother and sister turned to look at me, and I gave them a quick smile. "Sorry, wrong pipe."

"Oh!" Clarissa waved down the waiter for more napkins, and I dabbed up as much of the spill as I could.

When I looked up, my scalp prickled, and I started looking around. I knew only one person made me feel like that, and I whipped around, my breath catching when I saw Atticus standing at the door.

"What the heck is he doing here?" I mumbled.

Both Clarissa and Morgan glanced over where I was looking. Morgan whistled low. "Jesus, fucking hell. Is that what he looks like out of a suit?"

He was wearing a lightweight sweater over dark jeans. His hair was tousled, and I could see now that the curl he had in the mornings was natural. He looked far less coifed. And he sported some stubble on that stupidly square jaw, complete with a dimple on his chin and everything.

He glanced around the restaurant and then flashed a wide, wicked grin when he saw me. Clarissa coughed this time. "Jesus Christ, is that what his smile looks like?"

I sighed as my pussy fluttered. I was well acquainted with the effect that smile had on the populous. "Yeah, that's what it looks like."

My stepmother tittered. "Well, goddamn. No wonder you're not ready to get out of this whole deal."

I turned to frown at her. "Yes, I am. I just know that there isn't a way out."

"Honey, I don't blame you. Look at the man."

When he approached, he kept his smile in place. And wonder of wonders, it almost actually reached his eyes.

He greeted my stepmother first with a kiss on her cheek. "Clarissa, looking beautiful and radiant as always." When he went to Morgan, I didn't even realize I was holding my breath until he leaned over and gave her a tight side hug. No plastering his body to hers, no kissing her cheek. "Good morning, Morgan."

"Good morning, Mr. Price."

He winced. "Please, God, call me Atticus."

"Sure, *Atticus*." And then Morgan's gaze jumped from him to me, and back to him again. Atticus stood next to me, and his massive hand landed on my shoulder and then traced up my neck before cupping my face.

The flutter of butterflies tugged at my belly. I wished he would stop. When he was sweet, it was hard not to fall for it.

I had no choice but to look up at him. Then he leaned over and placed a very soft kiss on my lips. Honestly, who needed to breathe? Breathing was overrated. Because if you could hold your breath, the scent of heaven wouldn't tempt you.

Except my traitorous lungs didn't get the memo because they inhaled. And then I swooned. He deepened the kiss ever so slightly for a moment and then pulled back, grinning down at me. "My beautiful fiancée left without me this morning."

I gave him a tight smile as he sat, just inviting himself to join us. "I thought you had to work."

"Nope. Decided against it. I'm joining you for breakfast. Honestly, I wished you'd told me your plans. I would have loved to have your mother and sister up to the penthouse and let Magda cook."

Clarissa's eyes went wide. "You have a full-time chef?"

He nodded. "Yes. You know your daughter though. She will never take me up on it."

She sighed. "Yeah, well, Gwen is highly independent."

I bit the inside of my cheek. "Yes, I am."

Atticus leaned over to me and sniffed. "You smell delicious."

My stepmother and Morgan busied themselves chatting about where we were going shopping today.

"I'm not wearing any perfume," I said.

"That's not what I meant and you know it. You smell and taste good to me."

A shiver racked my spine. "You can't talk to me like that here."

"Why not?"

"Because we're in public, Atticus, and that's inappropriate."

His chuckle was low and smooth, and it felt like chocolate melting over my tongue.

"God, I'm just minding my business and trying to have a girls' day out," I mumbled.

"Yes, and I like your business. It's sexy. And your ass is a thing of beauty."

"Jesus Christ, Atticus, would you stop?"

"I haven't said anything inappropriate. I'm just talking about how delicious my wife is."

"I'm not your wife yet."

"You keep trying to remind me of that. I think one thing we should talk about is how to make the word *wife* a reality."

"I-I don't know. Let's not talk about that right now."

"Yeah, of course. But when we get home, we probably should talk about it before I lay you out on the bed and make you come again." A flush crept up my neck, and he grinned. "God, I love when you go just a little bit pink."

I smiled at him as the waiter delivered our food and took his drink order. "You can't tell that I'm going pink."

"Oh, I can tell. I've been paying attention. And God, I love to watch it. I'd rather see it naked, because then I know exactly where you turn pink."

God, the man was a menace. I sat clenching my thighs together through breakfast while he proceeded to spend the next hour and a half chatting with my stepmother and my sister. After breakfast, which was delicious as expected, and after he asked the staff to bring me a birthday dessert, which was breakfast crème brûlée, he insisted he was joining us on the first part of our shopping trip. I was wired, tight and tense, wondering what all the attention was about.

As we exited the restaurant, he wrapped an arm around me, casually walking next to me as if he belonged there. I was wearing a simple sundress with sneakers. Converse. I looked cute and fun as he towered over me.

Out on the sidewalk, as Morgan and Clarissa argued about which way to go first, he leaned down and kissed my temple. "See, I'm not so bad."

Then I heard a low voice behind us. "Oh look, the happy couple."

Fuck, why could nothing go well? We turned slowly to find Bronson behind us. His gaze swept over me, and all I wanted was a shower.

Atticus gave him a brusque nod. "Looks like everyone had the same idea for breakfast. If you don't mind, I'm in the process of spoiling her for her birthday."

Bronson lifted a brow. "So you two are genuinely attempting to pass this off as the real deal, then?"

My stomach twisted, but Atticus just held me tight and said, "Jacobson, I'm starting to get the idea that you're not happy for us. Why is that?"

I lifted my chin and met his gaze. He couldn't make me cower, and he couldn't make me run. What happened between us was a long time ago, and I was stronger now.

"No reason. You're not usually one to pick up scraps, Price, but hey, you do you."

I could feel the tension in Atticus's body, but he held it together. "I see you have a death wish."

Bronson's eyes went wide as if he hadn't expected Atticus to take that stance. "Wh-what?"

"You heard me. Gwen is my fiancée. See the ring on her finger? She's going to be my wife. And if you ever speak to her with anything other than the utmost respect again, you'll be missing your tongue."

Then he turned the two of us around to follow my sister and Clarissa as if nothing had happened. "You didn't have to do that," I muttered.

"Yes, I did. Are you going to tell me what the deal is with you two?"

What could I say? There was no way I was telling him the whole thing. It was too humiliating. Besides, I'd moved on.

Liar.

"We had one date. Not a big deal. I decided once was enough when I found out he was a major asshole. He obviously didn't take it well."

His gaze searched mine as if he knew that I was leaving something vital out. But he didn't press. Instead, he placed a gentle kiss to my forehead. "Come on, I think I owe you presents, don't I?"

He might have been calm and relaxed, but something told me that it wasn't over with Bronson Jacobson. Not by a long shot.

CHAPTER 27
GWEN

THE FOLLOWING MORNING, MY SISTER TURNED UP AT THE PENTHOUSE.

I was so confused when Manny buzzed up and told me someone was there to see me. I would have assumed Lance, but I had already texted him that I'd meet him at the park later after lunch for a run and a strategizing session. I had some plans for how to move team members around so they'd fit more seamlessly into Pendragon Tech. When I met her in the foyer, Morgan whistled low.

"Holy shitballs. I know I said I'd come by earlier this week, but there would have been no point as you were in the office. But had I known this place was so spectacular, I'd have invented a reason."

Morgan kicked off her shoes in the foyer, and I shook my head. "You want something to eat? A drink?"

I led her to the living room, and she froze, staring at the view of Central Park. "Holy shit, Gwen. Can I marry the view?"

"I'm glad you love it. As far as I can tell, no one else really seems to care here. Not Micah. Not Atticus. Sometimes I bring my laptop in here just so I can look."

"That's it, I'm moving in. Where's my room?"

"There are many to choose from. But I thought you loved your freedom and being downtown."

"I could learn to be an uptown girl."

"You love the West Village. Stop lying."

"Okay, you're right. But I shall be making a pointed effort to come up here more often."

I finally tugged her to the kitchen and found Magda packing some containers. Rice and chicken, pasta, the shrimp dish from the other day. "Hey, Magda, what are you doing?"

She smiled at my sister. "Hello, Miss, would you like some lunch?"

Morgan, ever the ham, grinned and then did a little twirl. "Are you offering me brunch? I'm in love with you."

Magda laughed. "I like you already. I'll feed you any time. There's some French toast here. I can warm it up."

Morgan just gave me the *Holy shit! French toast* face, and I laughed. "Magda, you don't have to cater to my sister."

She waved me off. "You won't let me cater to you, so I'm going to spoil her." She finished closing up what looked like leftovers.

"Taking some leftovers, huh?"

She shook her head. "No. Mr. Price wanted me to make sure I pack you lunches."

I frowned. "He what?"

"Don't worry, I mostly repurposed some of the dishes we had earlier. The shrimp from yesterday, you'll have tomorrow, since it's the freshest. And then I made you a few quick things. Some pastas and the zucchini that you liked the other day."

"I can't believe he asked you to do that."

"Oh, it's no bother. Besides, I like doing it. And since I'm making yours, I'm making some for him too. That way he won't eat out as much. It's not good for him, you know."

If I hadn't been so shocked and confused, I would have laughed. She looked after him like his own mother would. I frowned thinking about the older woman I'd met. How long had she been ill? How long had it been since Atticus had someone had to care about him?

Magda took out the warming plate and stacked on the French toast for my sister, warming it and giving it to her before she made herself scarce.

"Wait, let me make sure I have this right. You have a housekeeper who makes food for you. You never have to slave over your own stove again unless you want to?"

"Yes. Not that I have time to cook anymore anyway. It's been a little crazy."

My sister lifted a brow. "I mean, honestly, it's been a little crazy for a few years already. Things were supposed to get better for you once you took your company and joined Dad. But they never got better because you kept trying to show him that his investment was worth it, even though you didn't need to prove anything to anyone. He got the better end of that deal. You know that."

I massaged the back of my neck and said, "Can we not talk about that? I just... I don't want to."

"Okay." She spoke around a forkful of French toast. "Let me get to the reason I'm here then."

"Okay. You didn't just come for a visit?"

"Sure, I did. But I had an ulterior motive. The party planner is annoying me. She's not listening to anything I say."

"Morgan, I cannot deal with the details. If it's some insane, garish affair, fine, I do not care. None of that matters to me."

"Fine, then onto my other matter."

"I swear to God, if you bug me with something Lance-related, I will force-wrap your hair."

With a sharp gasp, she delicately patted today's wash-n-go style. "You wouldn't. It took me two hours this morning."

"I would. I love you, but I would."

"All right, fine, Lance is off the table. Which leads me to my final reason for coming."

"You wanted to see the view for yourself?"

"We have already covered the view. What I want to know is when the fuck were you going to tell me that you had boinked the hell out of Atticus Price?"

I coughed around the glass of water in my hand. "What?"

"Don't you *what* me. Those little touches yesterday, those weren't about putting on a show. The two of you have done the deed. The horizontal mambo. Why on earth wouldn't you tell me?"

"How could you know?"

"Because you're my sister. I will always know. Besides, you were walking with a pep in your step that wasn't there two nights ago.

So, that means something happened after I left the other night and before breakfast, and you didn't call me to dish?"

"Even if I wanted to, things got a little crazy. And then I woke up to meet you guys for brunch. I would have called you... eventually."

"Well, I'm here now, so spill."

"I'm not going to talk to you about sex with Atticus. Not here, where anyone could hear."

"Whatever. You will dish and you will dish now. Or the syrup goes in your hair and I start blabbing very loudly about the time that Todd Wilcox finger-banged you in the movie theater on the school field trip."

"Oh my God, you would not."

"I am ruthless."

"Jesus, Morgan, I was seventeen. And you weren't supposed to overhear that story anyway."

"Listen, eavesdropping on you and your friends having conversations was my essential awakening. Learning all about how you were trying to emulate the movie fear without the rollercoaster event had me running to watch that movie. And I have to tell you, Marky Mark... He was hot."

"Oh my God, Morgan, fine. We slept together."

"And? You can't just stop there. I mean, was it big? Was it any good?"

"Morgan, please!"

"All I'm saying is inquiring minds want to know. I'm inquiring. My mind wants to know."

I snorted a laugh. "It was..." God, just thinking about what we had done in the morning before I headed out to meet her and Clarissa, I flushed deep. "Let's just say he's more than promised."

"Hell, yes. I am happy for you. This is so exciting, and this is real. It's the real deal. This is love. I'm very excited about it, by the way."

"It's not love, Morgan. It just happened because he was upset I didn't tell him about my birthday."

She winced. "You didn't tell him, Gwen?"

"No, it didn't occur to me that I needed to."

"Gwen, maybe it's time to talk to someone. I mean, look, I know you've broken the seal. It might be good to speak to someone about everything that happened with Bronson. I definitely think that you should tell Atticus."

"I'm not doing any such thing."

"Oh, so you're going to continue to shove it down and pretend like it never happened?"

"I don't want to talk about this."

"Well, you need to talk about something. About anything. Hell, I would be satisfied if you told me that you're going to let Atticus Price spoil you stupid. That he's going to swoop in and give your employees all the bonuses, all the money, something to take the weight off you. I would be happy if you said that you are, for once, going to take a break, or if you said that we're going to celebrate your birthday properly. Not this bullshit thing where you try and ignore the day and then begrudgingly let Clarissa and me take you to brunch. I would be happy if you said any one of those things. But you keep saying nothing. I just want you to be happy, Gwen."

I bit the inside of my cheek. "I am happy. This is me being happy."

"No, this is you doing what you always do. Pretending and protecting everybody except yourself. And maybe by not talking, you think you're protecting yourself, but you're only holding yourself back. From the looks of it, you finally had an orgasm. Good for you."

I flushed again. "Morgan."

"What? It's an orgasm. If we're lucky, we all have them. And hopefully, yours was good. From the Ice King, no less. I am a little worried about the frost, you know, on the lady parts. But if it's big, then it's big."

I couldn't help myself. I picked up a piece of French toast and threw it at her. I didn't usually lose control. The splatter of syrup on her face made me gasp in shock. But instead of being irritated, Morgan just grinned. "There she is. I knew she was in there somewhere. Now, if you could let my fucking sister out more often, that would be fucking amazing."

I frowned. "What?"

"You just lost your cool. Old Gwen lost her cool. I want to see more of that. She was fun. She would throw fucking pieces of French toast at me. But I won't waste it and retaliate. I am going to eat this."

I shook my head at her silliness. Had I really changed that much?

Had I allowed working under my father's rule to make me meek?

"I'll drop it for now, okay?" she said with a smirk. "But you having orgasms now is really a big fucking deal for me. I just want you to know that I love you. And I know what you've been going through, so I'm happy for you. Though I expect to be told the details. And if you don't want to talk about it yet, that's fine. I'll let it go. But I want to be happy for you about something, not worried all the time. So let me be happy for you, even if it is a giant icicle." She grinned wickedly. "Tell me it's a *giant* icicle."

I snorted as I grabbed a paper towel and wet it for her to wipe the syrup off her face.

"Jesus Christ, it is. I fucking knew it."

And then, for the first time in a long time, I let myself relax as I told my sister something fun.

CHAPTER 28
GWEN

ON THE NIGHT OF THE ENGAGEMENT PARTY, MY SISTER SQUEEZED ME SO tight I couldn't breathe. "Oh my God, Morgan, let go."

"No, I'm not letting you go. You're my big sister, and you're about to walk out there to your engagement party. Why does it feel like I'm losing you?"

"That's ridiculous. You're obviously not losing me. I love you. Now, let go."

We were in the bathroom, double-checking makeup and things, and Morgan was hovering. "Are you sure you're okay?"

"Morgan, stop worrying. *I'm* the big sister."

"I know. I just know how this came about, so of course, I worry about you."

"You don't need to worry about me, honey. Things are good now. We've been slowly working our way toward each other. We're in a good place now, so don't start a fight with him on my behalf."

"First and foremost, I'm a lady. I don't start fights. Second, you deserve to be fought over. Remember that."

"When did you become the big sister?"

"I didn't. I'm just finally standing where I want to be."

"Yeah, I can see that."

"Excellent. Now go find your sexy fiancé. Let him shower you with orgasms. I'll be in the corner somewhere, yelling at Lance to get his sorry ass over here." My sister shoved the door open. "I'll see you out here in a minute."

"Hey, Morgan?"

"Yeah, Gwen."

"I love you. You know that, right?"

"Always and forever." Then she disappeared into the crowd.

I took a fortifying breath to steady the flutter of butterflies in my stomach.

Okay, then. I was going to become Mrs. Atticus Price. I'd asked Atticus if he thought his mother should come, but he said no. Besides, his father was more than likely to make an appearance tonight. And if he did, it was going to get ugly.

The door swung open again, and I laughed. "What did you forget, Morgan?"

But it wasn't my sister. It was a willowy woman, her skin like porcelain. Her hair was pale like a Nordic goddess, and her eyes were a startling blue, standing out in relief against the paleness of her skin and the fairness of her blond hair.

"Oh, sorry, I thought you were my sister."

"You're Gwenyth, aren't you?"

"Yeah, do we know each other?"

"No, I'm Lucy. Hello."

I shook Lucy's outstretched hand and attempted to place where I'd seen her before. "I'm sorry, but I don't think we've met. Did Atticus invite you?"

Lucy's expression froze for a moment before she grinned. "I'm sorry, it's just that Atticus has spoken so much about you, I feel like I know you already."

My heart started racing at the sound of his name on her voice. "Oh, I see. Well, it's nice to meet you."

"You too. Atticus is wonderful, isn't he?"

The way she said his name made my stomach turn. "Yes, he is."

"We used to be very close."

My stomach turned. I knew what she was saying. "I'm sorry, but Atticus never mentioned you."

Lucy's smile didn't falter. "Of course, he wouldn't. But it doesn't matter. I'm happy for him, truly. And for you, Gwen. You're a lucky woman."

I forced a smile. "Yes, I am."

Lucy's eyes locked onto mine, and I felt a chill run down my spine. "But just remember, Gwen. Sometimes the past can come back to haunt you in unexpected ways. I know it seems like it'll work, but it's not real. Men like him don't stay with mediocre. They like to elevate. So you have to ask yourself *why* he's chosen you."

Before I could respond, Lucy had turned and walked out of the room.

I couldn't breathe. My heart was beating a staccato pattern against my ribs.

It's not true. It's not true. He's chosen you. Because he needs you.

God I needed air. I tripped out of the bathroom. If I could just make it to the outside, I could breathe.

As I stepped out onto the balcony, I gasped for air, leaning against the railing for support. The cool night air felt like a balm washing over me and clearing my head. I tried to push Lucy's words out of my mind, but they lingered like a bad dream.

Why had Atticus chosen me? He told me he'd always made the deal for *me*, not for my sister, but I'd learned not to trust men. Especially men who wanted to make deals with my father. I shook my head, trying to dispel the doubts.

I heard the balcony door open behind me, and I turned to see Atticus standing there, a concerned look on his face. "Gwen, are you okay? I've been looking for you."

I tried to smile, but it felt like a grimace. "I'm fine. Just needed some air."

Atticus stepped closer, his hand reaching out to touch my arm. "Is something wrong? Did something happen?"

I hesitated for a moment, wondering if I should tell him about Lucy's visit. But then I shook my head, not wanting to start a fight at our engagement party. "No, nothing happened. I just needed a moment."

Atticus stepped closer, his hand still on my arm, his eyes searching mine. "Gwen, you know you can tell me anything, right? I'm here for you, always."

I nodded, wanting to believe him, but the doubt lingered in the back of my mind. "I know, Atticus. It's just... I guess I'm just feeling a little overwhelmed tonight."

"Two more weeks until we get married. You're not getting cold feet are you?"

I tilted my head up. "Are you?"

His wintergreen gaze searched mine. "Where's this coming from? I thought we were on the same page. We've been getting closer."

"It's just..." My voice trailed. "I met Lucy."

He blinked in surprise. "Lucy?"

"Your ex. She made it clear that she could take you back anytime and that I'm inferior."

"That's fucking bullshit." Atticus's voice was low and dangerous as his grip on my arm tightened.

He was always so calm, collected, and in control. But seeing him angry made me feel safe in a strange way.

"She's just jealous, Gwen. She knows what we have, and it's eating her alive. She wants what she can't have, and she'll do whatever it takes to get it."

"But what if she's right?" I whispered, afraid of the answer.

Atticus took my face in his hands, forcing me to meet his gaze. "She's not right, Gwen. From the moment you glitter-bombed me, I've been completely fascinated by you. Completely enthralled. Your father might have had other plans, but you are who I wanted. You are my little lioness. All fire and claws. There is nothing sexier. Not to mention I've never met anyone so genuinely selfless. I want *you*. I picked *you*. Don't let your father or Lucy or anyone else take that away from you. I would rather spend ten minutes arguing with you than a dozen life-times with some vapid, empty socialite. You have cracked my heart in two and nestled in there. I am not the same man without you."

"Atticus."

"I chose you because you're the only woman I've ever met who challenges me in every way. You're strong, smart, and beautiful. You make me want to be a better man. And I'm not going to let anyone, or anything come between us. Do you understand?"

I nodded, tears prickling at the corners of my eyes. "Yeah, I understand."

Atticus wiped away the tears with his thumbs, his eyes never leaving mine. "Good. Because I'm falling for you and there is no going back. I'm never going to let you go."

I felt a warmth spread throughout my body at his words. This was what I wanted. Someone who cared about me, who would protect me, who would never let me go.

"I'm falling for you too, Atticus."

"That's pretty handy since you're going to be my wife."

He leaned down for a kiss, and I tilted my head up to meet his. Our lips met, and I felt the passion and love behind it. It was like he was trying to convey all his feelings through that one kiss. I melted into him, feeling like I was the only woman in the world who mattered to him.

With a groan he tore his lips from mine. "What is it with us and balconies? Come on. Let's go enjoy our party. And then later, I'm going to show you just how hard I've fallen for you."

"You promise?"

CHAPTER 29

GWEN

The next two hours passed in a flurry of dancing, eating, and socializing. Atticus made introductions to friends and associates, but I knew I wouldn't remember any of the names.

In the car on the way home, Atticus was silent. He held my hand, stroking his thumb over my knuckles, but he didn't say much.

By the time Gavin dropped us off at the penthouse, I was a bundle of nerves.

We nodded to the doorman and walked in silence to the elevators. Once inside, I couldn't help it. I had to know.

"Okay, come on. What's wrong?"

Studying me intently, he asked, "What do you mean what's wrong?"

"Obviously, I did or said something wrong at some point. Was it that ambassador guy? He asked me a question when my mouth was full, and I couldn't answer right away. Or was it the redhead in the black dress? But that one's not my fault. I'm pretty sure she didn't like me because she wants you for herself. But I did try. I *am* trying. Are you already regretting this?"

As the elevator lifted us to the penthouse, he just studied me. "You're worried I'm angry with you?"

"Yes, of course I'm worried. I don't have much else to go on. We had that beautiful moment on the balcony, and it was perfect and amazing. And I'm so excited to be wearing your ring, and then you're silent the whole drive home. So please, just tell me what I did wrong."

"You're worried you've done something wrong because I haven't said anything?"

"Yes, exactly. You have to communicate with me somehow."

The elevator dinged as we reached the penthouse level. We just had to wait for the doors to open. "Did it ever occur to you that the reason I haven't said anything is because I have been trying to behave? There's a lot my mouth wants to do right now, but none of it is fit for polite company or at all related to *talking*. I've been trying to control myself until I had you alone to show you exactly what I want to do to you."

I blinked up at him as my brain clocked everything he just said. *Ohhhhh*. "You're not in the mood to *talk*?"

His tiny smirk had me pressing my thighs together. "No, I'm not in the mood to *talk*. But if you want me to communicate, then by all means, allow me."

He bent down and scooped me up, causing me to squeal. "Atticus. Oh my God, what are you doing?"

"Carrying you over the threshold."

"You're about a week early."

"Don't care. As far as I'm concerned. You already belong to me."

The penthouse was dark, save for the city lights twinkling in through the tall windows. He bypassed the living area then proceeded to carry me down the long hallway into our bedroom. Each footstep on the marble floor echoed through the spacious penthouse like thunderclaps.

He managed to kick the door shut with his foot before setting me down on the bed. He removed both our shoes before pushing me back on the bed and crawling over me until his face was inches from mine. Then he said, "You want me to communicate? All right then."

With the grace of a panther, he moved closer, his hands on either side of my face. His fingers tracing along my skin as if I was something precious, something delicate. His eyes never left mine as he lowered his lips onto my own.

It wasn't just a kiss—it was an affirmation of ownership, of understanding, of desire.

As our lips moved together, it was as if we were having an entire conversation without words. Every breath was an admission of need, every gentle nip a reassertion of his claim over me.

His hands found mine above my head, interlacing our fingers and pinning them down against the soft silk sheets.

"Atticus," I began, but words escaped me as his lips began exploring again.

"Um-hm?" He hummed against my skin, causing shivers to dance down my spine.

"I—" But my words were cut short as he captured my lips again.

"Shh," he quieted me, his voice a soft murmur against my mouth. "My turn to communicate."

His lips moved from mine and began tracing a path downward along the line of my jaw, the hollow of my throat. His hands, still entwined with mine, never left their place above my head, pinning me gently but firmly to the bed.

As his mouth drew closer to my breasts, I could feel my heartbeat quicken—the anticipation was palpable. He smirked up at me, his dark eyes brimming with promise. Then his lips found my nipple through the thin fabric of my dress. My head fell back as a moan escaped my lips.

"All good?" he asked as he traced figure eights over the swell of my breast.

"Yes," I whispered breathlessly. "Very good."

His hands released my wrists. "Stay," he murmured against the skin of my neck as he began to unzip my dress slowly. Every inch revealed more skin for him to kiss, to claim.

When he finally unfurled the dress from around me, leaving me in just my very tiny panties, his gaze was a mixture of hunger and adoration. He took in every inch of me as if I were a masterpiece only meant for his eyes.

His fingers danced down my body, teasing the edges of the lacy fabric of my underwear. His eyes, dark and full of desire, never left mine as his hands moved lower, tracing the line of my hips.

"Atticus," I moaned, my breath hitching as he teased the edge of my panties.

His smirk widened. "Just communicating," he murmured against my skin. His hand dipped lower, his fingers tracing over the wet spot in my underwear as a gasp escaped my lips. "You're so wet," he groaned.

"For you," I managed to whisper, my eyes fluttering closed as he applied gentle pressure through the fabric.

"Beautiful," he murmured. The word was heavy with sincerity.

I could only watch, breath hitched in my throat, as he stripped down. His body bore the perfect blend of strength and elegance, each muscle etched to perfection under his olive skin.

His cock bobbed insistently against his stomach, making my eyes go wide. Christ, he was huge. How the hell had we fit together before? How was I able to walk afterward?

He crawled back onto the bed, prowling over me once more. His gaze was so intense that it sent shivers cascading down my spine. His mouth moved back to my breasts, his tongue swirling around the pebbled nipple before gently sucking it into his mouth. A whimper escaped my lips as heat pooled deep within me.

"Do you like that?" he murmured against my skin.

I could only nod in response, lost in the pleasure he was giving me.

His free hand slipped between our bodies, cupping me intimately through the last piece of clothing separating us. I gasped as his finger pushed the fabric against my tight channel.

His fingers explored my wetness, the lacy fabric providing an enticing barrier to his touch. I bucked against him, a moan slipping from my lips as he found the right spot. My fingers gripped onto the silk sheets, the cool material a contrast against my heated skin.

He smirked against my breast, pulling away from my nipple with an enticing pop. "You like that, don't you?" His voice was a husky growl that rumbled deep in his chest, causing exciting tremors in mine.

"Atticus," I whimpered again, my hips instinctively grinding against his hand.

His eyes darkened further at my response, lust and desire etching deeper lines onto his handsome face. He slowly slid down, leaving a trail of kisses in his path. When his mouth met the apex of my thighs, I could only whimper in anticipation.

"Atticus... please," I begged desperately, my hands finding purchase in his hair. His hot breath against the soaked fabric of my panties made me writhe underneath him.

He looked up at me through hooded eyes, a wicked grin splitting his lips apart. "Patience, love," he murmured before nuzzling into the juncture of my thighs.

He nudged aside my thong but didn't remove it before delving his tongue into my folds. My body arched off the bed, a sharp gasp escaping my lips as he traced lazy circles around my clit. His large hands held my thighs apart, his fingers digging into my skin as my hips tried to buck against his mouth.

"Easy..." he murmured, his voice vibrating deliciously against my core. His tone was teasing, but his eyes were alight with an intense devotion that left me breathless.

His tongue danced along my sensitive button, each flick sending shockwaves of pleasure through me. My grip in his hair tightened as a moan tore through me, echoing off the room's tall windows. The sensation of his tongue against me was exquisite—wet and warm, rough and soft all at once.

With careful precision, he traced the shape of my entrance before diving in, lapping at my wetness like a man starved. My back arched off the bed again, and this time I screamed his name on my lips like a mantra. "Atticus... Atticus... Atticus..."

He moved lower still, toward my untouched hole. He blew gently on it before pushing a slick finger inside me. I gasped at the intrusion but didn't protest. I knew just how good this would feel.

The dual assault had me writhing beneath him.

My hands tangled in his hair, tugging on it as ecstasy washed over me, wave after wave. My breath came out in short gasps and pants, each one filled with his name. His tongue lapped at me greedily, drinking in every drop that I had to offer.

"You taste so good," he murmured before diving back in for another taste. His tongue instinctively knew where to stroke, how much pressure to apply. Each flick was calculated and precise, as if he knew exactly what I needed.

"You are so close," he murmured huskily. "Let go for me."

His words sent me over the edge. My body convulsed as an orgasm ripped through me. My vision blurred as I screamed his name, the sound echoing around the room.

He didn't stop until I was shuddering beneath him, every drop of pleasure wrung from my body. Then he gently pulled his fingers from me and licked them clean. When he crawled up my body, I shuddered against him and whispered, "You are... wow."

"And you are so beautiful when you come apart for me," he rasped, his hot breath fanning along the column of my neck before he fastened his mouth over it to nip lightly at the sensitive skin.

I kissed his pec before meeting his gaze. "You're not the only one who likes to communicate you know."

His soft chuckle sent a wave of need through me. "Is that so?"

"It is." I pushed him onto his back and straddled his hips, my hands splaying across his chest muscles. A low growl rumbled from within him as I slowly ground my wet pussy against his throbbing cock. He looked up at me, desire darkening his mesmer-izing wintergreen eyes.

"I want to taste you," I murmured against his ear, a shiver running down his spine at my words. His eyes held mine just as my fingers wrapped around his hard length. A gasp escaped him, the sound sinfully erotic to my ears.

I dipped my head down, trailing soft kisses along his chiseled torso. With each touch of my lips to his heated skin, he gasped and twitched beneath me. His breath hitching in anticipation was the sweetest melody to my ears.

As my mouth met the tip of his cock, he let out a long groan. His hands instinctively tangled in my hair, applying gentle pressure as encouragement. I teased his tip with the flat of my tongue before taking him into my mouth.

"Fuck Gwen... you... you're..." His voice broke on a grunt as he hit the back of my throat.

"I'm what?" I murmured against his skin as I pulled back. "Tell me."

"An angel... goddess..." His tight grip on my braids told me how I was making him feel. "Devil. Temptress. My ruin." Then he gasped as I took him deep again. "Fuuuuck."

The taste of him on my tongue was intoxicating, and I found myself relishing in it, trying to draw out every delicious moment for as long as possible. His cock throbbed in my mouth, each pulse an addictive rhythm that only spurred me on further.

"Fuck, Gwen," he gasped out through gritted teeth. His fingers tightened in my hair, pulling me down and forcing his cock deeper into my mouth. "That pretty mouth looks so fucking good stretched around my cock. You're such a good wife for taking all of me."

I tried to relax my throat, tried to take that last inch of him, but then suddenly he was tugging me off by my hair and dragging me up his body.

"Hey! I wasn't done!"

His breathing was sharp and ragged. "Yes, you were. The only place that's getting bathed in my cum tonight is your pretty pussy. Now come and sit on your throne." I tried to remove my panties, but he shook his head, his hungry gaze on mine. "No. Mrs. Price. Leave them on."

His command echoed through the room as his powerful hands immediately moved to guide me. I could see the desire burning brightly in his eyes. As I rose to position myself above him, the sheer intensity of his gaze only heightened my need.

"Atticus, it'll be easier—"

His fingers brushed against the delicate lace of my thong, the warmth radiating off his skin causing my heart to flutter. There was a certain undeniable edge to his voice as he demanded, "I said, leave them on."

With his thumb, he shoved aside the lace then fisted the base of his cock as he deliberately rubbed himself against my wetness. "Oh God, Atticus."

"You need to be wetter."

Instead of sinking inside me, he adjusted my panties so that they trapped his cock against me as he sat up to kiss me. He fisted both hands in my hair and drugged me with a kiss so good I thought I might melt into a puddle.

"Atticus," I moaned into his mouth, gripped with impatience. I was so ready for him, but he seemed to know just how to draw out the sweet torture of anticipation.

His lips left mine to trail hot kisses down my throat, igniting a trail of fire over my sensitive skin. He bit down lightly on my collarbone, eliciting a needy whimper from me.

His hands roamed from my hips to my breasts while our bodies were flush against each other, grinding. His firm chest was against my sensitive nipples, and every breath he took brushed them teasingly, sending waves of pleasure coursing through me.

"Open up," Atticus rasped, his hand falling lower.

I complied willingly, parting my legs wider for him. A soft gasp escaped my lips as his fingers brushed past the delicate fabric of my thong and found my clit again. He rubbed slow circles teasing the me in rhythm with the rocking of his hips against mine.

With every movement, I could feel him slide slickly against me, causing shivers to run through me.

"I need you," was all I could say.

His hands moved down to my hips, and he started to grind harder against me. The sensation of his hard cock rubbing against my sensitive fold through my soaked underwear had me crying out his name.

"Yes, Atticus," I moaned, throwing my head back in pleasure.

"That's it," he growled. "Fuck yourself on me."

He guided me again, encouraging me use his cock to tantalize myself. I rolled my hips, grinding down on him as he teased my clit. The friction was mind-blowing, making me whimper and gasp for more.

The wetter I grew, the more the tip of his cock slid through my folds to my rear entrance. With each brush of the ridge of his cock, I gasped, the sensation decadent and naughty and exciting. All of it adding to my desire, making my slide over his cock easy.

"Atticus... more," I pleaded, my hips rising and falling in a rhythm that matched his. He shifted one hand and I could feel him pressing against my puckered hole, each movement causing me to clench around him.

His eyes bored into mine, dark with lust. The sensation of his fingers, covered in my wetness and slowly circling my asshole, was maddening. He continued to apply pressure there, and despite the slight discomfort, there was an undeniable thrill coursing through me.

"That's it," he praised huskily. "So fucking tight... You like this?"

"Um-hmmm..." My words were nothing more than needy whimpers. And then he pushed a well-lubed finger up my ass just as his mouth closed over one of my nipples.

He sucked hard on it, biting lightly and swirling his tongue around it, making me gasp and arch my back. His cock was still trapped against me through the thong, rubbing against my dripping folds, sending shivers throughout my body.

"I love how greedy your little cunt is for me," he groaned out as he bit down on my nipple, causing me to gasp at the delicious sting.

His other hand was still busy playing with my asshole, pushing another finger into it and stretching me out. The sensation was foreign but addictive as he began to thrust them in rhythm with the rocking of our bodies.

My movements became frantic, my hips grinding against him as I begged for relief. "Please, Atticus... I need you inside me."

He smiled wickedly at that, "Only because you asked so nicely, Ness."

As he removed his fingers from my asshole, there was a sense of loss, but it was quickly replaced by anticipation. The lacy barrier of my thong was finally pushed aside, and I felt his hot, swollen cock nudge at my entrance. A choked gasp left my mouth as he began to sink inside me, stretching me deliciously.

"Fuuuck. So good. You fit me so well, baby," he groaned as he filled me, his hands clenching on my hips as he fought for control.

My lips found his again, desperate for the taste of him. Atticus welcomed it, his tongue brushing against mine in a heated dance that only added to the mounting tension between us.

Leaning back, he guided my hands back down to his taut abdomen and let me take control. I began to move rhythmically astride him, grinding down against the throbbing length of his cock, clothed only by a thin barrier of soaked lace.

The sensation consumed me. Each movement of my hips saw him sliding deliciously deeper, and every gasp and moan from Atticus made me even wetter.

His hands roamed over me, one playing with my nipples while the other kept a firm grip on my hip, guiding me as I rode him.

His gaze was wild yet focused, watching my every move as he murmured sweet obscenities to me. Each word sent a shiver running down my spine that pooled into a warmth radiating between my thighs.

"You're so fucking sexy when you're like this," he said, his words a husky growl. "Riding me so good... so damn wet."

He sat up abruptly, wrapping an arm around my waist to keep me impaled on him. His mouth descended on one of my nipples, sucking hard before biting down lightly. My scream was swallowed by the kiss he planted on my lips.

His hands moved to my ass, gripping me and guiding me as I set our pace. His finger again explored the sensitive ring of muscle at my ass. He continued to circle it teasingly before pushing a slick finger inside me again.

"Fuck, Gwen," he grunted against my skin. "You're so fucking tight. One day, I'm going to fuck you here. Would you like that?"

I rode him harder as I felt the coil tighten even further. "Yes. Oh God, yes."

"I wonder how hard you'll come for me this way. I wonder if it'll be so good I can make you beg for it."

I bit my lip to suppress a moan, whimpering in anticipation of his promise. "Please, Atticus," I begged. His dirty talk and the feel of his finger sliding in and out of my ass, alongside his cock thrusting inside me, had me on the edge.

He chuckled darkly. "That's it, baby, beg for it," he taunted, matching my movements with each deep thrust. The delicious sensation was making me delirious with pleasure as he continued to thrust into me.

He growled approvingly, the sound vibrating through me as he tightened his grip on my ass. His finger slid deeper into me, making me gasp and squirm. I could feel his cock throbbing inside of me, matching the pulse of my own clit.

His other hand moved from my breast to my clit, his fingers rubbing desperate circles around it while I bucked against him. His mouth continued to play with my nipples, alternately sucking and biting them as I rode him hard.

"Just like that Gwen... Don't stop." His command was ragged, his breathing as labored as mine. His thrusts up into me were becoming erratic, a clear indication of his impending climax.

My eyes locked with his, lost in the stormy sea of raw passion that clouded his gaze. The coil inside me was getting tighter and tighter until I felt it snap.

"Atticus!" I screamed out his name as waves of pleasure crashed over me. My entire body shuddered as he continued to thrust into my spasming pussy.

"That's it, Ness."

Pleasure washed over me in waves, my body still shuddering as I clenched around his cock. I cried out his name again, my voice breaking with the intensity of my orgasm.

Even as I came down from the high, Atticus kept moving beneath me. His hand on my ass was a steady pressure, guiding me through the aftershocks. He thrust up and into me a few more times before grunting loudly against my skin.

The sensations were overwhelming with his release. His cock pulsing inside me, a roar of his own mixing with my whimpers as he pushed deep one last time, releasing his hot seed inside me. His grip on my hip tightened as he rode out his orgasm with me still impaled on him.

Even through the haze of pleasure, I felt each spasm of his orgasm and swallowed his cries with a kiss.

"You're insatiable," he murmured huskily into my hair, kissing the top of my head lightly.

"And you love it," I retorted with a chuckle.

He hummed in agreement, stroking my bare back lazily. "Damn right, I do." He kissed me again, this time on the lips. It was slow and tender and filled with worship.

Minutes later, he disengaged and tucked me in the sheets before rolling out of bed and padding into the bathroom. I heard the water running for several minutes before he came back and tugged the sheets off. "Come on, Ness. Let's get you in the tub. You're going to be sore."

I was so sleepy. "I'm okay."

"I wasn't asking Mrs. Price." He gently scooped me out of bed and carried me into the bathroom. He'd dimmed all the lights and drawn a bath.

"Oh, I see what you're up to."

"Taking care of the woman I'm going to marry? Guilty."

CHAPTER 30
GWEN

LIFE WAS MOVING AT WARP SPEED. A FEW DAYS AFTER THE ENGAGEMENT party, I officially moved my team into the Pendragon Tech offices.

And true to his word, Atticus made everything seamless. From the movers, to the IT team, to the servers, and the database guys. Hell, he even had someone bring snacks around.

This is what it's like getting help.

Still, I nervously chewed on my fingernails.

Lance bumped shoulders with me as he mimicked my movements. "So, this is it? We are Pendragon now."

"Yeah, I guess so." I said with a smile and shrug. "It's not so bad so far. They have better tea options."

His gaze scanned mine. "Are you okay?"

"Yeah, I'm good." And I found it was true. Since the engagement party, I'd felt settled. Solid. And comfortable with Atticus.

"Okay, I trust you. I just worry, you know."

CHAPTER 30

"And I appreciate you worrying. But I'm good, Lance."

He nodded. I could tell he was dying to say something, but he didn't. He held his tongue because he was trusting me. But I was trusting Atticus, and that made Lance uncomfortable.

Atticus and I were making progress. After what he'd said to me on our engagement night, that he would be there for me and that I didn't need to do everything alone, I believed him. And for once, I was just going to let myself fall. It was easier with help. I wish I could say it wasn't, but it was. I had signed on the dotted line, and Atticus had taken care of the money and the interim things that we needed. He'd involved me in every meeting. I trusted him, and the way he made me feel in bed was unparalleled, but there was still a little part of me that was worried, still slightly unsure. But that was just my self-preservation kicking in. And I was allowed that, right?

You can't fall in love with self-preservation.

No, I couldn't. But I wasn't ready for love yet. Right now, just knowing that I had someone watching out for me was enough. And I wasn't really looking for love anyway. Love complicated things. Liking and respecting someone and having really good sex was enough, right? Except we'd both already admitted we'd started to fall for each other.

Christ. I was not unpacking those feelings right now.

Lance looked to the side. "That's my cue to go."

I turned and saw Atticus walk off the elevator. The smile that tugged at my lips was instantaneous.

And when his gaze met mine, the corner of his lips turned up slightly. My whole body tingled, and his gaze did not waver until he stopped in front of me.

"Mr. Price," I said.

"Fucking hell, I cannot wait until I can say Mrs. Price."

A flush crept up my neck. "I guess that will take some getting used to. Are you sure I can't hyphenate?"

"I don't care what you do. Keep your name if you want. I will still call you Mrs. Price." He took my hand, glanced down at the engagement ring, and brushed his thumb over it. "Everything going okay in here?"

"Yeah, your team is great. Carla over there with the snacks, she's a smoothie peddler. Every fifteen minutes or so, she comes out and offers me something. It's like you told her personally to make sure I'm well fed."

He shrugged. "I cannot confirm nor deny."

"Oh my God, you did not."

Atticus only gave me a shrug. "If you refuse to take care of yourself, then I need to make sure other people do it for you. And I have to make sure that your diet doesn't consist of just gummy bears."

I pulled a pack out from my back pocket. "Oh, really? You probably should have told Carla I'm not allowed to have these."

He growled low and tried to take them from me as I hid them behind my back, which only made him wrap his arms around me. My gaze skittered around. "Atticus."

"What? Everyone in here knows that we are getting married."

"I guess. It's just—"

He did not move his hands. Instead he gave me a quick peck on the nose. "What? It makes you nervous?"

"Yes, a little. It takes a little getting used to. It's not exactly like we've had a lot of time to get used to PDAs and stuff."

"That is actually a pretty good point. I'm guessing from the way you just stiffened that you're not down with that at work." He flashed that devilish grin that was mostly reserved for me, and well, there you have it, the panties melted.

I pressed my thighs together. "Atticus Price, I have work to do. I have to get my team settled in."

"I know, but I do have more questions."

"Yes?"

"Are your panties wet for me?"

I rolled my eyes and shoved at his chest, which didn't even budge. "You are incorrigible."

"I have been told that before. I'm afraid it's your fault if you're really looking to cast blame."

"My fault is it?"

"Entirely. I was thinking after work tonight we might go see my mother. Since she couldn't attend the engagement party, it might be nice to pop in and see her."

"Yeah, it would be nice to see her. I was disappointed she wasn't there."

"Something like that is not an ideal situation for her."

"No, of course, I understand."

He held on to me for a moment longer. "You actually understand?"

"Yeah. Being in a room full of two hundred guests, the chattering, the noise... Hell, I had a hard time myself. Now, if don't you mind, Mr. Price, I have work to do."

"You do. I will leave you to it so that you can get things sorted and make sure everyone is where they're supposed to be. I want to make sure that your team can manage without you for a couple of weeks."

"What do you mean, a couple of weeks? Where am I going?"

"Well, in less than two weeks, we're getting married, remember? You think I'm not taking you on a honeymoon where I'll have you all to myself? And you won't be allowed to use a computer or a phone. Hell, you won't be allowed clothes."

Another flush of heat hit me like a wave. "A-a honeymoon? I haven't, um, prepared." Just thinking about it made my body heat. But I had not planned ahead. "Oh God, I have to prep Lance to take over."

He gave me a tight smile. "Well, let's make sure you have lots of contingencies and redundancies in place, okay?"

"Okay. Now, can I get back to work?"

"Yes. But come to think of it, meet me upstairs in my office in two hours."

I shook my head. "I won't do that. You have that look like you want to bend me over your desk, and that's not what I'm here for."

"Just once, woman, can't you just go where I tell you to go?"

"No, I won't. I go where I want. And if it's urgent, you can come find me."

"Oh, you better believe that I will."

And I was entirely worried that he would.

CHAPTER 31

ATTICUS

"YOU WANTED TO SEE ME?"

I sat back in my seat, rubbing my jaw as Lance walked in. "Come in, have a seat."

He shrugged. "If it's all right with you, I prefer to stand."

Of course he would. He was Gwen's best friend.

Try to get along, asshole.

"Suit yourself." I watched him. I'd seen him watching me and Gwen downstairs. The jealousy was manageable. I had her, and he didn't. She was never going to choose him. He wasn't dangerous or even a threat. Gwen was mine. And she was staying fucking mine.

But I did need to do something with him. "I've been looking up your performance reports in the work that you've done while you were at Becks. Not to mention you have your masters in computer science."

"I know my qualifications. What about them?"

He crossed his arms, and I watched him. For all intents and purposes, he *was* better for her. He was accessible. He was easier. He was quick with a smile. He was simple.

I was a hard son of a bitch. I knew that cracking my exterior was next to impossible, but she'd managed to do it. And I was grateful. After the engagement party, we were solid. But I needed to be sure.

And if I was being honest, this opportunity *was* good for him. Not that I gave a fuck about that.

"All right, I'll get to the point. As you know, Gwen and I have been working on the best placements for the core teams."

He gave me a sharp nod. "Yes, we had recommendations. I assume she gave you the reports. If she hasn't yet, I can show them to you."

I just smiled at that. "I have them. I'm left with the job of determining what to do with senior leadership."

The muscle in his jaw ticked, and he rocked slightly from foot to foot. Ah, so he was getting the picture.

"Do you want a drink?"

He frowned at me. "What are you drinking?"

"Well, let's go with scotch. We can toast the move, the acquisition, my engagement, the opportunity for you, or all of the above."

He lifted a brow. "Opportunity for me?"

I pushed to my feet, walked to my bar, and poured two glasses. When I handed him his, he took it but only stared at it.

I deliberately took a sip of mine and seated myself on the couch with the view of the city. With a drink in his hand, he'd be hard-pressed not to sit.

When he finally joined me, I leaned back. "Look, I know you're not happy about my engagement to Gwen."

"Well, no one said you were an idiot." He took a sip and stared into his glass. "It's not bad."

"Macallan."

"Of course."

"Lakewood, I'm not going to pretend to like you, and you don't have to pretend to like me. We don't know each other, but your fascination with my fiancée is a problem."

He shifted uncomfortably. "We're best friends. Have been since college. That's never going to change."

Yeah, I read you, asshole. You're never going away. "And honestly, she needs you. I don't want that to change."

His brows puckered. "Okay?"

"There's one thing that *is* going to change though."

"Oh, excellent. What new delight have you cooked up for us now?" he asked sarcastically.

"I have a VP of Technology position available in Pendragon Tech's London office. Running your own show, essentially an R&D outfit like you've had, but there is no Gwen to answer to. Obviously, it's a significant bump in pay. The usual package, and it's a good fresh start. A young team with room to build, so you can mold them however you want."

He frowned into his glass. "That would be the offer, wouldn't it?"

"Excuse me?"

"You're dangling something so good in front of me that I have no choice but to go."

I sighed. "Let me lay this out for you. There is London, which means a new environment, a chance to grow and spread your wings. There, no one cares that you're a Lakewood. Research things that interest you. You're the major decision-maker. Or you can stay here where Gwen is still above you, she makes the decisions, and she's the one in the room, not you. Sure, she discusses things with you now and she likes your input, but she makes the choices, not you. If you want to stay in the position you have now, it's fine. I don't care. Because you are not a threat to me. You never were. But I do think your abilities can be put to better use in London."

I said that just as he was taking a sip, and he coughed into his glass. "Well, way to mince words there."

"It's true. How Gwen and I came together was not ideal. Her father has a lot to answer for. But she's mine to look after, mine to protect. You can stay here if you want, but you will only ever be her second in command."

"You don't know what we are to each other."

"No, I don't. I know that to her, you are invaluable. She loves you. She should. You've been best friends for years."

Lakewood swallowed hard. "What's your point?"

"You think I don't have eyes? You're in love with her. And if the rumors are to be believed about Lakewood Enterprises, you were going to bite that bullet for her, and she still said no, even though the one thing she wanted was to save her company."

"She knows what it would have cost me."

"That is Gwen. She is selfless to a fault. It's the thing that makes her heart so generous."

"You don't know her at all."

"I know that she will be my wife in less than two weeks, and she wants you there to stand by her side and watch her marry another man. I know that has to sting."

He drained his glass and gently placed it on the coffee table. "I think we're done here."

"We're not."

Lakewood glowered at me, stood, and crossed his arms. "Like I said, we're done. Thanks for the drink though."

"I'll expect your answer by the end of the day. Stay. Be here for her. Whatever. I don't care. She has already chosen me. But I'm just curious. Did you tell her that despite wanting nothing to do with your family, your granddad went ahead and put ten million into your account and that you could have bailed her out at any time?"

The blood drained from his face. "What?"

They called me ruthless for a reason. "Oh, wait, did you not know?"

I could see it in his eyes. He hadn't known about the funds being released. After the standoff he'd had with his grandfather for years, the old man had finally relented, but he didn't have a clue.

I told myself I wasn't a cruel man. But I needed to make sure that he got on the fucking plane.

"Oh, so you didn't? Yeah, you could have invested in Becks, or at least staved off the bleed for a couple of years, easy. You had the funds, but you didn't use them."

"I—I didn't know I had them." He sank back down into the couch and scrubbed his hands over his face.

"I know. You're between a rock and a hard place now, because if you stay you're going to be compelled to tell her that you could have saved her but didn't. And she wouldn't hold it against you, but you would hate every moment. Or you can go to London for a fresh start. Or you can leave Pendragon altogether. It's up to you. You've got the money to open your own shop now."

I tossed my drink back, swallowed, then pushed to my feet. "The thing is, you are smart. And you do love Gwen. And because you love her, I can't hate you. I mean, I wish you loved her a different way, of course, but she still chose me. So I want to do right by you and give you something I think you need. But the choice is yours."

He stared at me and shook his head. "You're a real son of a bitch."

"So I've been told."

"You think you know her. You think you *see* her. You have no idea the pain she swallows to get through every day. You have no fucking clue."

"All due respect, but nothing you say matters."

To my surprise, he laughed. "Wow, she didn't tell you, did she? About Bronson Jacobson? What he did to her?"

The room spun as my world tilted. "She said they dated once."

"Dated?" He ran his hands through his hair. "That fucker? He made her think he was interested in her. Interested in her work. He really poured it on thick. Her father already tried to marry her off to him. The 'perfect merger' he called it. Then that piece of shit tried to—" He stopped and dragged in a harsh breath. "He tried to rape her. She fought like hell. But she didn't escape unscathed. Some bruises and a broken hand from when she hit him. Not to mention the mental scars. She doesn't talk about it. *Ever.* But I know it's why she doesn't date. I know she still has nightmares. When she told her father and wanted to report him, her asshole father said he didn't believe her. And Bronson, well he told anyone who would listen, that he'd rather have had the hot sister. That the software wasn't worth having to fuck Gwen for years."

Bile churned in my gut. "Stop talking."

Rage flooded my blood stream and I was trying not to kill him, but lance kept speaking. "She didn't even trust you enough to tell you. So between you and me, who has it wrong?"

"Close the door on your way out. I expect your answer by the end of the day."

CHAPTER 32
ATTICUS

"WHY ARE WE HERE AGAIN?"

I rolled my eyes. Micah didn't get it. Sure, maybe I hadn't gotten it a few weeks ago either. The ring I had Leah pick out was service-able and fine, but it didn't reflect Gwen. And that's what I wanted.

Micah climbed out of the car behind me, and we approached the jewelry store on the corner of Canal.

When we walked in, an elderly black man beamed up at me. "Mr. Atticus."

"Jean Pierre. It's good to see you."

"It's been a long time."

Once upon a time, I'd thought I was going to propose to Lucy like my father wanted. *Bullet dodged.*

"How is your mother?" he asked.

I nodded and shrugged. "Some good days, some not great ones."

Micah looked at me curiously.

CHAPTER 32

"Micah, This is Jean Pierre. He's South African. His family owns a diamond mine. When Mom needed to get her jewelry fixed, she'd always come here."

"What's the occasion?" Jean Pierre asked. "Your mother's birthday? Anniversary of some sort?"

"No, I'm engaged."

Jean Pierre's eyes went wide, and they crinkled at the corners as a toothy white smile spread across his wrinkled face. "Oh, this old man loves love. Nothing better than a love story."

Micah turned to face me. "I thought you already had a ring."

"We do. But back then, I didn't care what it looked like. Well, I didn't care enough. I wanted to own her. And that's not what this is about now."

Micah lifted a brow. "You fell for her, didn't you?"

I shrugged. "It's hard not to. She's smart, she's beautiful, compassionate, she wants to help and fix everyone. But she's not a saint. She has quite a temper. Stubborn. Jesus Christ, she's so fucking mule-headed. Always thinks she knows best. Fiercely independent. And she's terrified of being rejected. And the next thing I knew, there I was fucking falling in love with her. I didn't even know what had happened."

My brother graced me with one of his biggest smiles.

Jean Pierre opened one of the cases with the keys from his pockets. "Let's look at settings, shall we?"

Micah had apparently always wanted an engagement ring, because my brother oohed and aahed like he was getting the ring slipped on his finger.

"Look at that one," he said excitedly. "Classic. You can't miss with classic."

I looked at the ostentatious design and laughed. "Well yes, I'd be able to find her in a crowd. I'm pretty sure you'd see anything in that setting from space. I don't think that's it for Gwen. She is elegant. Not really fussy. She doesn't wear a lot of jewelry."

Jean Pierre nodded. "I'll be back. I have some settings in the back I was working on earlier."

By the time he came back, Micah had already stalked several cases of women's pinky rings and was staring at them under the light.

"God help whoever you marry, brother. You're going to be obnoxious."

"Yeah, and what exactly are you looking for in an engagement ring?"

"Hey, I'm trying to get her the ring that screams, 'My husband-to-be is Atticus Price. All interlopers beware.' But if it was that easy, I wouldn't have any problems. Lakewood has continued making a nuisance of himself."

Micah rolled his eyes. "For fuck's sake. If that was going to happen, it would have happened already. Why can't you get it through your head that Gwen only sees him as a friend? But if you want me to get the fixers on it, Pierce will do it."

"No, I don't want this fixed. And what do you mean, Wade will do it? Do what?"

Micah grinned and shrugged. "Don't worry about what I just said. You just focus on getting the perfect bauble for my new sister-in-law, will you?"

So for the next hour, we worked with Jean Pierre. Micah finally started to focus when I was giving my design ideas. He'd interject, directing me several times, telling me that I was going too big and Gwen would like something more delicate.

"I need something big enough to hold the diamond."

Micah sat back, assessing. "Okay, I like how you think. It needs to be sturdy. Thick." When he said *thick*, his brows lifted, and then he fell over in a fit of laughter. The fool was laughing and I couldn't help but join in. When was the last time we'd laughed like this anyway?

Jean Pierre chuckled. "Don't worry. We'll find her the right diamond. Or jewel. Maybe she's a ruby girl."

I thought about her red lips. The way she always seemed to be wearing bright red lipstick of some color. Varying colors, actually. Sometimes it would be a darker red, and sometimes it would be a more muted shade, but it was always red.

"Hm, maybe a ruby. Is that too nontraditional?"

Jean Pierre smiled. "I do love a woman in red."

When I finally found the stone, I knew I had the right fit. The setting design was thin, with delicate diamonds placed around, and then the setting itself crisscrossed with white gold and rose gold. So she'd be able to wear both gold and silver, depending on her outfit. At least that's what Jean Pierre said. And the stone itself was a brilliant cut pink ruby. In some light, it was extremely pale, so it wouldn't flash too much. In other lighting, it was deeply pink, and in some it was red. It was perfect.

Now I just prayed she said yes... And not just because of the contract.

CHAPTER 33
ATTICUS

W̲ʜᴇɴ ᴡᴀs ᴛʜᴇ ʟᴀsᴛ ᴛɪᴍᴇ I̲ ᴡᴀs ɴᴇʀᴠᴏᴜs?

I paced back and forth, wearing a pattern in the middle of my living room as I waited for Gwen.

The soft *click-clack* of her heels alerted me, and I turned to watch her walk in.

I wasn't prepared.

Not. At. All.

She'd straightened her hair and smoothed it up mostly off her face, but she'd left some wisps to frame her sculpted cheekbones and jawline. The rest of her hair hung past her shoulders in soft waves. Instead of a little black dress, she wore red. Vermilion red. The kind of red that was brighter than a fire engine and would have everyone turning to stare at her.

Simple spaghetti straps led to a V showcasing the tits I wanted to plant my face between and never come up for air. Something seemed to push them together, hugging her waist but not too tight. Her gorgeous curves and ass led to ruffles around her mid-thighs. I could see her toes peeking out in her heels, and she smiled when she saw me.

"There you are. Which earrings? These or these?" She turned, showcasing a silvery-dangling one on the right that looked like dental threads and one on the left that was a simple diamond stud.

Unfortunately, all I could do was stare at her. "Yes."

She laughed uncertainly. "That's not an answer I can work with. These *or* these?"

"I, uh..." I couldn't fucking think. Did she know what she looked like? "Sorry, but I'm really just thinking that we might not leave the house tonight."

"Oh, we're leaving, sir. I got dressed. I left a meeting and a mountain of work. We are leaving this house."

I blinked rapidly. "No, of course we're leaving this house. I need to spoil you. You don't often let me."

"Right. The spoiling. I have to get used to that, don't I?"

"Yes." I walked up to her, gently brushing her hair off her shoulder, and I leaned in, meaning to give her a soft, chaste kiss. But Christ, that scent. Something with a hint of sweetness chased by spice. I inhaled, nuzzling the hollow of her throat.

A groan followed a soft, breathy catch in her voice. "Oh, my God, Atticus."

"God, you smell incredible."

"You still haven't answered my question."

"Fine. Dangly things. You can leave them on in bed."

"Atticus."

I cleared my throat and forced myself to pull back. Never mind the erection tenting my pants. I'd gone with a more casual suit because I figured we'd also maybe go out dancing if that's what she wanted to do. Fuck me, now I was really nervous. I couldn't fucking think. My brain cells were not coming online.

"Okay, let me get the other earring, then we'll go."

All I could do was nod as I watched her slink back to our room. Goddamn, she was absolutely gorgeous.

She was back in less than a minute with her clutch in hand and something gossamer looking that appeared to be a shawl.

"That's not going to keep you warm," I said.

"Isn't that what I have you for?"

Hell yes. "Abso-fucking-lutely. I just want you to know that I'm exhibiting a Herculean amount of self-control right now, because I am really thinking of picking you up and sitting you on that counter and eating you for dessert."

She gave me a blinding smile, and my heart stopped. Holy fucking Christ, she was so goddamn beautiful, and she was mine.

Our first stop for the night was this cute little spot that my friend Andre owned. It was tiny and nestled in the heart of Spanish Harlem, and you had to basically know it was there to even find it. But they made the absolute best mojitos I'd ever tasted. When we pulled up, I was worried she might be disappointed. After all, she'd gotten so dolled up. But her eyes weren't on the neighborhood or the restaurant. They were on me. "So, I'm completely in your hands. This will be fun."

"Absolutely."

Gavin opened my door and smirked at me. I lifted my brow at him, and he murmured. "She's too hot for you."

"Fuck off. I know that."

He chuckled again, enjoying himself far too much. That was the problem with having your friends work with you. They thought they were fucking hilarious. I walked around to Gwen's side, opened the door for her, and she took my hand delicately. Her lips looked even more inviting than they had when we left the house.

"I don't know how I'll make it all night and not fucking eat you raw."

"Well, you can do that later."

"Promise?"

Her giggle was like music to my ears. I led her inside, and Andre met us at the door. The interior was pure Cuban charm. The music was low, but I could hear the bongos and maracas that injected an urgency to move to the soft salsa music.

Andre gave me a tight hug. "Well, well, Atticus Price, good to see you uptown. I was starting to think you had forgotten I was here."

"Never. How could I? I like to check on your mother once in a while."

He rolled his eyes. "That woman. She's already back there cooking for you."

"I thought Mama Luz didn't work in the kitchen anymore."

"When she heard her favorite, Atticus, was coming by, she shooed the chefs out like it was her personal kitchen at home. That woman."

I laughed and then introduced him to Gwen. And being the charming fool that he was, he took her hand and bent over. Instead of placing a kiss on the back of her hand, he turned her palm over and kissed it.

Gwen gasped in surprise then laughed. "Oh, my."

"Forgive me. A beautiful lady should be seduced."

I took Gwen's hand from his. "Don't mind him. He was raised in a barn."

"It's nice to meet you, Andre. I haven't met any of Atticus's friends."

"That's because he has so few."

"Don't listen to him. He lies," I muttered.

"Yes, well, considering you're the first one I've met, I'm starting to think you might be right about that."

I rolled my eyes. "Not my wife-to-be and my best friend roasting me."

"Well, do you deserve to be roasted, husband-to-be?" Her eyes were dancing, and I could tell she was having fun.

Andre looked back and forth between us. "Hm, I think she's good for you. Atticus Price making gooey eyes at a woman. A sight I never thought I would see, but I love it. Come with me. Let's get you some drinks."

I was pulling out all the stops for her. I had a full night planned for us. But I also wanted to make sure she wouldn't be too tired. She'd been working non-stop, still burning the candle at both ends, but she'd made a concerted effort to be home on time for our date. I'd had a full day myself, but for her, I just got up and walked out on my last meeting. Micah had just looked amused. Normally, he'd have been freaking out.

Andre sent a platter of dishes, most of which I didn't even know what they were. And of course, he served his delicious mojitos. The delight on her face when she took a sip unfortunately had me thinking about her mouth wrapped around my cock.

She was happy. That was all that mattered.

"How do you know Andre?"

"Oh, him? Tales of a misspent youth."

"No, I'm serious."

"College. He went to Yale with me. His mother was hell bent and determined that he'd go to Yale, but after graduation, he was just as determined to come back and run the family business. We've just gotten closer over the years. It seems I couldn't shake him."

"I'm sure you tried."

"Maybe. I'm not used to making a lot of friends. But Andre stuck. When he was looking for investors for Cubana Havana, I threw money at him before he dared look elsewhere."

"So, you're an investor?"

"Yeah. He's already bought it back from me, but I keep a small one percent share just so I can say I'm one of the cool kids."

She watched me as she took another sip of her drink. "You look so relaxed."

"I am relaxed."

"Well, I mean in a way I have never seen you before. You're always so controlled."

"Not always," I said with a wink.

My mind offered up the oh-so-unhelpful memory of the two of us in her office. Of course, I was reminded of just what I'd done with that cake.

I cleared my head and shook it. "You make me lose control. Every time. I usually don't know what to do about it."

"I don't think there's anything you can do about it."

"Who are you, Gwen?"

"I'm just a girl, sitting in front of a boy, asking him to love her."

That little word. I was choking on it. And her eyes went wide. "Oh my God, you should see your face. I'm not asking you to love me. I'm just quoting *Notting Hill*. You know, the movie," she murmured.

"I have seen the movie."

"Oh, thank God. Because I'm not—"

I reached across the table and took her hand. "Oh, for fuck's sake, Gwen, be quiet. I'm going to kiss you now. Regardless of whether or not you're asking me to love you, I'm halfway there already."

Her hands were shaking. As was her smile. "I think I might have a little crush on you, too."

I took her face in my hands and pulled her closer. Our lips barely touching. "I think I know how that feels."

"You're not going to break my heart, are you?" she asked hesitantly.

I shook my head. "No, never."

"How can you be so sure?"

"Because I'm not just halfway there. I'm all the way there. I think I fell in love with you when you glitter-bombed me."

I watched her eyes close as my lips touched hers again. And I didn't think I'd ever stop kissing her, but I needed to do this before I lost my nerve.

I broke our kiss and lowered myself to one knee. "I figure I should do this properly."

She was staring at me in disbelief. "Atticus?"

"Gwen, I'm falling for you. Being with you feels more real to me than anything I've ever done. I *want* this to be a real marriage. Will you marry me?"

She smiled and nodded and then started to cry. "Yes, I'll marry you, Atticus. I'll marry you for real. Not because of a contract or a deal. Because of you."

I stood up and kissed her, and then I whispered in her ear, "I will do everything in my power to make you happy."

As the smile spread over her lips, I knew I had found my home.

CHAPTER 34
GWEN

WHEN WAS THE LAST TIME I'D BEEN ABLE TO DO A MARGARITA NIGHT? Things had been so crazy for so long, and I hadn't really wanted to go out or hang out. But being able to do margarita night with Morgan and Lance, I felt like I was finding myself again.

My ring glinted under the lights and there was no way I could hold the smile back. A few weeks ago, my father forced my hand, and now I was dopily in love. The warmth spread in my chest just thinking about him on one knee.

A part of me kept waiting for the other shoe to drop, but I was too damned elated to care. And knowing he'd had this ring made for me banished my worries. He'd made it to match me. He'd been paying attention to me. Of all the people in my life, *he* saw me.

Atticus had even kissed me goodbye and told me to have fun. He hadn't given me any of his usual 'Where are you going? Who are you going with?' questions. He just told me to go have a good time. Granted, I was only going back to my old apartment. When I let myself in, the doorman smiled at me, but I didn't recognize him. He must have been new. Considering I had a key fob, he had no reason to stop me. He just called out a bland, "Good evening, miss," and I didn't ask for his name because... Well, while I still had a place there, I didn't live there anymore. I'd have to eventually figure out what I was going to do with it. I certainly wasn't going to sell it. That was insane. I could rent it or keep it, just in case.

Just in case, what?

Ugh, why was I like this?

I let myself in to find Morgan and Lance already at it.

"For the love of God, Lance, that is not how you do it."

"I never had any complaints before. Wales women like it like that."

"Well, I'm not a Wales woman. Jesus Christ, move over. You're just doing too much. Use less."

"I'm not using less. Wales women want me to use more."

I snorted a laugh as I walked in on the two of them fighting over the tequila bottle.

"Honestly, from the door it sounded like you two were fighting about how much dick Lance was going to use."

Lance looked stricken. Morgan gagged. I just rolled my eyes.

One of these days, if I could just get them to stop fighting long enough, they might actually realize that they were a good match, but it was very unlikely. They were more likely to murder each other. Mutually assured destruction.

"Somebody margarita me. It has been way too long."

Lance handed me my margarita, no salt on the rim.

Morgan took hers, which was fuller than mine. "Hey, are you drinking?" I asked.

"Oh relax, it's virgin."

"Honey, you're in college. I doubt that's virgin."

"Well, I have to go and study tonight, so it *is* virgin."

I groaned. "Noooo, Morgan. This is supposed to be a night off. Now I'm going to want to hover over you and ride you about how you should be studying."

"Relax, I've been studying the whole week. I'm just taking part of the night off. I'll go back and do a little bit more light reading. But tequila is not conducive to reading. And you both have to work tomorrow, which Lance was apparently forgetting, because he was just pouring the whole bottle of tequila into his mouth."

I laughed. "Well, Lance will feel it just as much as I do in that case."

He winced at that and then took his glass. "All right, let's head out onto the balcony. I want to talk to you about something."

I sighed. For the last two days, I had known something was up with him. But he hadn't said a word. I just assumed it had been the whole move thing, being a part of Pendragon, and my impending marriage.

I knew I was going to have to do something about the fact that Lance didn't approve of Atticus and was worried about me.

It's more than that and you know it.

I didn't want to think about it. Our friendship had always been so easy. So simple. He was the one person other than my sister I could share everything with. And there was never any pressure. He'd never been my boyfriend. When Michael and I broke up, Lance had a girlfriend, and when they broke up a year later, we were fully entrenched in our, *we are best friends* vibes. More and more lately, I was feeling a shift in our connection. I hadn't thought much about it. I just thought we were evolving, and he was worried, especially after the Bronson thing. He saw himself as my protector, which I appreciated. And I knew that he needed me to need him. Which I couldn't do just to make him happy anymore.

Out on the balcony, I turned on the patio heaters and we shivered as we waited for them to warm up. Morgan groaned. "Really? The balcony? It's freezing. Why don't we just drink inside like normal people?"

Lance cut my sister a glance. "I didn't invite you out here."

Morgan rolled her eyes. "You know what? I forgot you have a ball sack. I'll be inside."

I frowned at him. "What's with you? Sure, you and Morgan snipe at each other, but you're never mean."

"She's mean to me all the time."

I rolled my eyes. "Okay, what is going on with you, Lance?" I wrapped my arms around myself and shivered as we stood under the warming light. "You've been acting odd ever since we moved to Pendragon a couple days ago. I know it's an adjustment, but come on."

He winced. "There's something I need to talk to you about that I've been holding back on because I didn't know how to tell you, and now I'm out of time."

"Whatever it is, you can tell me. Are you in trouble?"

He shook his head. "No. I just—" He swallowed hard. "I'm leaving for London tomorrow."

I blinked at him. "You have a vacation coming? Fuck, how did I miss that? I'm so sorry. Obviously, I assume you have your work covered. I know things are in transition with Pendragon, but anything you need, I'll cover. Why didn't you remind me? I've had my head kind of buried up my ass lately."

His expression softened. "Only you would think that somehow you forgot. And let me remind you, you were busy saving all of us. And it's why I love you the most."

"Well, I love you too. But I should not have my head buried up my ass. Hopefully now things will ease up a little bit. I mean, the whole move is going to be in adjustment, but if things calm down, I can be more present for you instead of you constantly running after me trying to save me from myself."

He chuckled softly. "You always say you never need any saving."

"And I don't," I mumbled.

"Well, you did this time, and Price managed to do it."

A warmth started in my chest and as it spread, I tried to bite back the smile. "He has been instrumental in making our lives a little easier."

Lance nodded. "Right. What I'm saying is I'm going to London tomorrow to start a job at Pendragon Tech's London office."

I blinked. And when that didn't work to bring my life into focus, I blinked again. "What?"

"Yeah, I took the job a couple of days ago, and it's been a whirlwind trying to get everything ready. Luckily, there's housing and everything. So I leave tomorrow, but I didn't know how to tell you. I knew I had to, so I figured I'd do it tonight, and here we are."

"You're going to London? You're moving? You're my right hand for the love of fuck."

"You're adorable when you swear."

My brow furrowed. "Don't you patronize me. You knew two days ago. My husband offered you a job?"

He swallowed hard. "Actually, I asked him for it."

CHAPTER 34

I rocked back on my heels. "You what?"

"It's a great opportunity, Gwen. I'll be a VP in Technology. It'll be just like R&D but with my own projects. Things I'm curious about."

"But why? Did you feel like I wasn't allowing you to spread your wings? I have always encouraged you to take on new projects."

"I know you have. And you've been the greatest boss, and partner, and best friend I could ever ask for. I wish I could have done more for you. I wish I could have saved you from all of this."

I shook my head. "Is that why you're leaving? Because you couldn't save me? Did you have twenty mil sitting around?"

He winced. "You know what I mean."

"Look, it's been a harrowing month or so. And you know, this isn't what we expected, but it didn't turn out half bad. I can't believe you're running away."

"I'm not running. I just need a fresh start. You don't need me anymore. It'll be nice to do something different."

"Fucking hell, Lance. You're serious about this."

"Yeah, I am."

I chugged the rest of my margarita and put the glass down. "I feel like you're not telling me something."

He shook his head. "I'm not hiding anything. I just need some separation. That's it. And I need a new opportunity. I'm excited. It's London, for the love of God."

"It is London. I just didn't know you were really interested in going away."

"I am. You can visit me anytime of course."

"Yeah, of course. I mean, it'll be kind of a pain in the ass for you to come back for the wedding though."

His gaze shifted from mine. "Yeah, about that. I won't be coming back."

And that's when a thought sliced through my heart. "What?"

"Come on, you've got Morgan and Macy," he said. "You don't even need me."

"Fuck that, I want you. You are my best friend. So, what? I'll just get married without my best friend?"

He squeezed his eyes shut and then let out a long breath. "I'm sorry."

I didn't even realize the tears had welled until they started to spill. "I'm happy for you, Lance. Honestly, I am. If this is what you want, then this is what I want for you. But it's just so rushed. And you didn't tell me. And—"

Morgan opened the screen door. "Oh my God, you two, if you just..." She took one look at my face and scowled at Lance. "For fuck's sake, what did you say to her?"

I frowned at her. "What? Morgan, no. Lance is moving to London tomorrow."

Her brows lifted. "What? You're running away?"

I was happy I wasn't the only one who thought that. Lance just rolled his eyes. "Oh my God. No, I'm not running away. I got this fucking job at Pendragon, for the love of Christ. It's a good opportunity, so I'm taking it."

"And he's not coming to the wedding," I ask.

He shook his head sadly.

Morgan, ever ready to slander him, pursed her lips. "Well, at least I don't have to see your ugly face anymore."

Lance gave her the kind of smirk Atticus sometimes gave me. The one that said he knew how pretty he was. "And you remain as beautiful and poisonous as ever."

My sister came to my side and wiped my cheeks. "We don't need him at the wedding. It'll be better without him, honestly, because he was driving the wedding planner up the wall."

His smile was soft. "Look out for her for me, would you, Morgan?"

Morgan rolled her eyes. "I was looking out for her long before you were."

"I know. But add on a little extra for me."

"I can't believe you're leaving," I said.

Lance reached out and smoothed a tear off my cheek with his thumb. "It's not like you're never going to see me again. Anytime you need me, I'll be right here, okay?"

And then while my heart was breaking in two, I wondered why on earth my husband-to-be hadn't shared this tidbit of news.

CHAPTER 35
ATTICUS

WAS IT BAD THAT I'D MADE SURE GWEN HAD AN ALIBI TONIGHT? MAYBE. Hell, Lance too. I may not have wanted him sniffing around Gwen, but he'd kept her safe when I couldn't. So I felt like I owed him.

Next to me, Gavin inclined his head at the dance floor. Bronson had strolled in with a pair of leggy blondes. When he took them to the bar, they were giggling as he ordered them drinks. In my earpiece, Micah's voice was low. "What are we doing with the girls?"

Gavin's voice was terse. "I'll handle them."

Pierce just watched me. "Are you sure you want to do this?"

"Yeah, I need to take him off the board."

"We can make it cleaner. Hire a specialist."

"No," I said firmly. "I need to do this one myself."

He sighed. "Right. Have it your way."

My brother, it seemed, had the best sleight of hand. When he joined Gavin at the bar, he accidentally bumped Bronson. During that quick exchange, he spiked Bronson's drink. It happened so quickly. If I hadn't been looking, I never would have seen it. Just a little reach, and there it was.

My brother, as it turned out, was terrifying.

I suddenly wondered about that boyfriend his mom had several years ago. The asshole died of a heart attack. Granted, he'd been knocking around Micah's mother, and then he'd started on Micah eventually. Two months after they met, 'the old geezer had a heart attack,' as Micah liked to say it.

Pierce sat back. "And now we watch."

Gavin was already on the dance floor with the blondes as Bronson started to nod off in the booth.

"Let's go scope him out."

The girls were so happy with Gavin they didn't notice that Micah, Pierce, and I had taken their date out the back door.

The bouncer was one of Pierce's guys, and he nodded as we carried Bronson out the back where there were no security cameras and shoved him in the back of the car. We drove around the corner, and five minutes later, Gavin joined us and climbed in.

"That was almost too easy. Good thing this isn't a habit of ours," I muttered.

An hour later, at a warehouse in Long Island, I sat back on the table as Pierce shook Bronson repeatedly to wake him up. His head lolled back, and he blinked rapidly and said, "Son of a bitch."

I *tsked* and shook my head. "His mother is not a bitch. She's lovely."

Pierce just grinned at me. "Thanks. She adores you too."

Bronson's head snapped to alertness. Then he realized his hands were secured. "What the fuck?"

"Easy does it, Jacobson. The way I figure it, you're going to walk out of here, provided some things happen the way I want them to."

He narrowed his gaze as his brain finally fired and came back online.

"What the fuck, Price?"

"Yeah, it's me."

"Are you insane? I will fucking end you over this."

"Oh, will you now? Who's to say that you'll be talking when this is over?"

For dramatic effect, Pierce had set up a whole bunch of tools of the trade that his much scarier friends over at Blake Security knew how to use.

When he told me what their old job was, it turned my insides just a little. I could have hired them. They would have dealt with Bronson, but this felt too personal.

Micah stepped forward with the syringes. "You want these? None of them will kill him, but he's not going to feel good. I took them from my mother a few months ago."

"Thanks, but I don't think we'll be needing them."

My brother almost looked disappointed.

"Don't worry, I'll leave some for you when I'm done."

Micah grinned, and it lit up his face. "Thanks. I consider Gwen a friend. I mean, she has an alarming gummy bear habit, but otherwise, she's a mate." He turned to Jacobson. "So if he lets you live, you have me to look forward to."

Bronson began sputtering. "I don't know what that bitch told you."

"That's the thing; you keep using that word referring to my future wife, and it's offensive."

"She's a bitch. A whore too."

Gavin wasn't going to let that one stand. He landed a devastating blow that I was sure cracked Jacobson's jaw. The idiot's head lulled to the side as he gasped, "Fuck you."

I grinned. "No thanks. Oh, but that's right. You have a problem with the word *no*."

Bronson lifted his head then, his gaze searching the room. "Is that what she told you? She's lying. The same deal you got, I got first. I didn't do anything she didn't want."

I pulled in a deep breath, trying to rein in my control, because if I didn't, I knew I was going to kill him. And that was not the objective.

I stepped forward and Micah frowned and said, "Maybe we just move on to part two."

I shook my head and leaned into Jacobson's face. "First, you called my future wife a bitch. And then you called her a whore. And you don't seem sorry for what you did to her, so I'm going to make you *really* sorry."

Bronson struggled. "No. I'll never talk to her again. I don't even like her. You know, darkies aren't—"

I popped him in the nose, fast, quick, and efficient, and it immediately gushed blood.

"See? The problem is you can't help being a pejorative racist cunt."

"Fuck. I'm sorry. I'm sorry. I didn't even want her."

"That's right. You're on the right track now, see, because Gwen isn't dumb. And she could see that a partnership with you wasn't going to be right."

"I chose to back out. She was so god damned prude—"

I hit him again. This time with my left hand. My trainer gave me equal practice on either side, so I was just as deadly.

He spat out blood, and was that... Oh fuck. Look, a tooth.

"Fuck. Fuck. I'll never touch her again. I won't even talk to her. Ever."

I nodded. "Of course you're not going to touch her because she is mine to protect."

I stood up straight, rolling up my sleeves.

Pierce and Gavin weren't even fazed. Micah was watching me closely though. He knew my temper and how hard it was to contain sometimes. And how much I hated a bully. The lengths I would go to in order to teach a bully a lesson.

"I won't tell anyone about this. I won't. Just please fucking let me go," Jacobson begged.

"Well, for starters, the next time you see her, and you will see her because I'll make sure of it, you are going to issue her an apology. A lovely one about how you were wrong. You are going to donate five million dollars to Hearts & Hope because it's her mother's charity. And then you're going to donate two million dollars to the Violence Against Women Coalition just because I say so."

He gasped. "Are you fucking serious? Seven fucking million? Fuck that. She was going to be a shitty lay anyway."

Micah sighed and shoved his hands in his pockets, and I glanced up at my brother. "Go for it," Micah said. "He deserves it."

And for once, I let loose my temper.

The next twenty minutes were a blur of unleashed rage and fury as I leveled blow after blow on Jacobson.

I had him by the hair and had knocked his chair over, when Micah stepped in and put a hand on my chest. "That's enough. We need him conscious enough to do the rest."

The haze of red over my eyes didn't fade quickly enough, and I struggled against Micah's hold. My brother held strong though. "That is enough, Atticus. He has to do the other part. Otherwise, there's no fucking point. He'll just go after her again."

That was it. Those words pulled me back.

Gavin and Pierce picked Bronson up. And with his bruised and bloody face, he still somehow managed to glower at me. "Fuck you," he said, though with swollen, bleeding lips and several missing teeth, it was barely coherent.

Pierce brought the laptop. "So, Bronson, we've been doing a little research on you, and we have discovered several complaints by various women. So you're going to drop another ten million to be distributed to several battered women's organizations to soothe the ache of what you've done to those women."

He gasped. "No."

"And one more thing. You are also going to sell me"—I looked up at Micah—"How many shares was it, brother? Oh yes, ten thousand shares of Jacobson Inc. stock."

"What the fuck?"

"That's right. I'm buying in with enough shares to cause a little trouble."

He shook his head. "That'll be more than I have. No, I'm not letting you have my company."

"Oh, you don't have a choice. You see, you're sloppy. Very sloppy. You leave evidence of yourself everywhere."

Pierce hit a button on the laptop and a photo appeared of Maria Klaus. She held the hand of a little girl who looked just like Bronson Jacobson. "See? Maria has evidence of what you did to her. She was more than happy to talk to us. That evidence keeps you paying child support and maintenance. We have a copy of it, and we're not afraid to release it, so you'll do as you're told."

His eyes went wide. "I'm going to make you pay for this."

"No, Bronson, you are the one who's paying. Go ahead, hit the buttons here and enter your account numbers."

He shook his head.

Gavin unclipped his right wrist. "Let me make it easy for you."

Bronson glowered at me. "Fuck you. You are a dead man."

"Then you should know that at my untimely death, all my shares in Jacobson Inc. will go to my wife, and then *she* will have you by the balls." I couldn't really tell if he paled, but his hand shook and he finally typed in the account numbers as I'd expected him to. Then Gavin unclipped his other hand and his feet.

I looked at Micah, and he nodded as he checked the accounts. "Yep, we have everything we need. The donations have been made to Hearts & Hope and VAW."

Bronson slumped in his seat. "I'm coming for you."

"You're welcome to try. If you ever think of going near my wife again, next time I'll stick you with whatever chemical compound

Micah has got in those syringes, and I'll let Gwen kick the shit out of you."

Pierce had men outside the door. They were going to take Bronson, clean him up, and put him in his apartment. A ploy like this was going to make me a permanent enemy.

I didn't care though. He had put his hands on Gwen. And while she didn't know what I was doing, I wanted to make sure that she got something out of it. Those donations would make her happy. As for Maria, I'd already set up a trust fund for her kid. She'd be able to go to school wherever she wanted. Bronson was a true piece of shit. And without someone willing to step forward with evidence, actionable evidence that we didn't steal, this would have to do, at least temporarily.

Now all I wanted to do was get home to my wife and wash off the stink of asshole.

CHAPTER 36
GWEN

I was slightly tipsy.

Liar.

Okay, I was more than *slightly* tipsy. But honestly, after Lance's bombshell, I had needed the drinks. I could see that it was tearing him up to have to tell me, so we turned it into a goodbye celebration.

I tried not to think about how he wouldn't be there at my wedding. That he wouldn't give me away. I sure as shit wasn't letting my father give me away either. He'd already done that. I would walk down the aisle by myself before I'd walk down it with him.

When the elevator dinged to let me into the penthouse, I peeled off my shoes, knowing there was no way I was going to navigate the Louboutins on the slick marble floor in one piece while I was tipsy.

The cool floor soothed my aching feet as I marched through the foyer, trying hard to stay quiet so I didn't wake Micah in case he was asleep. If I knew Atticus, he was still up and probably in the study.

I stopped short when I found my husband-to-be in the living area. "Oh my God. You scared me. What are you doing sitting here in the dark?"

He didn't turn to face me. Instead, he sipped a drink. "Did you have fun?"

There was a hollowness to his voice that gave me pause. "Yeah. I guess you know about Lance, obviously."

He turned then. The moonlight hit every curve of muscle just so, like a caress, enticing me to walk over and touch him.

I laid my purse on the couch and dropped my shoes on the floor next to it before walking over. I took the glass from him and took a small sip, letting the warm amber find its way down, warming me from the inside out. "I wish you'd told me."

He cocked his head and watched me carefully. "It wasn't my news to tell. He'll thrive in London."

I lifted my brow. "Did it have to be so far away?"

"It's a good option for him. And before you ask, I didn't *make* him take it. He could have stayed here, doing exactly what he does now."

I bit my bottom lip. I had wondered if Atticus had pushed him into it. But even I knew that a chance to head his own department was a huge career step for him. When he'd walked away from his family, he'd given up a lot. The chance for rapid advancement. This would be great for him. "I think it'll be good for him. But he's going to miss the wedding."

Atticus cocked his head then drained his glass. I could see the light hint of a smile playing at the corners of his mouth. "Is this the part where I pretend to be disappointed about that?"

I playfully slapped his chest, and he caught my wrist. It was only then that I noticed the bruised knuckles. "Atticus? What happened?"

"Will you leave it at I don't want to talk about it?"

"No, I will not. Did you hit something?"

"Yes," he said as he set the glass down on an end table. "Repeatedly."

I widened my eyes. "Christ. What? It looks like you've been in some kind of cage match."

He released my wrist and then wrapped his other arm around me, bringing me flush up against his body, the hard length of him pressing in the notch between my thighs. "Let's just say you don't have to be afraid of anything anymore. I took care of it."

Icy dread skated up my spine. "What did you do?"

"It's better you don't know. But Jacobson isn't going to be a problem. Not for you. Not anymore."

I felt like I'd been doused with a bucket full of ice-cold water. Bronson? How had he known? "What?" I swallowed hard. "W-w-who told you?"

He didn't answer. "I don't want to talk about that right now. Right now, I just want to hold you. Can I do that? Are you okay letting me do that?"

Tears pricked my eyes. He knew. He knew and he still wanted to hold me? He knew the worst thing about me, and he wanted me in spite of it.

His fingers eased away from my neck, sliding down along my jaw and tilting my chin up ever so slightly. And then he dipped his head to kiss me.

The kiss was a soft brush of his lips. Not at all demanding. It was designed to make me feel safe, to make me feel cherished. But right now, I didn't want to feel cherished. I wanted to feel alive. I wanted to feel *wanted*.

I pushed to my tiptoes, looped my arms around his neck, angled my head, and kissed him deeper, letting my tongue slide over his lips. Begging for entry.

The hand on my lower back slid over my ass as he pulled me tighter against him, and he growled low. "I'm trying to be gentle, Ness."

"Who said I want you to be gentle?"

He chuckled darkly before his lips crashed on mine again, rougher this time. His hand moved to tangle in my hair, pulling my head back, giving him better access to my neck.

I moaned as he sucked on the skin there. It would take a lot to leave a mark with my dark skin, but Atticus was determined to brand me as his.

I couldn't help but groan as his hand tightened on my ass.

I could feel his cock pressing against me, hard and ready, and I couldn't resist the urge to grind myself against him, wanting to feel more of that delicious friction. He responded by lifting me up, carrying me over to the couch, and laying me down on my back.

His eyes were so dark in the dim light they were almost black.

I held my breath as he peeled both stockings off, one at a time, letting his fingers slide up my thighs. His gaze followed. "I want to see all of you."

I stood, letting the dress fall to my feet, standing before him completely naked. I shoved the nerves down. I wanted him, and I could have him.

"My God," he whispered reverently. "You are so beautiful."

I slid my hand down between my breasts and past my navel. But his hand shot out, gripping my wrist. Making me pause.

"Only for you, Atticus."

He just stared at me for a long moment, like he was trying to memorize every inch of my body, trying to commit this moment to memory. "Say it again."

"Say what?"

"My name. Say it again. I need to hear you say it."

I laid my hand on his thigh. "Atticus."

He kicked off his shoes, then tugged his pants down and off before moving us back to the couch and settling into the space between my spread thighs.

"I want to hear you say it again."

I leaned my head back as he licked his way down my neck to my collarbone. "Atticus."

"Again," he moaned against my skin.

A jolt of electricity hit my clit at the sound of his hushed moan. "Atticus,"

"Again," he demanded.

His tongue flicked my left nipple, and I gasped, arching into his mouth. "Atticus."

"Again."

He sucked my nipple into his mouth roughly, and I gasped again. "Atticus."

"That's it." He said with a smile. "Again."

"Atticus."

"Again."

I gasped again as he sucked my nipple deeper into his mouth, harder. "Atticus."

"Again."

"God, please."

"Again."

I arched my back as he moved his hand between my thighs. He parted my slick pussy with his fingers and made a sound of satisfaction. "You're dripping wet for me."

"Atticus," I moaned as he sucked my nipple and stroked my pussy.

"Again," he demanded.

"God, Atticus, stop teasing me."

"Again."

I gasped as he sucked my other breast into his mouth. "Atticus," I moaned.

"Again," he ordered as he slid a finger inside me.

"Atticus!" I cried out.

"Again," he demanded as he slid a second finger inside me.

I panted. "Atticus."

He lifted his head to look at me, his eyes full of desire and lust. And then he leaned in and kissed me again. He pushed my legs wider apart as his fingers delved into the wet heat of me.

He groaned against my lips, and then his thumb began to circle my clit in a lazy rhythm that had me moaning.

"Tell me this isn't all in my imagination, Ness. Tell me this is real."

"It's real," I gasped as his fingers slid inside me. "It's so real."

"Tell me you want me."

"I want you."

"Tell me you want me to fuck you."

Scared about what I was feeling, I tried to pull away, but he held me tight.

"No running, Ness. Tell me," he said softly.

I kissed him quickly, reassuring him. "I want you to fuck me, Atticus."

"Good," He growled. Holding his cock in his hand, he rubbed the thick head through my wet folds. "Fuck, I love how you feel."

"God... Atticus."

"You are so fucking sexy."

And then his lips crashed down on mine, and the head of his cock dipped inside me.

"Oh, God." I gasped.

"Fuck, Ness." He moaned, going still.

"Please, you feel so good." I said, my heart pounding out of control. My body was desperate for him to fill me.

He swallowed hard. "Stop moving. I will fucking lose it."

"It's okay." I whispered. "I like it when you lose control."

When he groaned against my neck then slid a little deeper, I gasped.

"Fuuuck." He retreated, and that slide was so delicious. When he slammed back home, we both groaned.

"I-I trust you."

"Fuck, you're so tight," he whispered. He sank in again, another inch deeper. He was so thick, his cock stretching me. The sweet, delicious burn had me gasping.

"Holy fuck," he groaned. He slid back out again then back in. "Fuck."

"Atticus," I moaned. I could feel how soaked I was, and it was so sexy that I could feel him sliding through my juices.

"Say it, Gwen." He let out a feral growl.

"What?"

"My name. Say it again, damn it."

"Atticus." I bit my lip. "Fuck me. Please."

I was on the edge of something big and terrifying and exciting. I'd never said those words before. I'd never meant them. He was the only one I wanted. The only one I needed.

I tried to move my hips as he leaned down to kiss me. I tried to push myself closer to him and take him inside me, but he held me tight.

He raised his head to look at me. "Tell me again."

I panted. "I want you to fuck me, Atticus."

He surged forward, filling me in one thrust.

"Oh God," I gasped, trying to relax and get accustomed to his size.

"Fuck." He hissed, and then he started moving inside me in gentle, long strokes. "You feel so fucking good, Ness," he whispered.

GWEN

"I love how you feel inside me," I whispered back, feeling a little breathless.

His hips rocked against me, stroking while he slowly slid in and out of me. He dropped his forehead to mine, giving me the sweetest kiss, in direct contrast to how hard he was loving me.

"Harder," I moaned.

He thrust into me again and again. "Gwen." His voice was broken.

"Atticus," I panted.

"Come for me," he demanded. "Come for me, Gwen. Come around my cock."

"Atticus," I gasped, and then my body shattered. My back arched, my toes curled, and I cried out as my pussy clenched down on his cock.

It felt like my world was falling apart in the best possible way.

Then he arched his back and thrust hard into me. "Fuck, fuck, fuck," he cried out as he came.

He held me tight as we rode out our orgasm together.

It was so sweet and hot that tears pricked my eyes.

We stayed there for an eternity before he pulled out of me. Then he picked me up. With a giggle, I asked, "Where are we going?"

"To the bedroom to do that again."

CHAPTER 37
ATTICUS

In less than twenty-four hours, Gwen would be my wife. The turn everything had taken was a surprise. Yes, obviously, I had wanted her. But I hadn't expected her to worm her way into my soul. Hell, I hadn't even known I had one. But watching her care for my mother like she was her own, I couldn't shake that. That kind of thing didn't leave you.

I parked my car and marched into the elevator. I was only working this morning. Micah had already insisted that he and the boys, 'the lads,' as he'd said, were taking me out for drinks tonight on my last night as a free man. I didn't care about losing my freedom. I just wanted her by my side where she belonged, forever.

When I stepped out on my floor, a few employees were milling about, already hard at work. When I reached my office, Leah was there. "Mr. Price, sir, I've already got the files you requested. But there's a meeting on your calendar that I didn't put on there. The conference room."

I frowned. "Who does it say it is?"

She shook her head. "I don't know. I thought maybe you scheduled a personal appointment."

I frowned when she turned the monitor to show me. "No, but I'll take care of it." It was seven o'clock in the morning. Who was trying to meet with me this early?

I took the rest of my messages, and then instead of heading for my office, I turned out the door and made a left toward the large conference room at the corner. When I reached it, I paused. The back of the head was familiar. Too familiar. How the fuck had he got in here? Security knew not to let him in. I barged through the door and said, "What do you want, Dad?"

My father struggled out of his chair and beamed at me. "You know, I am very proud that you've taken the work habits I instilled in you seriously."

"I don't have a lot of time. What the fuck do you want?"

"Testy-testy." He put up his hands. "I'm just here to congratulate you on your upcoming nuptials. I am very surprised that somehow my invitation got lost in the mail."

"Are you? While you are a slimy, devious bastard, I never marked you for an idiot."

He lifted a brow and chuckled softly. "Touché."

"I don't have a lot of time. What do you want?"

"Well, on the eve of your pending nuptials, it seemed most appropriate to tell you to your face."

"What, that you're trying to come back? You think I don't know that?"

"I still have shares. I may be off the board, I might have been removed as CEO, but I still have voting rights. And I can bring up items for a meeting. I'm going to bring one up for a vote of no confidence against you."

"You can try. You won't have the votes."

He dug into his pocket and lifted his hand. "This flash drive is my ticket back."

"Fuck you. Whatever is on there, I don't want it."

"You might want to look at it before you make your decision."

"Stop being cryptic, old man."

"I don't need to be cryptic, Atticus. I'll tell you what's on it. But you're going to want to verify before you have Pierce and your baby brother take a look at it. How is my other son, by the way?"

"He says fuck you."

My father flashed a smile that was all too similar to my own. "That also sounds about right. So here's what's on this. That night five years ago when your mother had her unfortunate break from reality, she murdered someone. I have proof."

Those three words locked me down. Rooted me to the spot.

I knew what was on the flash drive, but how the fuck did he know? "Bullshit."

"You think I would do all this, make a play to come back if I'm bluffing? You must not understand how satisfying it is to prove you wrong. Honestly, I'd go to any lengths."

"Get out."

"Fine, but you and I both know the truth. That evidence will go to the police, and they'll come for your mother. They'll put her in prison or an insane asylum. I really don't care which because either way, she'll suffer, and that is all I ever wanted in life. Then they'll come after you and your little friends for covering it up."

"You fucking monster. What do you want?"

"I'm glad you asked. I'm not asking for too much. The girl. I know you're not marrying her because you believe in matrimony. You discovered your grandfather's clause. You think if you can convince everyone you're a steady family man, they won't bring a vote of no confidence against you. Well, you'd be wrong. I still have friends on that board. And in three month's time when you hit thirty and aren't married, your shares revert to me.

The dread slithered in my gut. "I am marrying her."

"Okay then. It's honestly sort of a relief. Knowledge of this murder has been weighing on me."

"Fuck you."

His maniacal grin gave me chills. "The mother or the fiancée? You can only have one. I'm being generous letting you keep one. If you save your mother, things go easier for you. In three months' time, you will vote for my return. You keep your voting shares, but Pendragon will be run by somebody who knows what they are doing."

"And if pick Gwen?"

"I expose the sham for what it is to the board. They vote no confidence on you, I get your voting shares. The prodigal father returns, remorseful and better than ever. Oh, and I kill her and you mother."

My blood ran cold. "You're insane."

"I could sit back and do nothing except watch you crash and burn. But God, I really want to come back knowing that I destroyed you, that you fell at my hands. It would be much more satisfying."

"So what... You think I'm going to let you come back?"

"No. I think you're still going to try to fight it. But do so at your loved ones peril."

I didn't even know what happened then. Time slowed, or sped up, or I lost the thread completely. Fuck it. All I knew was that I had my hands in his lapels, dragging him up, and slamming him against the glass. "If you fucking touch them, I will end you." My voice came out like shards of glass.

He grinned at me. That evil, feral grin that I had seen so many times when he abused my mother. "If you marry Gwen tomorrow, this evidence goes to the police. If you try and block me from coming back, this evidence goes to the police. So choose. The woman you were fool enough to fall for or your mother."

Fury had me vibrating . "You're a piece of shit."

"You're not the first person to tell me that."

He shoved against me, and I released him.

Gwen. I had to get her out of the city if she was on his radar. My mother. I had to get to her. Get her the fuck out of town. Away. We had a contingency plan for something like this, but fuck.

"Look, you can try and hide your mother all you want, but the evidence on there also points to the cover-up, so there goes your shot at running Pendragon. You have your board votes, of course. There's not much I can do about that. But she can't vote in your favor if she's not here. And if she is here, she'll go to jail. So it's up to you. Protect your mother, or get married tomorrow and fight me. But I will be pushing for a vote of no confidence, and you will have the fight of your life."

He dusted off his lapels. "I'm going to go now. You have until tonight to make up your mind. I am eager to see what you'll choose."

CHAPTER 38

GWEN

I was impressed with Morgan.

She'd actually kept the bachelorette night simple. She did make me promise her a full all-out party in Vegas after the merger was done, but there was no way I could handle that now. We went to dinner and then to see *Six*. God, it was so good. And she'd even resurrected some of my old friends who had been thrilled to get the announcement. She wanted to throw me a reception later, which was so beautiful.

See, you have people who love you.

I was happily buzzing from the few drinks I'd had. And when Gavin dropped me off, he made it a point to walk me to the elevator. I kicked off my shoes, padding through the foyer. "Is my husband-to-be here?"

Micah had made a point to tell me that he wasn't going to be home tonight and to feel free to shag all over the penthouse, so maybe I was going to do that. Yes, it was bad luck to see the bride before the wedding, but honestly, who even did that anymore? It wasn't like we were having the most traditional wedding in the world.

The light was on in the kitchen, and I turned to search the living room for Atticus, but he wasn't there. I eventually found him in the study. The lights were low, and he'd poured himself a drink as he stared at the computer monitor. "There you are," I said with a smile.

The light in the room glinted off the sapphire bracelet Clarissa had loaned me for tomorrow as my something old, borrowed, and blue.

"Did you have a good night?"

"Yeah. Shocker, Morgan actually listened and kept her promise. *Six* was fantastic."

He gave me our secret smile.

"Are you okay? You seem tired. Please tell me you actually enjoyed your bachelor party a little."

He swallowed hard and nodded. "You know, like Micah said, just the lads and some drinks."

"Okay, then why aren't you tipsier?" I nodded at his glass that looked untouched.

He lifted a dark brow. "Are you trying to get me tipsy?"

I sauntered over to him, moved his chair back, and planted myself onto his lap. "I would very much like for my husband-to-be to kiss me."

He swallowed hard for a moment, and then his hand slid up my arm, over my shoulder, and onto the nape of my neck before plunging into my hair. He held me steady. When he leaned forward, what I thought would be a slow, lingering kiss was harsh and desperate. His hand at my hip tightened like he was holding on for dear life. When he dragged his lips off mine, he panted, dropping his forehead to mine.

"Gwen," he whispered harshly.

"Hey, what's the matter?"

He swallowed hard. And then he released me, easing me off his lap to my feet. "I need to talk to you about something."

"Okay. You look serious. What's the matter?"

"We're not going to get married tomorrow."

I blinked at him, unable to process the words that had just tumbled out of his mouth. "What?"

"The wedding is off."

Suddenly, my world spun. The steady bedrock that I'd just felt in his kiss wavered, tumbling as the world tilted with tiny tremors and earthquakes. "I—I don't understand."

"There's nothing to understand. It's not going to work, you and me."

"What are you talking about, Atticus? You said—"

He swallowed hard and scrubbed a hand over his face before pushing to his feet.

I backed up automatically as he reached for me. "No, you said that you were choosing me. That we—" I couldn't finish. My words broke off in a sob.

Get yourself together.

But I couldn't. Something deep inside me cracked. "You said that you were choosing me regardless of the merger. You said that. You chased me down and you said that."

He winced and swallowed hard, avoiding my gaze. "It seemed like you needed to hear that."

The words hit me like blades, and I staggered backward. "What?"

"It seemed like you needed to hear that from me. For you to feel comfortable with me."

"So, those were just—" I couldn't even finish.

"Everything about this was designed to move you forward. But we won't be getting there tomorrow. You are already part of Pendragon. I've worked out another deal with your father."

"What? M-my father knew?"

"Why do you even seem surprised?" His voice was harsh, his words bludgeoning me in every sentence.

"Why would you do this, Atticus? Why are you doing this to me? I don't believe you."

"I'm telling you that we are over. I got what I wanted. I've already blended your team. Your father and I have an arrangement. I won't marry you. I don't want to."

Those last words hit me in the gut, and I wrapped my arms around myself, trying to hold on. This wasn't true. He was lying. This wasn't the Atticus I knew. This wasn't the man who had told me he loved me just a few days ago.

What is true?

"So you want me to believe that you don't care about me, that everything you said was a lie."

"Yes. I had another deal working all the time. Your father was bluffing."

I swallowed hard. "So that's it then? You got my algorithm, and I got what?"

"You have money, don't you? And obviously, you have a job."

CHAPTER 38

"So all my hard work was just for nothing."

"You are part of one of the largest technology companies in the world. You have saved your employees. You saved your sister. What more do you want?"

What more did I want indeed?

I staggered backward another step. "You never wanted me?"

"No. As a matter of fact, you should go be with Lance. He at least wants you."

"So you were faking it this whole time?"

"Yes."

I knew what he was saying, but his body language looked so rigid and stiff. He looked *broken*. This was a lie. He was lying.

I tentatively took a step toward him, reaching out, unwilling to believe what his mouth was saying. "Atticus..."

He took a step back from me. "Go be with Lance. Be with someone who actually loves you."

Then he marched from the room, leaving me to fall on my knees.

To be continued in Acquisition...

THANK you so much for reading TAKEOVER, book 1 in the KINGS of the BOARDROOM trilogy!

Desperate know how much groveling Atticus has to do? Can't wait to see how he has to make the up to Gwen? Will she actually marry him?

FIND OUT IN ACQUISITION————> Here!

. . .

WHILE YOU WAIT, dive in to Liv and Ben's story with **The See No Evil Trilogy:**

It began with a stolen almost-kiss.
And ended in revenge.
When Ben meets Olivia, sparks fly and danger follows. In a world where secrets reign, their forbidden attraction could be the key to survival or a path to destruction.

➜ Yes, you can pick up **Big Ben, The Benefactor** and **For Her Benefit** now!

Can't get enough ? Meet a cocky, billionaire prince that goes undercover in **Cheeky Royal!**

He's a prince with a secret to protect. The last distraction he can afford is his gorgeous as sin new neighbor.

Turn the page for an excerpt from Cheeky Royal...

ALSO FROM NANA MALONE

CHEEKY ROYAL

"You make a really good model. I'm sure dozens of artists have volunteered to paint you before."
He shook his head. "Not that I can recall. Why? Are you offering?"

I grinned. "I usually do nudes." Why did I say that? It wasn't true. Because you're hoping he'll volunteer as tribute.

He shrugged then reached behind his back and pulled his shirt up, tugged it free, and tossed it aside. "How is this for nude?"

Fuck. Me. I stared for a moment, mouth open and looking like an idiot. Then, well, I snapped a picture. Okay fine, I snapped several. "Uh, that's a start."

He ran a hand through his hair and tussled it, so I snapped several of that. These were romance-cover gold. Getting into it, he started posing for me, making silly faces. I got closer to him, snapping more close-ups of his face. That incredible face.

Then suddenly he went deadly serious again, the intensity in his eyes going harder somehow, sharper. Like a razor. "You look nervous. I thought you said you were used to nudes."

I swallowed around the lump in my throat. "Yeah, at school whenever we had a model, they were always nude. I got used to it."

He narrowed his gaze. "Are you sure about that?"
Shit. He could tell. "Yeah, I am. It's just a human form. Male. Female. No big deal."

His lopsided grin flashed, and my stomach flipped. Stupid traitorous body...and damn him for being so damn good looking. I tried to keep the lens centered on his face, but I had to get several of his abs, for you know...research.
But when his hand rubbed over his stomach and then slid to the button on his jeans, I gasped, "What are you doing?"
"Well, you said you were used doing nudes. Will that make you more comfortable as a photographer?"

I swallowed again, unable to answer, wanting to know what he was doing, how far he would go. And how far would I go?

The button popped, and I swallowed the sawdust in my mouth. I snapped a picture of his hands.

Well yeah, and his abs. So sue me. He popped another button, giving me a hint of the forbidden thing I couldn't have. I kept snapping away. We were locked in this odd, intimate game of chicken. I swung the lens up to capture his face. His gaze was slightly hooded. His lips parted...turned on. I stepped back a step to capture all of him. His jeans loose, his feet bare. Sitting on the stool, leaning back slightly and giving me the sex face, because that's what it was—God's honest truth—the sex face. And I was a total goner.

"You're not taking pictures, Len." His voice was barely above a whisper.

"Oh, sorry." I snapped several in succession. Full body shots, face shots, torso shots. There were several torso shots. I wanted to fully capture what was happening.
He unbuttoned another button, taunting me, tantalizing me. Then he reached into his jeans, and my gaze snapped to meet his. I wanted to say something. Intervene in some way...help maybe...ask him what he was doing. But I couldn't. We were locked in a game that I couldn't break free from. Now I wanted more. I wanted to know just how far he would go.

Would he go nude? Or would he stay in this half-undressed state, teasing me, tempting me to do the thing that I shouldn't do?

I snapped more photos, but this time I was close. I was looking down on him with the camera, angling so I could see his perfectly sculpted abs as they flexed. His hand was inside his jeans. From the bulge, I knew he was touching himself. And then I snapped my gaze up to his face.
Sebastian licked his lip, and I captured the moment that tongue met flesh.

Heat flooded my body, and I pressed my thighs together to abate the ache. At that point, I was just snapping photos, completely in the zone, wanting to see what he might do next.

"Len..."
"Sebastian." My voice was so breathy I could barely get it past my lips. "Do you want to come closer?"
"I--I think maybe I'm close enough?"
His teeth grazed his bottom lip. "Are you sure about that? I have another question for you."

I snapped several more images, ranging from face shots to shoulders, to torso. Yeah, I also went back to the hand-around-his-dick thing because...wow. "Yeah? Go ahead."

"Why didn't you tell me about your boyfriend 'til now?"

Oh shit. "I—I'm not sure. I didn't think it mattered. It sort of feels like we're supposed to be friends." Lies all lies.

He stood, his big body crowding me. "Yeah, friends..."

I swallowed hard. I couldn't bloody think with him so close. His scent assaulted me, sandalwood and something that was pure Sebastian wrapped around me, making me weak. Making me tingle as I inhaled his scent. Heat throbbed between my thighs, even as my knees went weak. "Sebastian, wh—what are you doing?"

"

Proving to you that we're not friends. Will you let me?"

He was asking my permission. I knew what I wanted to say. I understood what was at stake. But then he raised his hand and traced his knuckles over my cheek, and a whimper escaped.

His voice went softer, so low when he spoke, his words were more like a rumble than anything intelligible. "Is that you telling me to stop?"

Seriously, there were supposed to be words. There were. But somehow I couldn't manage them, so like an idiot I shook my head.

His hand slid into my curls as he gently angled my head. When he leaned down, his lips a whisper from mine, he whispered, "This is all I've been thinking about."

Read Cheeky Royal now!

Nana Malone Reading List

Looking for a few Good Books? Look no Further

FREE

Cheeky Royal
The Heir
Bridge of Love

Mistletoe Series
Mistletoe Kisses
Mistletoe Hearts

Gentlemen Rogues
The Heir
The King
The Saint
The Rook
The Spy
The Villain

Royals
Royals Undercover

Cheeky Royal
Cheeky King

Royals Undone
Royal Bastard
Bastard Prince

Royals United
Royal Tease
Teasing the Princess

Royal Elite

The Heiress Duet

Protecting the Heiress
Tempting the Heiress

The Prince Duet
Return of the Prince
To Love a Prince

The Bodyguard Duet
Bodyguard to the Billionaire
The Billionaire's Secret

London Royals

London Royal Duet
London Royal
London Soul

Playboy Royal Duet
Royal Playboy
Playboy's Heart

London Lords
See No Evil
Big Ben
The Benefactor
For Her Benefit

Hear No Evil
East End
East Bound
Fall of East

To Catch a Thief

Speak No Evil
Bridge of Love
London Bridge
Bridge of Lies
Broken Bridge

The Donovans Series
Come Home Again (Nate & Delilah)
Love Reality (Ryan & Mia)
Race For Love (Derek & Kisima)
Love in Plain Sight (Dylan and Serafina)
Eye of the Beholder – (Logan & Jezzie)
Love Struck (Zephyr & Malia)

London Billionaires Standalones
Mr. Trouble (Jarred & Kinsley)
Mr. Big (Zach & Emma)

Mr. Dirty(Nathan & Sophie)

The Player
Bryce

Dax

Echo

Fox

Ransom

Gage

The In Stilettos Series
Sexy in Stilettos (Alec & Jaya)

Sultry in Stilettos (Beckett & Ricca)

Sassy in Stilettos (Caleb & Micha)

Strollers & Stilettos (Alec & Jaya & Alexa)

Seductive in Stilettos (Shane & Tristia)

Stunning in Stilettos (Bryan & Kyra)

Tempting in Stilettos (Serena & Tyson)

Teasing in Stilettos (Cara & Tate)

Tantalizing in Stilettos (Jaggar & Griffin)

Love Match Series
*Game Set Match (Jason & Izzy)

Mismatch (Eli & Jessica)

Don't want to miss a single release? Click here!

About Nana Malone

USA Today and Wall Street Journal Best Seller, Nana Malone's love of all things romance and adventure started with a tattered romantic suspense she "borrowed" from her cousin.

It was a sultry summer afternoon in Ghana, and Nana was a precocious thirteen. She's been in love with kick butt heroines ever since. With her overactive imagination, and channeling her inner Buffy, it was only a matter a time before she started creating her own characters.

Now she writes about sexy royals and smokin' hot bodyguards when she's not hiding her tiara from Kidlet, chasing a puppy who refuses to shake without a treat, or begging her husband to listen to her latest hair-brained idea.

Made in United States
Orlando, FL
06 November 2024

53543381R00166